WOLF HUNTER

The entire fortress snapped to attention as console after console on the *Challenger*'s vast bridge leaped into life. Scanning and tracking systems identified the target for hundreds of cannons, and each cannon locked on. Over half the *Challenger*'s guns opened fire, shooting well ahead of their fast-moving target so that their bolts would intercept the Starwolves.

The two ships closed and exchanged a fierce barrage of fire. The Starwolf ship was rocked by an explosion so intense that she actually disappeared from the scan in the violent backwash of energy. The *Challenger* ceased fire. Its quarry shot past, still and lifeless, her course deflected by the force of the explosion. She was tumbling, her bow dipping as she began to roll end over end.

"We got her?" Commander Trace asked in the stunned silence that enveloped the bridge.

"An apparent hit on her main generators amidship," Marenna reported with her usual calm detachment. "The Starwolves are drifting out of control."

"Open fire!" Maeken snapped.

///////

STARWOLVES
BATTLE OF THE RING

Also by Thorarinn Gunnarsson

STARWOLVES

Published by
POPULAR LIBRARY

STARWOLVES
BATTLE OF THE RING

THORARINN GUNNARSSON

POPULAR LIBRARY

An Imprint of Warner Books, Inc.

A Warner Communications Company

POPULAR LIBRARY EDITION

Copyright © 1989 by Thorarinn Gunnarsson

Popular Library ®, the fanciful P design, and Questar ® are registered
trademarks of Warner Books, Inc.

Cover design by Don Puckey
Cover illustration by John Harris

Popular Library books are published by
Warner Books, Inc.
666 Fifth Avenue
New York, N.Y. 10103

 A Warner Communications Company

Printed in the United States of America

First Printing: October, 1989

10 9 8 7 6 5 4 3 2 1

1

The prey was a freighter of the D Class, not nearly as massive as the immense bulk freighters but far too large to land itself. Just under two hundred and fifty meters in length, it was shiny white with new paint and its boxlike hull was unusually trim for a cargo ship, although obviously too wide and heavy for a warship. Remarkable as well was its speed, for its drives developed the power of a freighter half its size. And it was a lure for any pirate who could take her.

The hunters were nine large freighters with down-swept wings, as black as space and as fast as death. These were wolf ships and their pilots were Kelvessan, the dread Starwolves. Exposed to stresses few other creatures—and certainly no human—could endure, they closed upon their prey with deadly purpose and accuracy. They could not see their target, but they sensed its every movement. They tracked their prey by the image they received in their minds from its tremendous power emissions, the low, echoing pulse of its stardrive marking it as a company ship and legitimate prey.

As the pack moved into range, the fighters broke formation to move into attack position. The lead fighter, that of the pack leader, moved in close behind the freighter for the first run, but hesitated. Velmeran knew that this run was his to make, and yet he had the vague, unexplainable feeling that he should not—that he must not. Not because this freighter was a danger in itself; in his short career he had sprung three traps already. But something was wrong. He had always trusted these feelings in the past, and yet he could see no cause to terminate this run. His one concession was to move slightly out of line to the position where he normally watched attack runs.

That move did not appear to surprise the others. They trusted him, perhaps more than Velmeran trusted himself. Baress moved up to take his place in line, maneuvering to align his cannons. The objective of the attack run was simple enough: the stardrive had to be wrecked to bring a ship out of starflight. A bolt had to strike and fracture the crystal of the drive itself, and that strike had to be on the very edge. A miss might do undesirable damage to the ship, while a strike too far inside would dissipate in the drive thrust. This ship was small and fast, and they would be lucky to get within ten kilometers of a target they could not see in the first place.

The ship executed a series of evasive maneuvers that did nothing to shake loose its pursuit. Before the helm computer could be set up for another set of dodges and turns, Baress seized the moment and rushed in. He fired a quick volley as he passed, missing the star drive by a fraction but raking the hull of the ship. As he dropped back to return to the pack, Tregloran moved up to make his own run. Although he would never quite equal his teacher in skill, he was learning quickly. He was already as good a pilot as Baress, who had flown special tactics for years; if one missed the target, the other would not.

"Scatter!"

At Velmeran's order, the fighters broke without hesitation and shot away as fast as they could. Velmeran had saved them from traps too often for them to question his judgment. Salran's pack, flying watch a short distance back, turned quickly away as well. And the Methryn, pacing the hunt, charged her main cannons as she closed. Curiously, the only one who did not follow that order was Velmeran himself. He continued to pace the freighter closely.

"Velmeran, what are you doing?" Valthyrra Methryn demanded over com. "Is that thing a trap, or not?"

"No, this is no trap," he answered. "That was the only way I knew to get Tregloran off her tail before he shot her."

"Then would you kindly explain yourself?"

"I doubt that I can. I am putting my reputation on the line."

"You already have. So, tell!"

"I want you to make contact with that ship."

On the Methryn's bridge, Valthyrra brought her camera pod around to stare in astonishment at the commander. Mayelna only shrugged both sets of arms and sat back in her chair to watch.

"You want me to talk to it?" she asked with obvious disdain. "It phases like a company ship. . . . Well, it has happened before."

She opened a new signal on the commercial band, trusting that she was within range of the weak achronic transceivers of Union technology, linking it to the channel she kept to the fighters for Velmeran to hear.

"Attention, unidentified ship!" she snapped in her best authoritative voice. "Identify yourself immediately."

There was a very long pause. Valthyrra was quick to grow impatient, mostly because she was afraid that he was right. "Well?"

"Give them a moment," Velmeran insisted. "They have been badly shaken. How would you feel if you found Starwolves on your tail?"

"Annoyed."

"Hello? This is Captain Garkelley of the Velka."

"Name your company and home port," Valthyrra demanded.

"No company. We are independent freighters."

Valthyrra swore privately before she reopened her channels. "Velka, drop to one quarter light speed and stand by to be taken on board. You are not under attack, but you will be destroyed if you make any hostile moves. What is your status?"

"Our hull is penetrated, near the engine compartment," Garkelley replied. "We do not have the crew to handle this situation."

"Do what you can," she told him, then muted that channel. "Velmeran, have you had a chance for a close look?"

"Good enough," he responded. "The good Captain told the truth. Baress clipped the cover of the engine housing and put some long tears in her hull where her engineering section should be. No real structural or mechanical damage, though. Their leakage is minimal, since my scanners detect only traces of escaping atmosphere."

"Keep an eye on that ship," she told him before muting that channel as well. She turned to Mayelna, who was watching it all with calm detachment. "Well, you certainly seem to be taking it all in stride."

Mayelna shrugged, unconcerned. "What is there for me to

worry about? He took care of the problem, and I have you to pick up the pieces."

"You are the Commander of this ship," Valthyrra reminded her.

"I have not forgotten. But we have worked out an agreement. I am the Commander of the Methryn as a ship. Velmeran is the Commander of the Methryn as a fighting force. You are the Methryn, and quite able to take care of yourself in the first place. That situation pleases me. He knows far more of what is going on out there."

"Yes, he does seem to know," Valthyrra agreed, glancing down at the lower bridge where officers hurried about their duties. "How does he know?"

Mayelna glanced up at her. "He is out there. He sees . . ."

"Yes, I know. He sees things that no one else can see. He bases conclusions on things that no one else would notice. He can devise foolproof plans on the most careful, precise logic and then avert disaster on the wildest hunch. And he is always right."

Mayelna looked at her in surprise. "That is what you wanted, is it not? You should be happy."

"Oh, I am happy," the ship was quick to agree. "There is nothing wrong, but something still bothers me. There is an alarm sounding in a dark corner of my memory cells, but I cannot remember. All I understand is that it is far more important than it seems."

By that time the Methryn had overtaken the damaged freighter and was closing to take it on board, opening her left holding bay to receive it.

"Captain Garkelley?"

"Yes?"

"I am going to take you into one of my holding bays for repairs," she explained. "There is a regular ship's atmosphere inside the bay, kept in by a restraining field even when the doors are open. It might be a little cold for your tastes, but you can live there. I want you to completely secure your ship as if you were already at dock at a station, all fields, drives, and major power systems shut down."

She did not wait for his response. She had already positioned herself so that the open bay was already over the small freighter, and began to descend on top of it. Two pairs of long

handling arms reached down to lock securely to the hull of the
Velka and draw it into the bay. The arms retracted into their
holding position and locked into place, and the vast doors began
to close. She had already ordered her fighters on board as well,
with special emphasis for Velmeran to get himself to the holding bay as soon as he could.

As soon as her ships were safely on board, the Methryn
turned and began to gather speed gently, so slowly that most of
her crewmembers were not even aware that she was moving.
This was special consideration for her human passengers, who
might not have survived her normal accelerations.

Velmeran landed as quickly as he could and hurried to the
holding bay, where Mayelna and Valthyrra waited as the docking tube swung into place. Mayelna was in the white armor of
an officer, a short cape of matching white snapped into place at
her collar to lend a look of authority. Valthyrra hovered nearby
in the form of one of her probes, the most lethal of her automa-
tions. A pack of pilots in black armor served as an impromptu
security force, while Dyenlerra and her medical remotes waited
behind. This looked to Velmeran more like a boarding party
than a group of rescuers.

"Ah, Velmeran," Valthyrra said, the retractable neck of her
probe bent well around to stare at him. "Do you expect any
trouble?"

"No, not really."

"None at all?" she insisted, still staring at him.

"I expect no violence, if that is what you mean," he corrected
himself. "Trouble is something you already have. All you could
want is waiting at the end of this docking tube."

"I was aware of that," Valthyrra said, drifting toward the
door of the docking tube as it snapped open. "Shall we go have
a look at it?"

She drifted quickly down the length of the tube and opened
the outer door of the lock, which revealed the closed docking
hatch of the Velka. A moment later they could hear the locking
mechanisms inside the hatch release with hollow clangs and
thumps, and the door began to move slowly inward as if under
stress. Outer hull doors always opened inward, so that internal
pressure kept them sealed even when mechanical locks failed.
That worked against it now, however, since the freighter kept a

slightly higher pressure. The Kelvessan were hit by a rush of what seemed to them warm air, and the door opened easily.

A small, thin man stepped forward in a very businesslike manner in the hatchway. The Traders were themselves a race apart, as adapted after many generations to life in space as nature would allow. They were nearly as small as the Kelvessan, thin and wiry and well-muscled against the stresses of acceleration. They were also shrewdly intelligent, especially so for humans in their declining age. There was something about the appearance and bearing of this man which suggested that a cold, almost hostile shrewdness was his major trait.

He made a brief gesture of acknowledgment. "I am Captain Larn Garkelley of the Velka, independent freighter."

"I am Valthyrra Methryn," the ship responded, and indicated right and left with her camera pod. "This is Commander Mayelna, and Commander-designate Velmeran."

Garkelley was shaken at the mention of that final name, turning visibly pale as he stared at the young pack leader.

"I must inquire as to the condition of your crew," Valthyrra distracted him subtly. "Does anyone require medical assistance?"

"No . . . No, we are all quite well," Garkelley answered hesitantly.

"Then we will assist you in patching your hull and replacing the damaged plate, and deliver you to your destination," Valthyrra continued briskly. "Also, we will ensure that your engines are recalibrated to phase at the proper levels."

"Oh, there is no need for that," Garkelley was quick to assure her. "We would not want to trouble you."

"You have already caused us more trouble than you are worth, and your ship will not be released until the modifications are complete," Valthyrra told him plainly. "You must be aware that your phase levels are how we are able to tell independents from company ships."

"Of course, but that is not important." His righteous indignation flared. "It seems to me that it is your responsibility to be more certain of the ships you pillage."

"You seem to forget that the Traders owe their very existence to our protection of their trade rights," Mayelna said in harsh warning. "The Union would not tolerate you if they could help it. We have always hunted them out of various freight lanes so that you can have the trade. The only responsibility you have in return is to properly identify yourselves."

"Of course, Commander," Garkelley was quick to agree.

"Why were your engines phasing out of sequence anyway?" Valthyrra asked.

"That is what we would like to know!" A young woman stepped from the hatch to join them. Angry mutterings of agreement from Velka's airlock indicated that she was the leader of a potential mutiny.

"We had a bad star drive that barely got us into Tarvan Station," the younger officer continued. "Garkelley was our freight and trade officer then. We had to leave Captain Wanesher to live out his last few days in the station hospital. Before we had a chance to refit, Garkelley arranged a deal with Dallord Trade for a new engine at a bargain price, free fitting and a five-year contract on a series of runs that their own ships would not dare to fight. It seemed a very good deal at the time, good enough for Garkelley to take the Captain's chair."

"You knew at the time that we were taking a risk," Garkelley countered. "We had to get under way immediately. There was no time to recalibrate."

"Yes, we did agree, but for just that first run. That engine was to be recalibrated at Laerdaycon Station. You told us that it was. But you put it off because you wanted to impress Dallord by making up the lost time on their schedule."

"You are out of line, Mersans!" Garkelley said hotly.

"You are out of line," Mersans retorted. "The crew is more than ready to call a meeting."

Garkelley regarded her coldly. "You will not find it so easy to depose a Captain."

"That is already decided, when a Captain nearly loses his ship to his own foolishness," she declared, then turned abruptly to the Starwolves. "Speaking for the crew of the Velka, I ask you to no longer treat with this man as the Captain of this ship."

"Your affairs are your own, and we want no part of it," Valthyrra answered. "We will deal with your new Captain when one is selected."

"That will not take half an hour."

"Half an hour, then," Valthyrra agreed as she turned to leave, followed by the Starwolves. Garkelley hurried back into the

Velka's airlock, upset but seemingly unconcerned about the outcome of this meeting.

But Mersans hesitated, then quickly laid a hand on Velmeran's shoulder before he was gone. Then, remembering who she had touched, she withdrew the hand as if it had been burned. "Forgive me. . . ."

"Do not be afraid of me," he assured her.

"I am sorry that we are such trouble," she began uncertainly. "I am Kella Mersans, helm and navigator of the Velka."

"And would-be Captain?"

"No, I want nothing for myself," she insisted sincerely. "Once we are rid of Garkelley, I intend to make my own nomination for Captain. But I must know, before this begins, if . . . when we were first aware of you, if we had tried to contact you instead of run, if you would have listened."

"Of course," he told her. "We are cautious, for our own safety. If you had not run, we would have stayed away until we found out why. Ships that do not run are usually traps. But when you sound like a company freighter and run like one, we can only assume that you are one."

"Our mistake was in running, then?"

"Certainly. We used to tell Traders from Company ships by whether or not they ran. Traders would drop out of starflight to give us a close look at themselves, while the company ships had no choice. Then the Traders began to use a distinctive phase level."

"Why do they not set their phase levels to fool you?" she asked.

"They still do for passenger ships, since we will not touch those. But that would not work very long, for we would go back to asking Traders to stop and identify themselves. Garkelley chose to run?"

Mersans nodded. "I was not on the bridge at the time, but I knew what was wrong when we began dodging. We must have been taking forty G's into those turns, so I could only make progress toward the bridge between maneuvers. By the time I got there, it was over. He said that you contacted him?"

"Valthyrra did."

"How did she know?"

"I told her," Velmeran said. "That was my pack on your tail."

"How did you know?"

"Trade secret," he answered simply. "I am a pack leader and Commander-designate, and that means something. Mostly it means that I am not allowed to make mistakes."

"That is something easier said than done," Kella observed, then hesitated even as she turned to the airlock. "Commander, were you the one who shot us?"

"No, that was Baress, my second," he said. "I would not have missed."

Kella had no desire to dispute that, and hurried on into her own ship. Velmeran turned and followed the others down the docking tube, joining Mayelna and Valthyrra at the end.

"Interesting group of people," Velmeran remarked, turning to the lift doors on the other side of the corridor.

"To say the least," Mayelna agreed. "What did she want?"

"She wants to be certain of her charges against her Captain," he explained. "She believes that he should have gotten on the com when he saw us coming, instead of running."

"That goes without saying," Valthyrra agreed.

"So I told her," Velmeran said. "She says that she does not want the position herself. But whether she wants it or not, I have the feeling that it is hers."

"Then we will consider that a fact," Valthyrra remarked cryptically.

Before Velmeran could ask for an explanation, the lift doors snapped open.

"I will see you on the bridge," she said quickly, and withdrew her presence from the automaton. The machine turned and drifted off, seeking its mounting cradle. Mayelna pulled Velmeran into the lift.

"Valthyrra is quite beside herself over something," Mayelna began as soon as the lift was moving. "And it has something to do with you. How did you know? There was nothing to indicate that it was not a company ship."

Velmeran shook his head slowly. "I do not know. It is not normal. . . ."

"Since when have you worried about being a normal, ordinary Starwolf?" she asked. "You can tell me. I am, at this point, prepared to accept anything."

"Well, there are times, more and more often lately, when I know things that I could not possibly know," he explained hesitantly. "It used to be that I was alert to clues that no one else could find. Now there are times when I know answers when even I can see no clues."

"You have already proven that."

"Also, there are times that I hear the thoughts of others calling out to me," he continued with even greater reluctance. "That is how I knew this time. It seems that I often hear thoughts of fear and desperation during a run. But this time I heard thoughts of indignation as well, that they were Traders and should be immune."

"Telepathy?" Mayelna mused, and shrugged. "Why the hell not? We have always had the ability to sense high-energy emissions. We generally do not think about it, but it must be some form of telepathy. Must be our Aldessan heritage. They are tremendous telepaths."

"But why should I be the first Kelvessan telepath?" Velmeran protested.

"Why indeed?" the Commander laughed. "Meran, it does not surprise me at all. I have always said that fate must have conversations with your subconscious, and now I see that it must be true. Why have you said nothing?"

"It was not the type of thing that I felt confident to talk about. Not until I gave myself away. When you are the first known telepath in the history of your race, you tend to keep it to yourself."

"Velmeran, I am going to arrange more matings for you," Mayelna said briskly. "It is now more important than ever to reproduce your traits."

That suggestion was a logical one, and with considerable merit. The females of their race, at those rare times when they knew that they were likely to conceive, often arranged a mating in the hope that desired traits would be passed on to their offspring. At that time there was no Kelvessan whose genes were in greater demand than Velmeran's. Nor was there a male more reluctant to mate.

"Consherra . . . ," he protested weakly.

"Consherra would be the first to agree," Mayelna insisted. He knew that it was the truth, but he had no wish to discuss it.

"I also want you to work on developing your talents," Mayelna continued. "Valthyrra might be able to help you with that. It will be interesting to see the extent of your talents."

* * *

"The object of this first exercise is simple enough," Consherra explained as she shuffled a deck of large, stiff plastic cards between her four hands. "I will draw a card and you will determine the symbol that is pictured on it."

"I take it that I am not shown the symbols on the cards?" Velmeran asked innocently. They were seated together on the floor of Consherra's cabin. The Methryn's helm was surrounded by various items that Valthyrra and Dyenlerra had helped her collect. A portable medical scanner was aimed at his back, although Consherra insisted that this was only an exercise, not a test.

"Concentrate!" Consherra ordered, drawing the first card so that he could not see it. He stared, she noticed, not at the card but at her. After an instant his expression became one of surprise.

"Where did you get these silly cards?" he asked incredulously.

She shrugged helplessly. "They are the only cards that I could find. Thrynna uses them with her first-level students—most of them have not yet learned to read. Just tell me what it is."

"It looks like a thark bison," he replied.

"You are not sure?"

"I have never seen a real thark bison."

She placed that card on the floor and selected another. "And this?"

"Terrestrial horse."

"And . . ."

"Quan rat."

"Do you have any idea how you know?" Consherra asked suddenly, her hand on the card she did not draw.

"I am doing it the easy way," he replied. "You are looking at the card for me. I see the image in your mind. In fact, you are thinking so hard that you are practically shouting at me."

"That is what I suspected," she remarked. "Can you guess the card before I draw it?"

"Now, that is harder," Velmeran said, and concentrated. "Tharnlak. Flordan. Sivan. Langie. And a very large dog."

Consherra glanced quickly at the next five cards and frowned. "Harder, you say? Because you have to probe the identity of the card itself?"

"I suppose so," he agreed. "All I know is that it is harder."

Consherra laid out several cards facedown, including a few that she had already used. "Find the Quan rat."

Velmeran indicated a card but did not pick it up. Consherra looked at the card, then glanced at him. "Find the langie."

When he indicated the stack of discarded cards, she made a disgusted sound. "And the wolf?"

Velmeran indicated a card without hesitation.

Consherra stared in surprise. "How can that be? I was making that up!"

She lifted the card and set it down again. "Damn! Well, so much for that."

Velmeran stared at her as she began to collect the cards. "What is wrong? How did I do?"

"You did perfect," she told him.

"But what about the wolf?"

She lifted the card for him, revealing it to be a wolf. "I had no idea what cards I put down. Either chance outsmarted me, or I have a touch of your own talent."

She set the cards aside and picked up a small cardboard box, which she placed on the floor in front of him. "There are several objects in the box. Name as many as you can."

Velmeran stared at the box a moment before glancing over at her. "More children's games?"

"No, not at all."

"I can see that." He stared at the box a moment longer. "There are five plastic figures that I identify as large reptilian forms, perhaps Terrestrial dinosaurs. Please do not ask me the type; paleontology was never one of my strong suits, although I do consider these ruling diapsids of the Mesozoic. There are several coins of various types, mostly copper and bronze although one is almost pure silver. There are four machine parts of types that I cannot begin to identify. There is a pan; a rubber ball, and . . . teeth?"

"Human dentures . . . that is Dyenlerra's contribution," Consherra explained. "And do not look so horrified. Our teeth might be self-repairing, but humans are not so lucky. Anything else?"

"There is a photograph," he said.

"Of what?"

"How should I know? It is dark in there."

Consherra rolled her eyes to indicate her impatience with

him. Velmeran frowned as well. He had little desire to be a part of this from the beginning, and now he was convinced that this was only more trouble for him, much more than it was worth. His new talents held no fascination for him. Instead they had frightened him from the first, not in themselves but because they were one more way in which he differed from his own kind. He was alone, and he would always be alone. Even Consherra, as much as she meant to him, could not fill that strange longing he had for someone just like himself.

"Velmeran, what is it?" Consherra asked, noticing his distraction. "What is it about this that troubles you?"

Velmeran glanced up at her, and was about to tell her that she could not understand. Then he caught himself. She had always made an effort to understand him, and she did know him better than anyone else could.

"I am not certain," he said at last. "Velmeran the Magnificent has grown somewhat, coming even closer to immortal status. Perhaps he is becoming a little too complex for me."

Consherra nodded. Velmeran the Magnificent was their own term for a living legend, his own alter ego, the great one who had lead the raid on Vannkarn and five more missions just like that. He was the person that Velmeran became when duty required. But the real Velmeran was simple, sensitive, and often insecure. Only she knew him as he really was.

"I understand," she said slowly, and glanced up at him. "Velmeran, do you still dream of what our race will become when the war is over and we are free?"

"Of course," he replied. "That dream gives me the courage to do what I must. If I lose that dream, then I will be no more than an ordinary pilot."

"Well, I believe that you are leading us along the path to what we will become," she continued. "You have many special talents, not all of them psychic. But being a leader, you are in front of the rest, alone and by yourself. I understand the sadness that is a part of your life, since you must pay for this greater dream with all your own personal dreams. I wish that I could make your sadness and hurt go away and still your longing, but I cannot. You need the understanding of someone like yourself, which I am not. No one is like you, but I think that you are not so different as you believe."

"Perhaps you do know me well," he conceded. "But if I am not Kelvessan, then what am I?"

"Something more," Consherra said, pointing to the medical scanner aimed at his back. "Dyenlerra wants to study you very closely. The suggestion has been made that you are a mutation, perhaps the first evolutionary step our race has taken since our creation. In short, you are the real Kelvessan. We are only the prototype."

2

The palatial structure in the mountains south of Vannkarn was called Rane Manor after its first owner, although the dynasty he had founded now bore the name Lake. This was not the original mansion; few things built by man could survive chance accident and natural disaster that long. In all those years, fifty thousand in all, only one thing had remained unchanged: the same family had ruled there in a line of descent that had remained unbroken. The family name had changed often and clan leaders had frequently turned to the offspring of near or distant cousins to adopt an heir.

Richart Lake had come to that high position with the sudden if not unexpected death of his grandfather hardly a year before. Richart was not the same sort of man Jon Lake had been, and the sector already reflected his changes. Jon Lake had been philosophical and reflective, while Richart was calculating and coldly efficient. He ran the sector as he had run Farstell Trade, as a business, a tool to control the population, with definite goals to be met and a profit to be made. And he was in his own way even stronger.

Donalt Trace, the Sector Commander, was like neither of those two. He disdained both government and business; according to his own philosophy, a society existed primarily to serve the needs of its military. His whole life had been shaped around the single, all-important task of defeating Starwolves. Richart, on the other hand, had been taught that the Starwolves were a threat that could not be effectively countered, a problem that could be quietly worked around but never eliminated. That was perhaps their main difference. Donalt would have them always fighting, while Richart knew that they could not win. Neither of them had an effective solution.

Until now.

Jon Lake had divided the two great tasks of his life between his two successors. Donalt had inherited the problem that the Starwolves represented, but Richart had received the greater responsibility of ensuring the survival of their race. The human species was in rapid decline, too long apart from the rules of natural selection that had shaped their very being. Weak and defective traits had polluted the genetic resources of the entire species. A large portion of their race was impaired physically or mentally beyond the ability to function normally. This escalating problem was a drain of resources that the Union would be unable to afford before long.

Richart Lake was the key supporter of a daring, even dangerous plan to correct this problem. His grandfather had first proposed to trim back the population of the Union by at least half. Forced sterilization would be employed on a large-scale basis, having already begun on those with severe mental or physical impairments. But those standards would slowly be increased to include everyone below a certain intelligence level or a victim of any physical defect, a subsidized return of natural selection, while genetic enhancement would be used to predispose groups of people to certain tasks.

The problem of enforcing that plan was obvious. The implement of the first phase, four months earlier, had led to unrest on every Union world, rioting on twenty and the complete overthrow of Union authority on one. Before the next phase could be put into effect, the full force of the military would be needed to intimidate or punish the general population into compliance. And for that, the problem of the Starwolves must somehow be eliminated. That last point was vital, for the Starwolves would quickly use the Union's troubles to defeat it.

And that was Donalt Trace's specialty.

Trace had been nervously pacing the hall outside Richart Lake's office in Rane Manor for the past half hour. Now he straightened his back cautiously and eased himself into a chair. Circumstance had not been kind to him these past two years. He had just finished with a series of operations to reconstruct his ruined back, blasted by a bolt from a Starwolf's gun. Nor had his reputation survived the raid on Vannkarn unaffected, in spite of his uncle's best efforts to protect him. Then the old Councilor had died suddenly, leaving him to fend for himself while still immobilized by his injuries and his new weapon only half built. As the new Councilor, Richart had shown him little support and had gone so far as to consider his replacement.

But now that they needed him for their purposes, they could not be nicer. The door to the inner office opened and Richart Lake stepped out. Trace rose as quickly as he dared, hoping that he was not betrayed by the pain in his back. His real condition was such that, had it been an officer in his command, he would have restricted the man from space travel and certainly combat duty.

"Hello, Don. I'm glad that you could make it," Lake greeted him cordially enough, almost enthusiastically.

"No problem," Trace assured him, stepping into the office as the other held the door for him.

"Please excuse the mess," Lake said as he pulled the door shut, indicating the boxes, files, and temporary access terminals that littered the room. He showed Trace a chair in front of the desk and hurried around to take his own seat behind. "I'm afraid that we are only now getting matters straightened up and back into working order. Next week we move into the new government building, but it will be at least a year before we return to the same level of efficiency we had before the Starwolves brought the roof down on top of us. Farstell was a lot easier to put back together."

"Farstell had the advantage of duplicate records as shipping and receiving ports and factories," Trace pointed out. "There was a lot gone from the government and military offices that can never be replaced."

"True enough," Lake agreed, and leaned back in his seat. "I have received a full report on the space trials of your new ship."

"So? What do you think?"

"It is slow. . . ."

"It was never meant for speed," Trace replied. "Just as long as it can get itself where it needs to be."

"Then you are satisfied with the machine?" Lake asked.

"Yes, I am," the Sector Commander replied without hesitation. "It is everything that I had hoped it would be. It accelerates and handles perfectly. The computer network and channeled power grid work as well in real life as they did on paper."

"And the sentient command computer?"

Trace shrugged. "Again, it was perfect in its operation. It is no more or less than it needs to be. As you know, it has intelligence, independent reasoning capabilities, and self-awareness. it can take care of itself, but it will also follow orders without question. It is not a living, thinking, feeling being like the Starwolf carriers, but we did not want that in the first place."

"No, we did not," Lake agreed thoughtfully.

"And it can fight," Trace continued. "We ran it through twenty-eight simulated attacks by Starwolves. Everything we know they have, we threw at it. It survived every attack, and won more than half of the engagements that we played through."

Lake glanced up at him. "No problem for you, I trust? I mean, you are still fairly fresh from your last surgery."

"No, no problem," Trace assured him. "As you pointed out, the machine is no light cruiser. We took at most a momentary five G's, otherwise no more than sustained three."

"Then you will be along for its first mission?"

"Yes, I must. I expect that we will have no problem the first time that we meet Starwolves, since they will not be prepared for what my beauty can do. Assuming they survive, they are likely to run crying for Velmeran to slay this dragon for them. And Velmeran is the one unpredictable element. If he shows up, then I want to be there."

"Well, that is just the problem," Lake said, leaning back heavily in his chair. "The Fortress is a strong defensive weapon. Put one of these in a system and you are drawing an imaginary line that you dare any Starwolf to cross. I do not like having to use our only Fortress as a combat lesson. But we need that ship at Tryalna if we are going to retake and hold that system. The Starwolves know what the revolt and secession of a major system will mean for the Union, and they are going to fight to keep it free.

"We have to do something about the Starwolves if we are going to be respected. They have been having their way with us ever since they broke into Vannkarn. And you can bet that

Tryalna would not have been so quick to revolt if they had not been certain that the Starwolves would protect them."

Richart Lake sat back for a moment, deep in thought. Trace knew that he was being lectured one last time before being sent off to complete his assigned task, but he accepted it in good grace. The unfortunate reality was that if he wanted the High Council to give him more of these very expensive ships, then he had to listen attentively to a certain amount of advice and words of wisdom.

"Do you believe that you can defeat a Starwolf carrier with this machine?" Lake asked after a moment.

"Yes, I know I can," Trace replied quickly and certainly.

"Just stay away from Velmeran, if you can. He has a bag of tricks for every situation. His is a problem that we must work around, for now."

Trace looked up at him. "Quite to the contrary, I should think. Velmeran is a problem that we cannot ignore; if we can eliminate him, the rest will be comparatively easy. This is my best chance to defeat him, before the Starwolves can develop any strategy against this new weapon."

The Councilor considered that. "You might well be right. But you must also take whoever comes your way. I'm glad that you were able to get Maeken Kea to captain your ship, especially since the Krand sector helped us put up so much of the cost."

"She is the best that I could find. True military geniuses are few and far between these days."

"Geniuses of any type are few and far between anymore. That is why the situation is becoming so critical. We have to save ourselves while we are still smart enough to be able to do it. You will be on your way, then?"

"We have to get to Tryalna in time to do some good."

"Then I must allow you to be about your business," Lake said, and leaned over the desk to shake his hand. "Good luck, Don. I cannot tell you how important this is. But if you lose this ship because of your personal grudge against Velmeran, I'll hang you out to dry when you get back."

"Don't worry about that. Besides, if I don't win, there probably will be nothing left of me to send back."

Maeken Kea was not at all sure she liked this. She had arrived on a military courier late the previous night, shown to a room—a suite—that was opulent beyond even her rank and reputation, and then pushed on board a small passenger shuttle the next morning to find herself in the company of no less than Sector Commander Donalt Trace. Now they were on their way back into space with an air of calm stealthiness that left her very uneasy.

Maeken was smart enough to figure a few things out for herself, since the Sector Commander sported a self-satisfied wait-and-see attitude toward this affair. She had been relieved of her command while she had still been trying to get her battleship into dock, informed that she was now attached to Union High Command. Her orders vaguely mentioned a new command. Well, she had heard a rumor that Donalt Trace was off his deathbed and running trials on a new ship that was supposed to be a match for a Starwolf carrier.

She did not much care for the prospect of commanding a ship designed to equal a Starwolf carrier, since it implied that she would be fighting Starwolves. She had once fought Starwolves and won, holding on to a very valuable piece of property her sector had wanted for a long time. A short but successful career bore out the fact that she was probably the Union's best tactical genius. But she had no false pride in that regard. She knew that she could not take on the likes of Velmeran or Tryn or Schyranna and hope to win. And she certainly did not want to fight Starwolves under the command of someone like Donalt Trace. Rumor made him out to be either a fool or a madman, and either one was dangerous.

"What led you to choose the military?" Trace asked suddenly. Maeken glanced up, startled from her own thoughts.

"I hesitate to mention it, but it is really just an indulgence of my childhood fantasy," she explained. "I love big ships."

The Sector Commander laughed. "I might just have a ship for you! Would you be willing to fight Starwolves?"

Maeken shifted uneasily. "Do you mind if I do not answer at once? Yes, I would fight Starwolves if I had the right weapon. Do you have one to offer?"

"Your judgment of my new ship will be your answer?" Trace asked.

"If I think that I could defeat Starwolves with it, I might just be willing to try."

Trace nodded. "That is reasonable. Of course, the burden of responsibility will not be yours alone. I will be going along with you, at least this first time out. The two of us together should be as smart and any Starwolf Commander."

"Including Velmeran?"

"I hope so. But it is not our business to track down Velmeran or any other Starwolf. We are on our way to Tryalna to secure the planet against a Starwolf counterattack while our forces reestablish firm control."

"Your weapon has such power?" she asked.

He nodded. "You see, the Starwolves were designed for a specific purpose, a very specific set of rules, and our mistake has always been in playing according to their rules. This new ship is designed to bring the advantage to our side, forcing them to play according to our rules. Their high-speed attacks, their swift reflexes, and ability to endure crushing stresses will no longer be of worth to them. We now have shields to counter their big guns, guns of our own powerful enough to pierce their shields. Look."

Maeken brushed back her pale brown hair and leaned toward the window to see that they were overtaking a temporary station of some size. Temporary stations, as the name implied, were meant for temporary use, able to move where they were needed under their own power and be ready for immediate service. This one was clearly meant for military use, for she could see at a glance that it was heavily armored and sported cannons inside retractable turrets large enough to swallow their shuttle. But it was also dull black, nearly invisible against the stars in spite of its vast size. Starwolf color. Then she understood only too well.

"Your ship?" she asked simply.

Trace nodded. "This is what we call a Fortress."

"Impressive," Maeken remarked, recovering from her surprise. "Of course, I know that you are too smart to believe that simply building a bigger battleship than they have will give you any special advantage. What does this beast have that makes it so special?"

"Look at its design," Trace said. "Begin with the engines. Notice that it has no main drives, just clusters of stardrives."

That much she could see. The engines were arranged in hexagonal clusters of seven large drives, six on the outside with one in the center. The engine clusters were themselves arranged in a flattened hexagon on the rear of the drive housing, six outside with two, side by side, inside. They were large engines, at least half the size of the immense crystal drives that the Starwolves somehow synthesized for their carriers. And like the

Starwolf ships, they had armored plates that closed like doors to protect them. Each engine also had a protective flaring that made shooting out a running drive very difficult.

"Each engine is a self-contained unit," Trace explained. "Each is a module that contains its own generator, drive system, and controls. The same is true for each major cannon, which consists of generator, gun, and retractable focusing turret. These modules simply slip into sockets in the hull, where they merge with the central computer system. It is possible to change out every engine and cannon on this ship in only five hours' time.

"The hull is composed of heavy armored plates, sloped to shed heavy bolts by deflection. Each plate is covered by a thin sheet of quartzite which, when infused with a defensive shield, becomes impenetrable to any bolt or missile the Starwolves can throw against it. In that way the body of the ship serves as an indestructible platform for its engines and cannons, which are the only vulnerable points."

"And, as such, you have designed those areas for rapid damage control and repair," Maeken observed.

Trace nodded approvingly. "Exactly. A convoy of tenders will follow the Fortress—at a discreet distance. Engines and cannon modules are transported end to end in special racks that have their own drive units.

"This ship has the firepower and shielding of a major planetary defense system. Its cannons have nearly the power and range of those of a Starwolf carrier. But we have more guns; we can inflict more damage, and endure more damage, in the same amount of time. And, if a battle breaks out for a short time, we can repair our damage, while they cannot."

"I like it so far," Maeken said. "But I see one flaw. What about their conversion cannon? They might hesitate to use it on a planetary target, but it would be the ideal weapon against this machine."

"It would seem so, yes," Trace agreed. "They can convert enough mass to destroy a world in a single shot. But the Fortress can divert the energy of all its generators into a single defensive shell of tremendous power. Even damaged guns and engines can supply power, as long as their generators are operative. Simulations have shown that it can turn even that."

"And this beast can move?" Maeken asked, staring out the window as they rounded the nose of the Fortress. The main forward battery was located here, as well as two more engine clusters to provide reverse thrust.

"Yes, it accelerates and handles as well as a Class A bulk freighter. Not all that fast for a warship, but that can get it where it needs to be."

"But it cannot actively chase down a Starwolf carrier." Maeken stated the obvious. "Then what is to keep them from simply ignoring it? If it was in my way, I would simply go around it."

"I suppose they will, when they simply want to get past. But it cannot simply be ignored if it is guarding an inner world we want protected, or in orbit over a colony they want us to leave alone. Then they will have to deal with it first."

Maeken considered that for a moment, and shrugged. "You seem to have thought of everything."

"So, what do you think?" Trace asked. "Do you believe that you could fight Starwolves with this?"

Maeken looked at him sharply. "Are you giving me any choice?"

"Of course," he insisted. "If you think that this is not right for you, that you cannot use it to best advantage, then you are completely free to return to your former command and tell your Sector Commander that Donalt Trace is as mad as rumor makes him out to be."

Maeken leaned back in her seat and sighed heavily. "You are mad. And so am I, for that matter. Crazy as Treyvestrian Knock Beetles, so I guess that we were meant for each other. Who wants to grow old, anyway?"

"Well, they are safely gone," Velmeran observed. The Velka, flying again under her own power, was cruising into the system as if she had made the entire run herself, rather than suspended in the belly of a Starwolf carrier. The Methryn held back; she had business elsewhere.

"I was beginning to wish that you had blasted them when you had the chance," Valthyrra told him quietly, turning her camera pod away from the main viewscreen.

"Have they really caused that much trouble?" Velmeran asked. "They never even came out of their ship."

"All the same, that is the last that I want to see of Traders," Valthyrra insisted. "I have never before had a murder on my decks."

"Attempted murder," he corrected her.

"A very near miss."

"Well, Kella Mersans is their Captain now, just as I expected she would be, and she will keep them under firm control."

"You expected?" Mayelna asked, looking up from her monitor for the first time. "Was that a premonition?"

"No, just an intelligent guess," he insisted. "I refuse to believe in foretelling. The future is a variable. It can be predicted, in the honest sense of the word, but I cannot believe that anyone can actually see visions of what will come to pass."

"Still, I wish that you would keep an open mind on this and any subject," Mayelna said. "That is the only way to find out what you can do."

"I cannot help wondering what we will do if these talents turn out to be fairly widespread," Valthyrra added. "I suppose that we could carve up old drives to make crystal balls."

"I hope that the two of you enjoy your fun at my expense," Velmeran said coldly, and turned to Valthyrra. "And yes, I have had others come to me about developing their own talents. In fact, I already have two promising students."

Valthyrra's lenses nearly popped out of her pod. "How did you know what I was thinking?"

Velmeran looked at her in mock surprise. "I thought that we had already established that."

"Yes, but I have chips for brains . . . as the Commander phrases it. How can you possibly read a mechanical mind?"

"How should I know? I am a simple telepath, not the Oracle of Delphi."

"Wait a minute!" Mayelna said, calling him back. "Who are these promising students of yours?"

"Well, Consherra is becoming fairly good at her own card game. In fact, she is nearly as good as Tregloran."

"Tregloran?" Valthyrra asked. "Of course. He is in many ways not unlike a lesser copy of yourself."

"I cannot comment on that," Velmeran said, obviously reluctant to make the same comparison. "But he is a cunning little sneak; even I am not aware of all of his schemes. And on his good days he can already outfly Baress."

Just then the Methryn threw herself into starflight. Valthyrra's camera pod glanced around cautiously, as if checking to see if she had made the jump intact.

"Ah, it feels good to run at normal speed again," she remarked, and turned back to Velmeran. "I know that we should not tease you for your special talents. We have already learned that we must trust you, so please keep your ears open."

"And what happens when I am wrong?" he asked.

"There is no need to worry about that," she assured him. "As you pointed out, you are not the Oracle of Delphi."

Unfortunately, Velmeran did not see it that way. As he took the lift back to his own cabin, he reflected that this was why he had kept his talents secret for the past two years. Now, if he gave warning and nothing went wrong, he would seem the fool and his reputation as a leader would suffer. And if something happened when he failed to give warning, he would be held accountable for his failure . . . or so it seemed to him.

He was surprised to find someone waiting for him in his cabin, and even more surprised to discover that it was Baressa. He could not imagine why she would seek him out now, unless something was wrong or she needed his help.

"Hello. Have you been waiting long?" he asked hesitantly as he paused just within the door, still astonished at finding her sitting at ease in his favorite chair.

"Not long," Baressa replied, stretching her arms. "Consherra told me to come up a few minutes ago."

"Oh? Is there something that I can do for you?"

"Well, to put it bluntly, I want you to get me pregnant."

That was certainly putting it bluntly! Velmeran's first impulse was to turn and run. He could not refuse flatly; by Starwolf custom, this was his duty, not a self-indulging privilege. And he knew that he could not come up with an excuse in time to save himself. But Baressa was prepared. Consherra had taught her well what to expect, and now she closed for the kill.

"You do not seem very willing," she remarked, unobtrusively moving to place herself between him and the door. "Do you have some objection to accepting me as a mate?"

"No, of course not," Velmeran insisted, retreating even farther into the room. "It just seems so . . . impersonal and contrived."

"Impersonal? I am going to let you mate me until I turn up pregnant. That seems very personal to me," she declared. "Meran, you have your chosen mate, and I have mine. And, to tell you the truth, I would prefer that Baress consider this his child, since he does not know that we can never have one of our own. Just remember that I have done this before. Treg and Ferryn have no more idea of who their father is than you or I know of ours."

"Yes, I know that," Velmeran admitted reluctantly. "But I still find it very embarrassing."

"Why? Because you know me?" Baressa asked.

"Yes. And because I do not want you to know that I really am not very good at this."

Baressa shook her head in weary resignation. "Velmeran, I am not keeping score."

Maeken Kea tried to settle herself in the Captain's seat, which had obviously been made to accommodate the Sector Commander's long frame. This chair was a throne of sorts, from which the Captain commanded his ship. She knew only that she felt like a little girl in this immense seat, her legs dangling and her small body almost lost between its massive arms.

Unfortunately, this chair was not her only obstacle in her command of this ship. She was at a disadvantage from the start, coming unprepared on board a ship that already had an experienced crew. So far she knew how to use the intership com and the lift, and most of the buttons on her console. A second major distraction to her effective command was that she was not certain just how much authority she possessed. In theory he was along only as an observer; that did not mean that he might later decide to start giving orders. At least her name and reputation commanded enough respect; Maeken Kea had once fought Starwolves and won. Not even Commander Trace could claim that. And on a ship designed for the sole purpose of fighting Starwolves, that meant a lot.

Actually, the crew was a surprisingly small concern. There were just over a hundred crewmembers in all, three teams of bridge officers, a medic, and a small cooking staff. That was a very sparse population indeed in twenty-five kilometers of ship, but it needed no more than that. The army of technicians and mechanists needed to keep this hulk in repair followed with their parts and equipment in the tenders.

"All primary and secondary functions are powered up and ready," a disembodied voice announced. The voice was female, not dry and emotionless but unmistakably mechanical. "All systems are ready."

"Very well," Maeken replied uncertainly, ill at ease since there was nothing she could physically address. "Your destination, course, and speed are listed in your records. Have you scanned your flight information?"

"Yes, Captain. We are clear to proceed."

"Then you may get under way when ready," Maeken instructed. "Please inform your support convoy to follow at the prescribed distance."

"Yes, Captain. I am beginning acceleration now."

The beast was moving? Maeken glanced about the bridge, wondering if they were going to maintain this leisurely pace all the way into light speed. Officers were seated at their consoles on the main bridge, several steps lower than her own raised platform, watching attentively as the machine ran itself.

"We are under way and moving toward our assigned flight path," the ship reported. "System control reports all clear. Do you have any additional orders?"

"No, that is all," Maeken replied, hoping that she had told the beast everything it needed to know to get itself under way. "Get me Commander Trace on the com."

"One moment."

"Trace here," he answered almost immediately.

"Yes, Commander, the ship informs me that we are under way," Maeken said, leaning over the microphone in the arm of the chair. "Everything seems to be functioning perfectly."

"Excellent! What do you think of her?"

"Ah . . . ask me again when I have seen if it can fight."

Trace laughed. "Too slow for a warship? I'm afraid that the Starwolves still have us beat in that regard. If she gives you any problems, just tell her to explain herself."

"Yes, Commander," Maeken answered, and hoped that she did not sound too dubious in that reply. She shrugged to herself and leaned back in her oversize chair, watching numeric and graphic displays flash across the main viewscreen superimposed on the starfield that was the ship's forward view. Most of it was beyond her present understanding.

"Computer?" she asked suddenly, remembering one important omission.

"Yes, Captain?"

"Do you have a name?"

"Yes, Captain. I have a name for my own use, as does the ship itself," it explained. "I am Marenna Challenger."

Maeken nodded to herself. This ship was a perfect anthithesis of a Starwolf carrier. She was impressed, although not greatly. But she was hopeful. Soon they would see if the theory behind this ship was as sound as Commander Trace obviously believed. The Fortress was going out to hunt.

3

Consherra knew that something was wrong when she saw Velmeran enter the bridge, fully dressed in armor. The Methryn was hunting, laying in wait beside a major lane, and her on-duty personnel had to remain suited and ready for battle. But that did not include Velmeran, since his pack was not due to go out. She slipped out of her seat on the middle bridge and hurried to him, leading him back from the bridge into the outer corridor. She was surprised when he responded to her attentions by holding her close and kissing her. Velmeran turned to her in open affection of his own initiative only when he felt troubled and insecure.

"Trouble?" she asked, reluctant to end this rare moment.

"The worst," he answered. "Do you recall when I was laying plans for our raid on Vannkarn? I was uncertain that anyone would believe in me."

"I remember," Consherra said. "Valthyrra came to your rescue."

"Well, she might not support me so willingly this time, since what I am going to say is even more outrageous. Sherry, do you believe in me?"

"Of course," she assured him.

"Then turn down your thermostat and follow me."

He led her quickly to the upper bridge, where Mayelna and Valthyrra were conferring on some matter. They both looked up immediately, well aware that something was wrong by the purposeful manner of this delegation.

"Is there some problem?" Valthyrra asked.

"Perhaps," Velmeran said. "A ship will come into scanner range in about five minutes, a freighter of the new Class M type and a very tempting target. Although you will find no indication of a trap, it is a tremendous danger to us. We must let it go or we stand a very good chance of losing ships—perhaps even you."

"And how do you know this?" Valthyrra asked without a pause.

"Do not ask me how I know," he snapped, irritated and desperate. "I do not believe in precognition—I cannot. And yet the fact remains. I know that if we capture this ship, it will blow up in our faces. Do you believe me or not?"

Valthyrra did not answer at once. She glanced at Mayelna, but the Commander offered no advice. After a long, uneasy moment she came to some decision, for her camera pod moved in a negative gesture.

"No, I do not," she said. "I know that I encouraged you to explore your talents. But there will be times when you are wrong, and it seems to me that even you are reluctant to believe this. I cannot afford to indulge your whims and hunches."

Velmeran looked hurt and betrayed. He had thought that Valthyrra believed in him, even loved him in her way. He was not prepared for her to so quickly judge him a fool and tell him so to his face. But if he was hurt, Consherra was outraged.

"You listen to me, you steel-plated ass!" she declared, approaching the pod menacingly. "His untried and oh-so-inexact talent has already saved you from one incident when your befogged scanners could not tell an independent freighter from a company ship."

Valthyrra considered that. "You are right. Very well, I will make this concession. If a Class M freighter sails past in the next few minutes, then I will scan it as thoroughly as I possibly can. If I detect nothing wrong, then I will permit you to run guard. That way you can be out there in the middle of things, where you might be able to tell us just what is wrong. And when you can explain a little better, then I will listen."

"Good enough," Velmeran agreed. "I think that I can get us out of the trouble that you are determined to get us into. I sent my pack on to the landing bay. I trust that you will have our fighters sent down to the deck."

"It is so ordered," Mayelna said softly, glaring at Valthyrra.

Velmeran turned and walked away without a second glance.

Consherra seemed likely to follow. She hurried to the edge of the upper bridge to watch him until he left through the lift corridor. Then she turned to Valthyrra in raw, unrestrained fury.

"What do you think you are doing?" she demanded. "What could have possibly gotten into your circuits for you to turn against him like that, after all that he has done for you?"

"Now you just wait a moment," Valthyrra returned with equal force. "I cannot for one moment believe that he can see the future. It may be that trying to deal with his frightening new talents has unsettled him. I can only hope that he will recover from these fantasies, but I certainly cannot afford to indulge him."

"Well, you just suit yourself," Consherra replied. "I am going to take Velmeran to another ship as soon as I can arrange it."

"You can do that, and I will be rid of both of you. But I can tell you now that no other ship . . . Oh, dear!" Valthyrra ended ominously. The others looked at her questioningly, but she offered no explanation. Instead her lenses unfocused as her concentration shifted elsewhere. "Velmeran, are you still near a com?"

"I was just getting off the lift," he replied. "So, you finally found that Class M freighter. Will you let her go?"

"No. Not unless we find a good reason. I suppose that I will have to learn the hard way."

"Very well, then. I expected no more."

"Do you still refuse to believe?" Consherra demanded.

Valthyrra turned her camera pod to look at her. "If Velmeran is going to start making predictions, then he is going to have to prove his accuracy before anyone can trust him completely. Even when it means taking a risk."

Part of the reason that Velmeran found such reluctance to his call to let this one go lay in the fact that Starwolves dreamed of catching Class M freighters. These unique vessels were the freight versions of the big colony and passenger ships. They were rich prizes in themselves, for they carried only the cream of the company trade, as well as bringing a healthy ransom.

Velmeran's pack was to fly guard for Barthan. That, in Velmeran's estimation, only complicated matters all the more. Barthan was the youngest pack leader except for Velmeran himself, and he was as well the only pack leader on the Methryn who opposed Velmeran's appointment as Commander-designate. Their enmity, although strong for Kelvessan, was relatively tame by human standards. But it was enough that Barthan would be recklessly eager to prove the younger pilot wrong.

"My scanners detect nothing to cause any concern," Valthyrra reported as the two packs closed on the unsuspecting freighter. "No bombs. No missiles. Not much in the way of rich cargo, either. Barthan, are you willing to go after this thing?"

"Of course," Barthan replied. "I am not concerned with false prophets."

"Just remember that he has not been wrong yet," Valthyrra reminded him.

"You have nothing to worry about," Velmeran answered. "They are going to drop out of starflight and abandon ship the moment you show yourself. You will not have a chance to fire a shot."

Barthan did not answer, since he was already moving in on the freighter's tail. The ship's crew must have been aware of the pursuit, but they did nothing to evade. Instead the big ship began to drop speed quickly, falling out of starflight. That was the age-old gesture of surrender, the crew offering the ship intact in exchange for their lives. Barthan honored the request, falling back slightly from his attack position. Taking a ship intact was a rare and welcome occurrence, but this once Barthan regretted it. He disliked having to see Velmeran's prediction prove true.

"They are giving up without a fight," he reported. "Have the capture ships move in."

"No, let it sit!" Velmeran interrupted. "It is going to explode if we try to move it."

There followed a long, uneasy silence as Valthyrra considered that. The odds were getting uncomfortably high against her now. Velmeran had called it twice in a row on this ship, and it seemed logical to suppose that he really did know what he was talking about. Logic also told her that he could not possibly know. The unavoidable fact that she was ultimately a machine was to her disadvantage in this matter. In the end she could trust only what she could see.

"Velmeran, I am not going to argue with you," she decided at last. "You have given your warning, and that is the limit of your responsibility. I am bringing it in."

"Now I know how Cassandra felt," Velmeran muttered in disgust.

And, like Cassandra, he was ignored to the end. The crew and a fair number of passengers had just escaped in a pair of launches, and now the Methryn's capture ships approached. Two of the curious machines moved in to either side of the silent drive housing, unfolding their three pairs of handling arms to lock themselves tight against the hull. Velmeran remained close the entire time. Valthyrra might have relieved him of responsibility in this matter, but his own conscience had not. The two capture ships, working in unison, used their own engines to accelerate their burden gently back toward the Methryn.

"Clear out!" Velmeran ordered suddenly. "That ship has a sentient computer system, and it is waking up to carry out its final orders. Get away from it now!"

His warning was no longer necessary, for every Starwolf inside the Methryn and out could sense the main generators of the ship as they powered up. A moment later the freighter fired its engines and began to fight the capture ships for control. In spite of their best efforts to turn it away, the freighter began to accelerate straight toward the Methryn.

"Get clear!" Valthyrra ordered. "Get away from that thing so that I can blast it."

The two capture ships needed no warning; their crews had begun the task of casting loose the larger ship the moment they realized they could not control it. One of the capture ships leaped clear immediately, but the second had only just released its hold as the freighter came about to orient on the Methryn. Pinned against the freighter, it slipped down the length of her hull, fending off actual collision with its three pairs of handling arms. Suddenly it was brought up short as one of its arms became firmly trapped in the open hatch of a launch bay. The mechanical arm was too tightly pinned to pull free, and too powerfully constructed to rip loose at its joints.

"Methryn, hold your fire!" the pilot of the capture ship called frantically. "I have an arm caught in something. I cannot pull free."

"Valthyrra, keep your distance from the thing," Velmeran advised. "Try to get it to chase after you. Buy us time. Capture ship, maneuver around to stretch that trapped arm out to its full length. Retract the others out of the way, and stand ready to run."

Velmeran darted in beside the massive drive housing of the

freighter, orienting on the relatively small shape of the pinned capture ship. As he closed, he sighted on the outstretched arm that pinned the capture ship and fired. Bolts from his fighter's cannons bit into the hard metal of the arm, blasting through in an explosion of superheated metal. Velmeran knew that he had run out of time; the freighter had cut acceleration, which meant that it was working its generators to a forced overload. The capture ship shot away as the arm snapped and Velmeran circled around to follow. In the next instant the freighter exploded with a force that would have shattered a small planet.

That blast of raw energy expanded outward in a fiery sphere, for an instant assuming the size and brilliance of a star before it began to dissipate rapidly. With nothing left to feed those flames, it was gone in almost the next instant. The freighter itself had been vaporized in that blast, leaving only a scorched capture ship still running under its own power, and the battered shell of a single fighter. It tumbled end over end, its wings and fins ripped away and its hull cracked and broken, so hot that twisted portions of it glowed dull red.

"Velmeran?" Valthyrra called anxiously.

"Is that him?" Mayelna asked softly, watching the image on the main viewscreen. The entire bridge crew waited motionless and silent for the reply they did not expect to come. That explosion had taken a wolf ship and thrown out only a twisted mass of broken metal, with little chance that anything could have remained alive. Valthyrra knew that Consherra was watching her, silently demanding that she do something, but she did not dare look at the girl.

"Yes, that is him," she answered. "Velmeran, do you hear me?"

"We are going in to get him," the pilot of the undamaged capture ship said.

"Hurry, then," Valthyrra replied. "Velmeran, do you hear me? Help is on the way."

"Will you stop pecking at me, you tin-plated bitch!" Velmeran snapped in return. "I am doing the best I can."

Valthyrra brought her camera pod around so fast the gears creaked. "Meran? Are you alive?"

"I seem to be," he replied. "No damage that I am aware of, but I must have taken my limit of G's."

Mayelna leaned back in her seat and sighed heavily, while Consherra was already running toward the lift that would take her down to the landing bay. Valthyrra watched her go, then brought her camera pod around to look at the Commander.

"You have been very quiet," the ship observed.

Mayelna rolled her seat back from her console, then shrugged as she rose. "What can I say? I had no idea how matters would turn out, so I had to allow it to remain between you and him."

"Do you think that he will forgive me?" Valthyrra asked cautiously.

"Knowing Velmeran as I do, I suspect that he blames only himself in the first place," Mayelna said, pausing on her way to the lift. "I will probably forgive you in a day or two. Consherra is quite another matter. I suspect that she will remain in an unforgiving mood. And you might do well to court her forgiveness, or you may find that she has the power to take him away from you."

The capture ship brought Velmeran's fighter directly into the landing bay and deposited it gently on the deck before passing on out the forward door. Those who saw it brought in could hardly believe that Velmeran could have ridden it through the blast unharmed, for the little ship was nearly ripped apart. It began to smoke lazily as it was brought through the containment field into the atmosphere of the bay; Valthyrra had to direct a blast of icy air at it from a pair of blowers for two minutes before it was cool enough to approach. Only the cockpit area remained reasonably sound, and the windshields, although cracked and glazed, were intact.

As soon as they could, Benthoran, the crew chief, and an assistant moved in to open the ship by simply breaking the canopy free and lifting it away. A good deal of smoke poured out and continued to do so until Benthoran blew it out with a heavy dose of carbon dioxide. When Consherra would have rushed in to aid her mate, Dyenlerra was there first to wave her away. The medic helped Velmeran remove his helmet but indicated for him to remain where he was while she opened his chestplate to attach the leads of a portable medical scanner. The machine needed only a moment to decide that he was sound enough to get out under his own power. The interior of the cockpit was burned out and his suit was badly scorched, his last line of defense against that terrible heat.

Consherra tried to take hold of him as soon as he was out,

only to find that he was still too hot to touch without the gloves that she had left on the bridge. Dyenlerra waved her away a second time and made Velmeran stand beneath one of the cold-air blowers until the damaged suit was cool enough to remove.

Valthyrra had been hovering nearby in the form of one of her remotes. Now she brought the machine in cautiously. "I am sorry, Meran. I should have believed you. I knew at the time that I should have, but the machine in me could not. This is new to me, and I handled it badly."

"That is something of an understatement," Consherra remarked coldly, moving in protectively beside her mate. Dyenlerra, oblivious to all else, was busily checking the joints of Velmeran's armor to see if the suit beneath, which was exposed only at these points, had been penetrated.

"He warned me. I refused to listen," Valthyrra admitted, aiming her remarks at Consherra. "I am not infallible, although I have been around long enough to learn from my mistakes. I will not make that mistake again."

"You may not have a second chance," Consherra said darkly, taking hold of Velmeran's left arms as if to assert her claim on him. "Perhaps another ship will have greater respect for his abilities."

Dyenlerra impatiently slapped her hands away, forcing her to release her hold on Velmeran. "You people can air your grievances later. Just now he is on his way to the medical section for a complete scan."

She physically turned her bemused patient and led him toward the lift. Consherra followed uncertainly; she was well aware that she would not be allowed inside the medic's examination room, but she meant to stay as close as possible. Valthyrra remained where she was, watching, and equally aware that she was not welcome.

"Well, I really screwed it up this time," she said softly. "I have not been in this much trouble since the time Dveyella was going to take him away from me."

"Maybe not," Mayelna said as they turned toward the lift, getting out of the way as the bay crew began to remove the wreckage of the fighter. "Velmeran will not want to leave, and I trust him to say so."

"Why would he not want to leave?" the ship asked bitterly.

"Because you are still the best fighting ship in the wolf fleet, in spite of yourself," the Commander insisted. "He needs you as much as you need him."

"I was not exactly helpful when he needed me this time," the probe's camera pod sagged, the mechanical equivalent of a dejected sigh. "Just now I feel old and useless."

Mayelna glanced at her and smiled. "You know better than that. And, if it is any consolation, I will tell you that he makes me feel very old from time to time."

The medic took Velmeran to a private diagnostic chamber and locked the door, forbidding even Consherra to enter. She cautiously removed him from his scorched armor, sometimes having to force catches that were now reluctant to open, then set her naked and nervous patient on the table and gave him a very thorough examination with her most accurate and sensitive scanners. She was soon satisfied that he was neither burned nor had suffered internally from shock or buffeting. She finished by bringing up a very large and intimidating microscopic scanner and, to Velmeran's astonishment and profound embarrassment, aimed it at the portion of his anatomy that made him most nervous.

"The monitor in your suit controls says that you took a sustained heat of over twenty degrees above body temperature," she explained without looking up. "We can take a surprising extreme of temperatures, even heat, for limited periods of time. But you were in that overheated suit for some time, and too much heat for too long can damage the genetic code you carry, perhaps resulting in sterility."

"Sterility?" he asked cautiously.

"Which, fortunately, you do not have to worry about," she said as she switched off the machine and pushed it out of the way. "At the very most, you might be unable to have a successful mating for several days."

"And there might be some danger of genetic defect?" Velmeran inquired.

"No, of course not. Have you ever heard of a Kelvessan with genetic defects? It cannot happen." She secured the machine in its storage cubby and tossed pants and shirt to her patient. "You recall what happens in cell reproduction? The DNA chain splits in half, and a special molecular machine runs up each half, pulling out amino acids and sticking them in the proper place to form two identical chains. In most natural organisms this little machine occasionally makes mistakes, sticking pieces where they do not belong.

"But our little replicator is smaller than that. It has the ability to check itself. When it finds a mistake, it will either back up and correct it or break the DNA chain to prevent cell division. In our species, an uncorrectable defect results in termination of the pregnancy at the time of conception. After the first few cell divisions, the loss of one or two defective cells at a time has no lasting consequences. Neat trick?"

"I suppose," Velmeran agreed. "They must have thought of everything when they made us."

"Perhaps. There are certain failings in character that could have been corrected genetically, but I have no real objection. If they had tried to make us absolutely perfect, we really would have been machines." She paused and shrugged. "Speaking of conception, Baressa tested out pregnant this morning. She was impressed with your efficiency."

"Efficiency is one of my strong points," Velmeran said as casually as he could, although he did not hide his dismay well. In fact, he was fortunate to be sitting down when he heard that. "Who knows?"

"Well, I do, of course. Consherra knows. I am sure that Valthyrra knows, and Mayelna might."

"That is quite enough. This is supposed to be Baress's child," Velmeran reminded her.

Dyenlerra frowned. "I wish that I could understand your objection. Any other male would be delighted to be in your position."

He shrugged hesitantly. "When . . . when Consherra first came to me, I made a promise—to her, I think, and certainly to myself—that I would never compare her to Dveyella or do anything to make her think that she is not my first choice."

"And this is the simplest way to prove it?" the medic asked. "I guess that I can understand that. But have you ever thought that this is a selfish act on your part? Consherra wants you to mate, and it does not worry her. What does worry her is your refusal. She blames herself."

"Then I have no real choice, do I?" he asked.

"That is for you to decide," Dyenlerra told him.

Consherra herded the entire pack before her, sending them firmly and quickly into the common room that served all their cabins, sparing one hand to pull Velmeran behind her. There were, however, several others besides just the Helm and the nine pack members. Three other pack leaders were there as well: Shayrn, Daeryn, and the redoubtable Baressa. This was clearly a council of war—perhaps even a mutiny. Just yet they were not sure which, and they were waiting for Velmeran to tell them what to do. And, if it seemed that he was still undecided on the matter, Consherra was not.

"Pack your bags!" Consherra told the younger pilots. "We are leaving here as soon as we can if we have to pack a very large dinner and depart in our fighters."

"Wait a moment," Baressa said firmly. "Meran, I stand with you in this. But first I want to know just what did happen out there. As I understand it, you warned Valthyrra of a trap and she ignored you?"

Velmeran shrugged helplessly. "I told her that I could predict the future. Naturally, she found that difficult to believe."

The older pilot looked startled. "Indeed? If I may dare to ask, can you predict the future?"

"He made three predictions in a row, and they all proved true," Consherra answered for him. "He said that we would find a Class M freighter long before it came into scanner range. He said that her crew would abandon the ship intact, and that it would explode."

"Explode?" Daeryn asked.

Velmeran shrugged. "Once it was close enough to get a fix on the Methryn, it drove itself straight at her in the hope of getting close enough to blow itself up in her face."

"With what?" Baressa asked. "A conversion device that large should have scanned."

Velmeran glanced up at the others for the first time, roused from his own thoughts. "There were three conversion devices of tremendous size. Valthyrra saw them, I am sure, but simply assumed them to be the ship's generators. Which they were."

"But generators cannot be made to explode," Baress protested.

"Any generator is a conversion device that can be made to explode," Velmeran said. "Class M's have limited sentience, apparently enough to override their safeties."

"That is so," Baressa agreed. "But where does that leave us? You knew what was going to happen, and Valthyrra ignored you. She is still at fault in this matter, since it could have been avoided."

"I do not know," Velmeran said uncertainly, once again seemingly unaware of the others as he retreated back within his own thoughts. "It might be tempting to hold Valthyrra to blame, but I cannot. Even I could not believe completely until I had proven myself."

"That is still no excuse for her to treat her best pack leader like that," Consherra said hotly. "Any other ship would consider herself very lucky to have Velmeran, and willing to pay him the attention he deserves."

"It is up to Velmeran," Baressa said, gently reminding them of who was the real leader of this group. "If he goes, then I will go with him."

"Me, too!" Shayrn agreed enthusiastically.

"And me," Daeryn added.

Velmeran glanced up, confused, as if suddenly aware of what was going on.

"Wait a moment!" he protested. "Who said anything about taking half the packs on this ship and going anywhere?"

"You did," Shayrn insisted.

"I did?"

"Actually, Consherra is the only one I recall having anything to say on the subject," Baressa said. "What do you have to say?"

"The matter is already resolved, it seems to me," he said. "My ability to predict has been tested and successfully proven, and I came out the hero because I happened to be right. As I see it, I have won and I have already gotten all from it that I can expect. Whether or not Valthyrra and I will ever again be on close terms is beside the point. I am Commander-designate of this ship, and here I must stay."

Baressa shrugged. "How can I argue with that? I cannot believe that today's mistake will be repeated. Just remember that we will always be here when you need us."

At that signal the others withdrew as quietly as they could, the younger pilots retreating to their cabins while the pack leaders departed. Obviously the matter was not completely resolved; Velmeran now had to make his peace with Consherra before he could mend his affairs with the rest of the ship. And Consherra still had a great deal to say on the subject. Taking

Velmeran firmly by the hand, she pulled him inside his own cabin and locked the door behind them.

"Meran, do you really know what you are doing?" she demanded. "I can get you on board another ship, one with greater appreciation for your talents."

"One that would allow me to command and be meekly subservient to my every order?" he asked, seating himself on the bed as he watched Consherra pace nervously. "I cannot leave now. Valthyrra needs me."

"Valthyrra needs to have her circuits checked!" She declared explosively. "And so do you, if you hold any false loyalty to that ancient automaton. You had no business going out there and risking your life. . . ."

"Will you slow down and at least try to be reasonable," Velmeran said with more firmness than he had used with her in a very long time. "I am Velmeran, and this is my decision. Not yours. Not Baressa's. Valthyrra Methryn might have her faults, but she is still the best fighting ship with the best group of pilots in the wolf fleet. This is what I have to do."

"Why?" Consherra insisted, only slightly daunted.

"You know well enough. I want to make an end to this war, and my battles will be fought here, with Donalt Trace. He is looking for the Methryn."

"Well, he can just as easily look for you elsewhere," Consherra said calmly but firmly. "And I would be just as happy if he did not find you. Why do you think he has to be your special problem?"

She paused, surprised to realize that he was sitting on the edge of his bed, crying silent, calm, lethargic tears of desperation and weariness. She realized then just how selfish her own position on this matter had been. Shamed by her own behavior, she hurried to comfort him.

"Meran, what is it?" she asked with gentle anxiety.

"What do you think it is?" he asked in return. "I am tired of it all. I am tired of having to be responsible for every move this ship makes, of being accountable for every life on board. I am tired of always having to be right and watching out for everyone else's mistakes. I am just tired of being me, Velmeran the Magnificent. It never gives me any rest."

"Yes, I suppose you are," Consherra said as she sat down beside him. "There is never any rest for you. But you took this burden upon yourself."

"Yes, I know," he agreed, and sighed in resignation. "I never knew how easy I had it when I was still chafing against my inabilities. And yet, as difficult as it can be, at least my conscience is clear. Ability brings its own responsibility. But I am so tired. And I am afraid."

"Why?" Consherra asked suddenly, glancing at him suspiciously. "Meran, what is wrong? Is there trouble?"

Velmeran hesitated, then nodded wearily. "Yes, terrible trouble. Sometime within the next two weeks the Methryn is going to have to fight something that we have never seen before, and she is not going to win. I will have to do everything I can to save her."

"Meran, no!" Consherra cried, knowing that he had no choice. "Why does it always have to be you?"

"Because this is my game," he answered. "Donalt Trace is looking for me. He is going to use his new toy to rip our carriers apart until I stop him. I have no choice."

Consherra nodded slowly. "I know, and I will help you all that I can. What can I do?"

"Love me," he replied simply. "Help me to forget that I am frightened and alone. That is all you can do for now."

That was a bold request for him, and one which worried him. Always before he had needed love, even longed for it, but he had never asked for what, in his own belief, could only be given freely. But his time was short, and the future he saw frightened him. The Methryn would live, but at the price of a life. And he knew the price. Within the next two weeks he might finally be free of the burden of responsibility, for he would quite likely be dead.

4

Maeken Kea had accepted the command of the Challenger knowing that she did not particularly like the idea, but she did not have time to regret it. By the end of her first shift on the bridge, however, she knew that she both disliked and regretted it. This beast was all ship, a relatively small and superfluous crew, and two captains. No, it was not even a ship, just a mobile planetary defense system. Maeken was smart enough not to be impressed by technology for its own sake; therefore, she was not impressed. If it could fight and defeat a Starwolf carrier, then she would be impressed.

The theory behind this ship was sound, she did have to admit that. The possibility remained that it might just be able to defeat a Starwolf carrier in equal combat. But Commander Trace was after big game: he wanted Velmeran and the Methryn. And Velmeran was too smart for him, smarter even than herself, Trace, and this ship altogether. She knew that Trace meant to force a confrontation with the Methryn, and she had strong doubts about their ability to win that battle.

Marching the halls at a furious pace, Maeken turned onto a main corridor and ran straight into a monster. Since her diminutive human form was no match for this towering hulk of quasi-reptilian flesh, she promptly bounced off and fell on her rump in the middle of the floor. Startled, her first reaction was to reach for her gun. Then she recognized this massive obstruction as a Kelfethki warrior and paused. The massive saurian head cocked inquisitively, the enormous green eyes regarding her.

"Pleesh ekshuz me," the Kalfethki hissed. He reached out with a hand that could have encircled her waist and lifted her as easily as if she were a small pet to be picked up and held.

"And you are?" Maeken demanded as he assisted her to stand. She weighed thirty-eight kilos, while the Kalfethki weighed perhaps three hundred. But authority carried its own weight, and she assumed this talking dinosaur to be part of the crew.

"Ahee am Kramthk, af dee Kalfethki foorze." His reply was prompt enough, if unenlightening. "Eeyu air dee Kapton?"

"Of course," she said less sharply. She did not at all like this talk of a Kalfethki force, but she thought it best to remain on good terms with a potential army of the beasts. "Are you an officer?"

"Hay schmall hwun," Kramthk replied sociably. "Ahee vash up to dee bridgsh to schpeek weth dee Schector Kommandor."

"Very good," Maeken responded promptly, not at all sure what the Kalfethki had said. He stepped carefully aside, opening a passage for her to continue. But she hesitated a moment and looked up at him. "If you would, what is your duty?"

"Ahee am en interpretor," Kramthk replied proudly, flashing a toothy grin.

Maeken only shrugged and continued on. At this point, nothing surprised her.

What was Trace thinking of, bringing a Kalfethki "force" on board this ship? The Kalfethki were a saurian race, higher than true reptiles even though they laid eggs and had no fur, but lower than true mammals despite the fact that they were warm-blooded. They were immense beings, three meters tall and five from their nose to the tip of their powerful thrashing tail. But they remained dull-witted and primitive, still as much animal as intelligent being. Their warrior code and complex religion of demons and prophecies were their only vestiges of civilization, for they possessed few ethical and moral virtues.

It was that fierce warrior code that made them useful as fighters, and yet their worship of a demanding and bloodthirsty god made them too dangerous to keep in useful numbers. One of their many cherished prophecies held that they would someday cleanse the stars of all aliens, murdering entire races for the glory of their god, and they looked forward to that day with eager anticipation. Maeken could imagine the Kalfethki in revolt, having convinced themselves that this unique ship was the divine gift they needed to wage their holy war.

Maeken entered the semicircular area of the bridge, crossing to the raised central portion of the Captain's station. The Challenger's bridge was a vague copy of that of the Starwolf carriers, although there was no middle bridge for helm and weapons officer. She was not surprised to find Donalt Trace in the Captain's seat, only annoyed that the chair had obviously been made to his size. Even as she climbed the steps to the central bridge, he signed some report and returned the board to Lieutenant Skerri, the ship's second-in-command, who hurried on his way.

"Why was a Kalfethki walking down the corridor of this ship?" she demanded unceremoniously.

Trace only shrugged. "To get to the other side?"

Maeken rolled her eyes. "Ho, ho. We are a wit today."

Trace folded his hands behind his head as he leaned back in his seat. "I try to be. Otherwise I would be totally lacking in any social graces. To answer your question, however, the Kalfethki serve this ship as a boarding party."

"Boarding party?" she asked. "Boarding what?"

"Starwolf carriers, if we are fortunate enough to disable and capture one intact," he explained. "We put them in self-contained armor, like Starwolves. And they can carry guns powerful enough to open Starwolf armor. If we link up with a disabled carrier, we send them in quick with most of our sentries as a secondary force."

"And how long will they last?" Maeken inquired. "A carrier holds a crew of two thousand, as well as defensive automatons like their probes."

Trace shrugged, unconcerned. "The carrier's crew will be scattered and disorganized, with wounded and young to protect. And their best fighters, their pilots, will be gone. Against that, I have two thousand Kalfethki warriors, as well as five thousand sentries. And given time, I can also bring in the troop transports."

"Two thousand Kalfethki?" Maeken demanded. "That isn't a boarding party, that's an army! And what do you do if those fanatical dragons decide that your fancy fortress is a present from their great demon-god Harraught?"

"Simple enough," Trace said, always pleased with his ingenuity. "Dead Kalfethki are very easy to control. They are all housed together—alone—in their own section of the ship. Their armor and weapons are sealed under lock in another section. And the computer watches them constantly. If they do get out of hand, we seal off that section and vent their air. Even Starwolves have to breathe."

"Not quite," she pointed out. "They can take ten to fifteen minutes of full vacuum."

"True, but we are not talking about Starwolves. Kalfethki are amazingly tough, but space vacuum rips up their lungs and kills them in seconds. I know. I had it tested."

Maeken tried to betray her surprise at that. Union High Command, of which she was a part, privately subscribed to the belief that all life except their own was of no real worth except in service of the Union. She could not accept that herself, but she had learned to pretend.

"Take over, Kea," Trace said suddenly, rising. "I will be in my cabin."

With that he was gone, marching from the bridge with a

long-legged stride that she would have to run to match. Maeken watched with mild interest. She was sure that, when they had first met, he had still been moving cautiously, even painfully, favoring his reconstructed back. Now he moved with such quickness and grace that he might have never sustained such injuries. Thoughts of revenge were proving to be a strong cure.

Maeken had no sooner situated herself in the oversized seat than she saw Skerri returning quietly to the central bridge. She knew his type well enough, ambitious but not quite smart enough to make his own opportunities, and she knew just how to use him to best advantage. Just now there were two Captains on the bridge, and Skerri wanted to be sure that he was good friends with both. He was kept so busy that he was in danger of falling off his fence.

"Two thousand Kalfethki?" she muttered, as if to herself. That was bait to get the game rolling, and Skerri leaped at it.

"With friends like these, who needs enemies?" he asked jokingly. "I take it that you do not care for the idea?"

"No, but Commander Trace is already aware of that," she answered, always careful that she never said anything that could be quoted against her. "Perhaps I should have asked to go for a ride before I agreed to accept command of this ship. It seems I find something I should have already known every time I look."

"True," Skerri agreed. "But at least you have a choice."

Maeken glanced at him inquiringly. "You did not?"

"Me?" Skerri asked incredulously. "I'm not Union High Command. Like everyone else, I was assigned."

"I see," Maeken commented politely. Then she leaned closer and continued in a soft voice. "What happened to him, anyway? Did Velmeran really shoot him in the back?"

"You had better believe it!" the first mate declared. "That was during the raid on Vannkarn, of course. Trace knew what they were after and went running to stop it, then ran in the other direction when he realized his mistake. You do know of Velmeran?"

"Who doesn't? He led a two-carrier raid in our sector not six months ago and didn't leave a ship in the sky. So he expects to fight Velmeran again?"

Skerri frowned. "We are going outside the Rane Sector and Velmeran's usual hunting grounds, so we are not likely to meet up with him first time. But you can bet that he is going to come running when he learns of this ship. Trace is counting on it."

"Can we beat him?"

"Well, we have a good chance. A Fortress and a Starwolf carrier are supposed to be evenly matched, so it depends upon whether you and Trace can outmaneuver him," Skerri said, and looked at her. "They say that you have fought Starwolves before and won. Can you do it again?"

"That depends, I suppose," Maeken said with exaggerated casualness. "I have never fought Velmeran before, so I cannot say."

"How did you do it before?"

"Trade secret," Maeken said with irritating finality. "I will tell you one secret, however. If you want to advance, you have to collect as many command secrets as you can and hoard them jealously. Have you heard the saying that there must be a secret to doing that?"

"Yes."

"Well, there is. A fair number of secrets, and you need to collect as many as you possibly can."

"I see," Skerri replied seriously, believing every word of it. "But how do I go about getting these secrets?"

"Oh, you get secrets from those who have them," she explained officiously. "Your superior officers have the secrets you want, of course. Be loyal and helpful, and you will be rewarded with a secret or two. Also, secrets can be bought with other secrets. But you have to know the difference between real secrets and gossip. Gossip is fool's gold; it sounds good to other fools, but it has no value to those who know better."

"I see," Skerri said thoughtfully. "How do I learn any secrets?"

"You already have," Maeken assured him. "I just told you the most important secret of all."

"Yes, I see what you mean," Skerri agreed with growing enthusiasm. "Thank you, Captain!"

The first mate hurried off, leaving Maeken to bite her tongue to keep from laughing aloud. But her purpose was accomplished; she had certainly impressed him and won his admiration and loyalty, and he would prove to be a mine of useful information.

"So I ask you, was there ever a ship's Captain smarter than me?" she inquired aloud.

"Not in my experience," a mechanical voice replied promptly.

Maeken glanced up impatiently. "Who asked you?"

"You did, of course," the ship responded in a voice that seemed to hold a note of self-satisfaction. Maeken was wise enough to avoid responding. Controlling people was an easy matter, but a computer was something altogether new. How did one apply psychology to a machine?

Velmeran stirred, waking suddenly but gently. He opened his eyes but saw nothing, for the cabin was completely dark. But other senses told him that he was not alone. Consherra lay wrapped in his arms, her warm body pressed tightly against his own, while he lay in her comforting embrace. Although he could not see her, her face was so close to his own that their small noses touched. He snuggled even closer against her, feeling very comfortable and secure.

When Consherra did not respond, he began to suspect that she slept as well. That surprised him at first, until he considered how worn she must have been from worrying for him . . . and from that first-rate fit she had pitched. He ran his lower hand gently over the firm muscles of her double shoulders, down the bony inward curve of her back and the softness of her rump, then nuzzled her gently and kissed her in the darkness. She stirred, then tightened her own embrace, returning his kiss while running one of her own hands down the tight muscles of his hip and upper thigh.

"Sherry?" Velmeran asked, almost cautiously.

She laughed. "Who did you expect?"

"I am never certain anymore," he teased.

Even though they could not see a thing, Velmeran was sure that Consherra was glaring at him. The long moment of silence that followed was certainly ominous. But, in truth, she was really just amazed at him for saying such a thing.

"Oh, ho! Our good pack leader thinks that he is funny!" she exclaimed in mock sarcasm. "I suppose that you have been making comparisons between me and your duty mates."

"Of course."

"Indeed? And what have you determined?"

"That you are the only one who can make me happy," he said with that peculiar innocence he possessed, assuring her that he made a statement of fact of what would have been simple flattery from anyone else. She nestled closer against him, touched by his sincerity.

"Well, you have better luck with your duty mates," she said as casually as she could. "I have been wondering why we have no child of our own."

"I was not aware that you desired a child," Velmeran said simply. Female Kelvessan found it nearly impossible to conceive if they did not desire it. They could, in essence, practice contraception by force of will. If Consherra was not pregnant after two years, it was only natural to assume that she preferred matters that way.

"For a long time I did not," she answered.

"Then what is the problem?" he asked with frustrating simplicity.

"I just wanted to know if you desired a child. A child that would be your own as much as mine, different from your duty matings. And so your decision as well."

"So? Do you recall the first time you took me to bed two years ago? I knew then that little wolflings could come of it."

"Does that mean yes?"

"If that is what you want," he said, and laughed at himself. "I really do know better than to say 'I want what you want.' But sometimes that is a valid answer, like right now."

"The prospect does not frighten you?" she asked skeptically.

Velmeran laughed again. "You know me well! Of course it frightens me, with my talent for worrying. I worry about the ones that are not even supposed to be mine. Still, the one thing that does frighten me most . . ."

"Yes?"

"That I might turn out to be the type of nagging, overprotective parent my mother is."

Consherra laughed, aware that she was being teased. Velmeran jested about the things that were important to him. She thought that he was privately delighted with the prospect of a child that he could call his own, much to her relief. She pulled the heavy blanket tight about them. Shipboard temperatures were low, uncomfortable by human standards. And the Kelvessan themselves found it a bit chilly when their powerful metabolisms were running low.

"Now?" she asked uncertainly. "I know that it might not be the right time. . . ."

"No, there is no better time than now," Velmeran insisted with sudden urgency. She had reminded him of his own predictions, and especially the part that he had not told her. He knew his duty, that he needed to sire as many little ones as he could in case he did not return. And he wanted to have at least one child by his chosen mate, the child he thought would be most like himself.

"You! Come with me!"

Consherra glanced up from her console, startled, as Dyenlerra ascended the steps to the upper bridge. Consherra knew trouble when she saw it, but she could not imagine what this could be about. Dyenlerra was politically neutral as far as the management of this ship was concerned, and Consherra was herself the only serious troublemaker among the senior officers. Mystified, she hastened to follow.

"Well, what brings you into my domain?" Mayelna asked, equally mystified, as she glanced up from her own console.

"Business, of course," the medic replied promptly. Then she turned to Valthyrra, who had folded her boom to rotate her camera pod around into the upper bridge. "I recall hearing some time ago that you were in need of a visit to an airdock for overhaul. Is that true?"

"Ah well. So it is," the ship admitted regretfully. "I have been planning to make the arrangements soon."

"Make them now, immediately," Dyenlerra ordered sharply. "Consider that a medical order, if you prefer."

"Indeed?" Valthyrra said, at a complete loss. "Since when has my health become a matter for your concern? It is usually Tresha's province as chief engineer to bore me with the details of my decline."

"I am not concerned with your health, you pretentious pile of scrap metal!" Dyenlerra snapped. "I am thinking of Velmeran. He is about to blow a gasket under the stress of his demands. Those months in airdock will give him the freedom to rest."

"Is it that bad?" Mayelna asked.

"Commander, Kelvessan are not easily knocked out of their orbits by anything, but it can happen," the medic explained. "Velmeran is under tremendous pressure, dealing with the responsibilities of command as well as trying to make some sense of his new talents. He is also his own worst enemy, as seriously as he takes his responsibilities, both assumed and real."

"Yes, of course," Mayelna agreed. "I have always thought that he takes too much upon himself, but we are fortunate that he does."

"Well, it is not at all fortunate for him," Dyenlerra declared, and frowned at her own thoughts. "This accident gave me a chance to run a final series of tests on our good Commander-designate, and I was able to confirm something that I have suspected. You see, our race has been in existence for quite some time now, and it is about time for something to happen. Our genes might be protected against deterioration and random mutation, but we are still subject to the forces of evolution. And, while our strongest do not often survive, the practice of taking duty mates has ensured that they do reproduce. . . ."

"Of course!" Valthyrra exclaimed suddenly. "Of course! That is what I have been trying to remember. Deep within me are certain instinctive memories that were given to me when I was first made. One told me to wait and watch for the Dvannan Kelvessan, the High Kelvessan, who will be different from those who have come before. When Velmeran pulled his tele-pathic trick, something had been trying to push that memory to the front of my mind."

Dyenlerra nodded slowly. "Of course. And you would have saved me a fair amount of trouble if you had called up that information when you were supposed to, instead of losing it in that scrap heap of data you call a memory."

Valthyrra's camera pod struck an indignant pose.

"Wait a moment," Mayelna interrupted. "You mean that Vel-meran . . ."

The medic nodded again. "Dvanna Kelvessa. He is not like you or me."

"And just how is he supposed to be different?"

Dyenlerra shrugged. "I am not yet certain of every smallest detail, but we do know the important points. His psychic abili-ties are the most obvious difference. Others are more apparent, once you recognize them as racial differences. Dvannan Kel-vessan are slightly taller and a good deal stronger than the old model. The indication is that they are smarter in certain ways. And they live longer. Our life expectancy has increased from three hundred to three hundred and fifty years. I am sure that Velmeran, barring accident, will live to see three or four thousand—the Aldessan live thirty-five hundred. But his regenerative powers are such that he may be functionally immortal."

"My Velmeran?" Consherra and Mayelna asked at the same time, and glanced at each other.

"Yes, our Velmeran," the medic continued. "Also, early Kelvessan did not look that different from modern humans. Now we are very hard to mistake for human. The High Kelvessan, although very good-looking by our standards, are diverging even more. The elfin qualities are taking on a curious feral appearance. His eyes are larger, and his skull is elongated. Humans have their brains mostly above their eyes, and high foreheads. Our brains are retreating somewhat behind our faces, the way the Aldessan or Feldenneh are. Our brain shapes are changing: our areas are becoming more compact and efficient. I wish that I had kept Dveyella for autopsy."

"She was Dvanna Kelvessa?" Valthyrra asked.

"Certainly. Dvanna Kelvessa have been around for nearly a hundred years now. Velmeran is just so unique that his differences cannot be overlooked. I have already positively identified five others on this ship. That oldest duty child of his certainly is. Baress is Dvanna Kelvessa, as his sister was. As well as the twins Tregloran and Ferryn. However, their mother Baressa is not."

"Who is the fifth?" Consherra asked.

"You are, of course," Dyenlerra said, confirming her suspicions. "The rule, with no exceptions that I have yet seen, is that High Kelvessan are natural telepaths. There are also readings on the medical scanners that cannot be denied. And, as I indicated, you can tell by sight once you know what to look for."

"Then, if our race is beginning a transition period, how long will it take for the Dvannan Kelvessan to replace the old ones?" Mayelna asked.

"The process should proceed fairly quickly now," Dyenlerra explained. "You see, they have the genetic advantage. A mating of the old and new always produces a child of the new variety, never one of the old or even a half-breed."

She paused, for everyone was watching Consherra closely, for the first officer was preoccupied with feeling the shape of her skull. She found it rather unsettling to be told that she was something other than she had always believed herself to be. It made her feel very alien and alone, and she could well imagine how Velmeran was going to react to this; he felt alien and alone as it was.

"Shall I send for a mirror?" the medic asked. "Dear girl, you are not going to turn into a Faldennye."

"Besides, what do you have to complain about?" Mayelna asked. "I feel like an obsolete model, out-of-date technology."

"Returning to the matter of Velmeran," Dyenlerra reminded them. "He needs our help more than ever just now. To begin with, our other telepaths need to develop their own talents. Velmeran needs Kelvessan he can relate to on his own level. Velmeran did tell me that you are the most promising psychic on this ship."

"Yes, although a child compared to him," Consherra admitted. "Tregloran is a better pure telepath, but he has less luck with related talents."

"He also needs to be trained by someone who knows what they are doing, which means the Aldessan of Valtrys," Dyenlerra continued. "If Valthyrra would be good enough to call Home Base and have them pass the word, I have no doubt that they would send someone out in a hurry to take over his training. And a few months in airdock would be the perfect time for that."

"Unfortunately, it will have to wait a while longer," Consherra said dourly. "There has been another prediction."

Valthyrra's camera pod snapped around to face her. "Now what?"

"He said that he is going to have to fight Donalt Trace again. He said that the Methryn is going to fight something that we have never seen, and Valthyrra is not going to win. He said that he will have to fight hard to save her."

"And why does it have to be his problem?" Dyenlerra demanded.

"He said that if he does not fight it now, then it will destroy other carriers until he does," Consherra answered. "I do not like it either. But if his foreseeing is true—and I certainly hope that no one cares to dispute it—then we have no choice."

"I have no problem with that," the ship replied. "I simply applied a little old-fashioned logic to the problem."

"How is that?" Mayelna asked suspiciously.

"Well, the problem arose from the basic assumption that it is impossible to predict the future," she explained proudly. "But I have observed that Velmeran can indeed predict the future. Therefore, Velmeran can do the impossible."

The others stared at her in astonishment.

"There are certain inherent fallacies in your logic," Mayelna said. "But if it makes you happy, then I am not about to argue. Consherra, when is this supposed to happen?"

"Sometime in the next two weeks. Velmeran indicated that we will be called first. Trace will catch another carrier first and thrash it soundly."

"Wonderful," Mayelna said sourly. "That implies that it will not even be in this sector. At least he can have as much vacation as time allows. Valthyrra Methryn, where is the nearest likely port?"

"Kanis?" she asked after a moment's consideration. "I can be there in three days."

"Good enough."

For once in her career as the Commander of the Methryn, Mayelna did not try to look busy when someone entered her private office. She had always thought that she should look busy, as if to impress upon others that she really did serve a vital function on this ship. But not for Velmeran, certainly not this time.

"I am not disturbing you?" Velmeran asked apprehensively, glancing about the room as she let him in.

"No, of course not," she insisted, directing him toward a chair before her desk. "I asked you here."

Velmeran nodded absently as he seated himself. "I guess you heard that there is trouble."

"Yes, Consherra told us everything you told her," Mayelna said as she took her seat behind the desk.

"And you believe me?" he asked fearfully.

"Yes, we believe you," she assured him. "All of us. Do you know where and when this will happen?"

"No, not with any certainty. It will be soon, and in another sector. We must go to him when he makes the first move."

"The first move?" Mayelna asked. "Will we lose a ship to him just to learn what he is planning?"

"No, I am sure of that. He will fight Starwolves and win. But they will flee. And they will call for me. Until then, I can only wait."

"And until he reveals his schemes, would you prefer to do your waiting on extended port leave?"

"Kanis?" he asked immediately.

"How did . . . ?" Mayelna paused, and shook her head. "I should not have to ask. We will be there in three days. You can go down immediately, and then forget that you are a Starwolf until you are called away."

Velmeran leaned back in his chair, his arms folded on his chest. "There are times when I wish that I could forget. But it is a very difficult thing to ignore."

"No, not really," Mayelna said. "Have you never pretended to be human on port leave?"

"Human?" he asked in disbelief. "How could I possibly pass myself off as human?"

"Look at this." Mayelna pulled a photograph from a drawer of her desk and handed it to him. Velmeran recognized it as his mother only because he had been forewarned; in those days of mutant stock, it might have been a human girl of some divergent race. Her lower set of arms were obviously folded behind her back and hidden within the folds of a heavy cape, drawn around her upper shoulders. The dark color and heavy material of her clothes helped to hide any revealing shadows, while a hat disguised the fact that her ears were large, pointed, and not even in the right place. There was nothing that she could do about her immense eyes and tiny nose, but those features were not as noticeable as he thought they would be.

"When others look at Starwolves, all they ever see is the armor," Mayelna explained. "Take away that and the second set of arms and they do not know what they are looking at."

"Amazing," Velmeran agreed as he handed back the photograph. "But I do not think I want to play such a game."

Mayelna shrugged. "I was only suggesting a diversion. Once this battle is done, you will have all the rest you want. Valthyrra is taking herself into airdock for an overhaul."

Velmeran paused a moment, and nodded slowly. "Yes, then I can rest. But Valthyrra will have no choice in the matter. After Trace is finished with her, she is going to need more than an overhaul."

"That sounds ominous."

"That is no prediction, but a statement of fact," he said. "She cannot fight this thing without getting a few dents in her nose.

But I would not tell her that, since she will not refuse this fight."

"No, I imagine not," Mayelna agreed, and frowned. "Did Dyenlerra talk to you? About what you are?"

"Yes, she did."

"And it does not bother you?" she asked cautiously.

"Bother me?" Velmeran asked. "It comes as something of a relief. Now I feel that I am exactly what I was supposed to be, rather than some type of freak. But I also feel very different from everyone I have ever known."

"Not everyone," Mayelna reminded him. "Do not forget that Consherra is like you, and she will always be with you."

Velmeran smiled. "I do not believe that I could ever forget that. She will make certain of it."

5

Among the most ancient legends of the Faldenneh there exists the story of the creation of life. In the earliest days there was just the universe itself, the stars and the empty worlds, and the gods knew a happy existence, free from worry and concern. But in time they came to think that they were lacking something, and so they created all life so that they might have something to worry and care for. It was not long before they realized their mistake.

Somehow that story came to mind while Velmeran was preparing for port leave. He was beginning to appreciate a few universal rules that governs all life. On the whole, life is a complicated, disagreeable, and largely disillusioning affair, not at all what it was made out to be. And yet all creatures cling desperately to life, perhaps because the alternative appears less attractive. Just now complication was the key feature in his own life. He had no real desire to take port leave, but he could not refuse.

Standing in his cabin, Velmeran moved his arms around to

check the articulation of his new suit. Since he was also the leader of the Methryn's resident special tactics team, Valthyrra had been very careful about the manufacture of his suit. Consherra, standing nearby, nodded thoughtfully.

"Good enough," she said, and retrieved the helmet. "You recall the operation of the new features."

Since the chestplate was still open, Velmeran looked down into the folded-down mirror at the controls. Valthyrra had incorporated two special features into his suit. One was a two-way system that allowed him to hear and speak with those outside while his helmet was on. The other was a control device that, when activated, gradually equalized pressure within the suit with that outside. Sudden pressure changes caused a temporary muffling of his acute hearing; during his last raid, he had nearly been shot by a mechanical sentry he should have heard.

"Everything works fine," he assured her. "Are you certain that you will not come with me?"

Consherra shook her head sadly. "I cannot. We will be getting the Methryn battle-ready. Any advice?"

"Yes, two things. Do not take anything apart that will take more than an hour to put back together again. That is all the warning we will get."

"That is understandable," she agreed. "What else?"

"Make certain that the conversion cannon is ready for firing."

Consherra paused, startled. The Methryn's conversion cannon possessed the destructive potential to reduce the planet below them to dust. Valthyrra had never fired the cannon in actual battle, since there was rarely any need for such power. If Velmeran planned to use this weapon, then he expected a battle such as the Starwolves had not seen since the ancient days.

"Yes, it will come to that." Velmeran knew well enough what she was thinking. "We will be facing something quite capable of destroying us if we are careless or unlucky."

"I will keep that in mind," she promised. "And you watch out for yourself while you are down there."

"I will. Without you to keep me company, I will probably be too bored and lonely to get into trouble."

Velmeran hurried down to the landing bay, where he knew that his pack members would be waiting impatiently. They were already in their ships and ready to fly, and he dashed to his own. But he slowed as he neared the centermost of the nine fighters, savoring his first look at his new ship. It radiated newness in the deep matte black of its finish, unscratched by debris and handling and unfaded by cannon flash, hot engines, or the extremes of space.

Velmeran took his pack out of the bay and, without warning, led them on a wild chase as he tested out his new fighter, defying them to keep pace with him. They were real pilots now, far from the mere students they had been only two years earlier. They were the best pack on the Methryn by far, perhaps the best pack in the entire wolf fleet.

Although he knew that his days might well be short, this was not a time of sad reflection on what might have been. He was content with what he had accomplished; he would have said at peace, but that suggested a stoic but resigned surrender to one's fate. He was by no means ready to surrender; his fate was not sealed and he meant to fight for his own life as hard as he fought for the Methryn. But in his own order of priorities, the Methryn had to come first.

Velmeran knew that he could save his ship, but saving his own life in the process was problematical. He looked upon his apparent ability to glimpse the future as a method of forewarning, not a pronouncement of inescapable fate. There were always alternatives, and most of his forewarnings were self-defeating because they revealed those alternatives. Just because he had not yet seen those alternatives did not mean that they did not exist.

Such thoughts occupied his mind for the flight down to the port, but his first look at the mountainous landscape rising swiftly beneath him chased away such brooding thoughts. Kanis was a second home for the Starwolves. In terms of their balance of power, Kanis was Starwolf property, one of several worlds deep within Union space that enjoyed the freedom and independence that Starwolf protection brought. In practice, Kanis was an independent world, an empire self-contained in its own system, self-governed and free of the economic tyrany of the trade companies. Its governing council did treat with the Union as one nation dealt with another, making trade concessions and treaties. Small allowances, but it kept the Union placated.

Still, no one doubted that the Union would arrive in force if the Starwolves relaxed their voluntary protection. In return for this service, Kanis was a strong supporter of the Starwolves. The Kelvessan enjoyed port leaves here such as they seldom knew, free from danger and at liberty to be their true selves, not their carefully maintained image of armored death.

Kanis itself obliged by being climatically ideal for the physical requirements of the Kelvessan. Most of its two major continents were extremely mountainous and situated in thick bands just below the polar seas. Thus the climate was cool at best, the summers short and pleasant and the winters long and harsh. The native population had been there long enough to adapt somewhat to the adverse climate, and they found it no hardship. For Starwolves, Kanis was something of a paradise, one of the very few inhabited worlds where it was both safe and practical for them to come out of their armored shells.

Kanis remained a frontier world, very sparsely populated, lacking in vast reserves of natural resources that would attract settlers and industry. Most of the natives were "Rangers," keeping vast herds of langies—indigenous beasts of vast size, sharp wit, and evil temper—in the high mountain plains. Langie wool was a luxury item throughout the Union, so high in demand that trade companies argued among themselves for a share of the limited market. The wool was so profitable that the animals were seldom slaughtered, although a good langie hide was nearly worth its weight in gold. "Ranging" was a harsh life for the natives, but rewarding.

Velmeran brought his pack down in the port field—such as there was. Kallenes was the only port, and even it saw little traffic except in late spring when scores of company freighters would descend upon it for their share of the thousands of bales of langie wool brought in from the highlands. Otherwise there was one ship in port at most, importing machines and luxury goods the Kanians could well afford.

The main business district was near the port, for the convenience of the members of ship's crew and for the rangers who came into port to sell their wool. The main part of the shopping district was the Mall, several blocks of the port's best shops and restaurants that had been enclosed under a protective roof. It made no pretensions toward the domed cities of the inner worlds, a crude frontier flattery of the wealth at the Union's heart. A simple wooden platform on heavy posts stretched between the roofs of the buildings. No attempt was made to enclose a warm, comfortable environment beneath. It was meant only to keep away the worst of the local weather, the harsh winds and volumes of snow that fell more than half the year.

Indeed, there had been a serious attempt to preserve the frontier appearance within the Mall, for Kanis could afford better. The shop fronts were dressed out in rough-cut wood and large windows of framed glass, while the narrow streets were paved in brick, stone, and planks of seasoned wood. Velmeran was not certain just who the natives were trying to impress with this touristlike atmosphere where there were no tourists, although his own suspicion was that they simply preferred things this way.

Velmeran first took his pack to a local jeweler, where they could sell the pieces of jewelry they received as pay for local money. Their business concluded, he dismissed his pilots to enjoy their port leave as they desired. The Mall was large enough to swallow up an entire ship's portion of pilots so well that a glimpse of black armor became rare, and he wanted to be alone. Or so he thought, until he looked around and wondered what he was actually going to do with his port leave. If this was how he proposed to spend what might be the last days of his life, he would be better off to return to the ship, retire to his cabin, and read Shakespeare. Or Kipling, for all the good this did him.

Still pondering this problem, Velmeran began to walk slowly down the street, peering inside each shop as he passed. There were few people in the narrow streets; with winter coming, the rangers had long since returned to the highlands. Even beneath the protective canopy, the morning air was sharply frigid. After only a moment he came upon a tailor's shop, an oddity that was more than enough to distract him. He knew what a tailor was, but he had thought that such an occupation had long since ceased to exist.

What captivated his interest even more was the fact that the tailor was a Feldennye, for that defied all reason. The Feldennye were a canine race, in appearance not unlike large wolves walking on their hind legs. Since they wore no clothes except for their own natural fur coats, it was unimaginable that one would choose such a profession. The Feldennye saw his staring and hurried to open the door.

"Is there something I can do for you?" he asked eagerly in a thick accent that indicated that he had come from a Feldenneh colony.

"Surely not, I suppose," Velmeran replied. "I could wear nothing of yours."

"Oh, there you are wrong!" the tailor insisted, surprising Velmeran again by taking him by the hand and pulling him into the shop. No one dared to touch a Starwolf, but Velmeran was so bemused that he went along willingly.

The interior of the shop was in keeping with the rustic appearance of the Mall. The floor was crude wooden planks and the interior walls were paneled with polished wood. The lights overhead hung from iron chains and the counter and other furnishings were constructed from real wood. But there was nothing simple about the merchant's wares. Velmeran saw from the first that, while the tailor might undertake special orders here in his shop, he sold for the most part the very best this world had to offer. Most of the clothes were of the extreme of the local fashion, almost a native costume. The rest were less distinctive, reflecting off-world tastes.

"It happened that I was approached by a Starwolf several months ago," the tailor explained as he stopped before a small rack in a remote corner of the room. "He asked me for clothes, shirt and pants, such as he could wear on port leave. I made him a set, all very fine, and he was most pleased. Then I made another, thinking that he or another might come back.

"I am a merchant, Starlord, and I cannot afford to have clothes on my rack that I cannot sell. And when I saw you, I thought that you might be tall enough to wear those clothes. Of the tags that you see, you may take away half."

"That is generous," Velmeran agreed. "But I do not know what I would do with such clothes."

"Ah, but look at these!" the tailor declared proudly as he pulled the tunic and pants from the rack. The tunic was soft velvet, the pants of some hardier material that Velmeran did not recognize. Both had been dyed to a color that matched perfectly, a violet so deep that it graduated into black in the shadows of the folds.

"Surely you do not have clothes such as these," the tailor insisted. "These are real clothes, not the armored suits that you hide yourselves in or the half-uniforms that I see. Surely there are times when you are not a Starwolf, just yourself. Clothes like these would be for such times."

This furry merchant knew all the right words, Velmeran had to admit. His own thoughts were on the photograph that Mayelna had shown him, how easy it really was to make a Kelvessan into something that might just pass as human. The old fantasy, so long pushed aside for more important matters, began to stir. Just once in his life, even for only a very short time, he would like to pretend.

"Try it on, at least," the tailor urged, his eyes seeming to glow with hope. "If it does not fit, that question at least is answered."

Unfortunately, it fit perfectly. The tailor must have known, judging with an experienced eye that had not been confounded by armor. And he must have known as well that, once inside those clothes, his client would not be able to part with them. Velmeran emerged from the changing room, looking for a mirror.

That did not show him anything that he had not seen before; it was still Velmeran, even if the clothes were richer than he had ever known. But the costume was not yet complete. The tailor came up with a pair of low half-boots, having trouble finding a pair small enough, and a matching belt. A dress cape, deep black, was wrapped around his upper shoulders and hung down just below his rump. Since the main part of his body was rather small for his height, it was too large for him. He folded his lower arms behind his back, adjusting the folds of the cape to hide them.

"Ah, good!" the tailor crowed with delight as he beheld the vision. "You would play at being human? It is often done, and no one knows but me."

"I had considered it," Velmeran admitted cautiously, wondering if he really did dare to do such a thing. "I will have to do something about my ears. Do you have a hat?"

"No, not the type you would need." The Feldennye paused a moment to consider the problem. "I think that braids would look best on you anyway."

"Braids?"

"Yes, let me show." Taking a brush, he parted Velmeran's long, thick hair down the middle and deftly tied it on either side into thick, loose braids. Gold clips from under the counter tied off the ends, with the last ten centimeters left free and brushed into thick, plushy tufts. His heavy bangs, too short to be brought into the braids, remained in front. Although the braiding started low, it still brought a thick curtain of hair down over each of his ears. Velmeran rather liked the effect, lending him a rather handsome barbarian look. The Feldennye obviously knew what he was doing.

"This will do for you," the tailor said. "Everything else you wear will be the same half off, because you are a Starwolf. Also, I have a little closet in back that I keep for Starwolves. You may put your armor inside, lock the door, and keep the key until you return. Is that fair?"

In the end he did as the tailor suggested, leaving his armor locked in the closet while he went out into the city wearing his new clothes. And he would not have been less ill at ease if he had been naked, since that was exactly how he felt. He still wore both his guns, hidden beneath his cape, but he was without the protection of his armor. He could only think how every loyal Unioner wished him dead, and a few would be willing to try their best at making that a reality. He hoped that his special senses would keep him safe.

When he stepped out of the tailor's shop, however, he found that no one seemed to notice. He hardly resembled the tall, rugged natives, but he could pass as a member of some mutant branch of the race. Encouraged by the fact that he was completely ignored, he started down the street to his right. The morning air was chill enough to be comfortable, although he wondered how he would be able to endure the heated shops. If he did give himself away, he reflected, it would be from passing out from the heat.

Once again he did not make it very far. Two doors down from the tailor, in a corner shop, was an art gallery. Being a casual artist himself, he stepped inside for a quick look. He paused at the door as a blast of hot air struck him. At least there was no one in the front of the shop, although he could hear voices in the back. He looked about briefly but soon decided that most of what he saw was just tourist fodder and investments for healthy collectors, and he was not particularly impressed.

He was about to leave when something curious caught his eyes. It was a landscape much like any other, a deep glacial valley with a high, rocky peak in the background. It was definitely a painting, not a photograph. But as he watched, much to his surprise, a dark band of clouds began to rise behind the mountains, sweeping over the ridge to obscure it behind a white veil of falling snow.

"Like it, do you?"

Velmeran nearly jumped out of his new clothes at the sound of a voice immediately behind him. A human girl stood there, watching him with the same expectant stare the tailor had employed when anticipating a sale. Dressed in a stylized version of the local costume, she was small and slim, slightly taller than himself with a slender, bony build that was best described as lean and gawky. She was definitely not a child of the highlands but, curiously enough, of Trader stock. A small nose and large eyes peered out beneath a long, full mane of brown hair. From a distance, she might have passed for another Kelvessan in disguise.

"Have you ever seen the like of this?" she continued. She might look like a Trader, but she spoke with the thick, rolling local brogue. "All the rage, it is, in the inner worlds. The frame, you see, is actually a flat-screen monitor. Down here is the computer and disk drive that runs it. The artist assembles the work from a fixed feature, the subject itself, and a series of variables. The variables exist in groups; in this case time of day, season of the year, and weather. You can set it to run in sequence, or the computer selects variables at random. And with multiple drives, you can also alternate several different works over a period of time. The hard microdisks will last forever."

"And you sell the disks as you would prints?" he asked.

"Exactly so. You put out, say, fifty to a thousand disks of each work, each one with a certificate of authenticity. So what do you think?"

Velmeran shrugged. "It is very interesting, but still just a toy."

"Sure, but it is!" the girl declared, laughing. "But collectors are paying a lot for these toys just now. But then, that's all art has ever been to most collectors anyway."

Velmeran laughed at the obvious scorn in her voice. "You must be the artist."

"And you obviously are not a collector," she said in return, and nodded politely. "Lenna Makayen."

"Er . . . Rachmaninoff. Sergei Rachmaninoff." Unprepared for that question, he had to think fast . . . and he could have done better."

"So, what brings you to a place like this, anyway?"

"Business, of course."

"Business?" she asked. "You're not a wool merchant, that's for certain. What other kind of business would bring you to this hole?"

"I am in . . . salvage and redistribution, you might say," he replied cautiously. "I am just passing through . . . on business."

"And how long will you be here, do you suppose?"

"Now that I cannot say. I will just have to wait and see."

"Wait and see when the Starwolves are ready to move on?" Lenna asked sharply. "Salvage and redistribution indeed! You manage their loot for them, don't you? You're a Trader, aren't you?"

Velmeran smiled. "How did you guess?"

"My mother was of the Traders," she explained proudly. "I've got her looks. And you look like me, only more so, if you take my meaning. Traders are small and tough, with big eyes and small noses. You stand about five feet tall, as they say locally, about a hundred and fifty meters tall, and I'm not two centimeters taller. Not quite human, they say. So, what will you be doing until the Starwolves move off again?"

"I do not really know," he admitted. "Just waiting."

"Then you can wait with me," Lenna said decisively. "My buyer has been in port, and he payed me a small fortune, so I was going to celebrate. Come along and I'll buy you a beer."

They were outside and marching down the street at a furious pace before Velmeran knew what was going on. Lenna's energy and enthusiasm was a bit overpowering for a sedate Kelvessan; she made even the extroverted Consherra seem quiet and shy. Still, Velmeran thought that he might go along with it. There was something of a challenge to it; he wondered how long he could keep up this game without giving himself away. He also wondered what Lenna's reaction would be to discovering that she was flirting so energetically with a Starwolf.

"You would be hard-pressed to entertain yourself two days in this place, much less two weeks," Lenna continued briskly. "You need someone to show you around. What do you say?"

"I might agree," Velmeran replied. "If you tell me what happened to your accent."

"Ah, but my local tongue's just to show my clients," she said, the accent back and thicker than ever. "Said I was of Trader stock. Born and bred on a freighter, so I was. But I've lived here half of my twenty-five years."

He resorted to a fairly standard question. "Do you enjoy your work?"

"The truth is, I fly a freight shuttle for the Trade Association, and I love flying too well to give it up. I'd leave here in an instant to go back to the Traders, but that isn't likely."

"Why not?"

"No formal training," she said bitterly. "My father saw to that."

Before Velmeran could question that, Lenna directed him into a small restaurant, hardly more than an indoor café, and sat him at a table by the front window while she went to get drinks for the two of them.

"My father was local," she began as she sat down. "But he had no land and no herd, and there's not much else you can do in this place. But our treaty allows us to hire on in their military as civilian technicians. Got his training that way, in drive mechanics. He stayed with them four years, then came back here, married, and had a son. But the money he'd saved soon ran out and his first wife left him. Then it happened that an independent freighter came in and got stranded at port for want of repairs her crew could not do, so he fixed her up. Being Kanian, he could take G's better than most, so they gave him a contract. Soon it looked like he was settled in to stay.

"Then, one day, their ship was rammed by a tender as they were coming in to station. Damage was slight, but my mother was gone. And my father was very bitter about it. He flew back here and did his best to forget about space . . . which was hard enough with me around, looking like a Trader. I was too young to understand, and it seemed to me like he brought me here just to make me miserable. Especially once my older brother came to live with us."

"You could get the training you needed, just like your father did," he suggested hopefully.

Lenna shook her head sadly. "You have to be twenty-one to get Union training, but you can't travel off-world without parental permission until you are twenty-one. Naturally, my father wouldn't sign. I did get flight training locally, enough to convince the Trade Association to hire me on as an apprentice for a year until the old pilot retired."

"Surely your father's old texts . . . ?"

"Do you really think my father kept his books?" she asked. "I was able to get the texts for helm and navigation, and I taught myself. I know enough to get a ship from here to there. I'm certainly ready for an apprenticeship on a Trader."

Velmeran pointedly refused to answer that, for he knew only

too well what she was asking him. She thought him to be a Trader; in his rich dress and manner, perhaps a senior officer or even a Captain. She was desperate, and she hoped that he would give her what she wanted. And Velmeran felt guilty, since there was little he could do to help her.

"Treck is back in town," someone behind him said suddenly.

Velmeran had no idea what that could mean, but Lenna obviously did. Her eyes widened and her face turned from lightly tan to chalky white. Whatever else it might mean, it was obviously a threat and intended as one.

"So what's that to me?" Lenna demanded.

A pair of rangers, fresh from the highlands, appeared from behind Velmeran to stand at either side of the table. They were young and a matched pair of second-rate bullies, the one to his left short, stocky, and stupid, while the other, the speaker, was tall and lean. They were ragged, dirty, and fairly rank. Kelvessan had no sense of smell, but he could guess that part. But they must have something of a reputation, judging by the way the rest of the patrons were slowly retreating.

"You know the answer to that," the tall one said, sneering. "Treck Lesries has put his name on you, and he doesn't like for his girls to run around on him."

"I'm not afraid of Treck Lesries," Lenna declared.

"No, I'm sure you're not. It's your little friend here who'll get his neck broke," the tall one said, his threat now aimed at Velmeran. He put a hand on the Starwolf's shoulder and did his best to knead the muscle painfully.

Velmeran reached up and took hold of the offending wrist, applying pressure until both bones snapped loudly. The tall ranger gasped in pain and sank to his knees, for Velmeran did not let go. "If you are Treck Lesries's messenger, then you can take him this message. Tell him to get out of town."

"Lesries can take care of you!" the ranger threatened, his voice sharp with pain. "He's half Starwolf, you know."

Velmeran laughed aloud. "Do not be a complete idiot! No one can be half Starwolf."

"He'll show you what he can do!" the other squealed.

Velmeran laughed again. "I have enemies that make your Treck Lesries seem like a child. Now go."

He squeezed the wrist until the ranger screamed in pain, then gave him a shove. The stocky ranger caught him, him under the arms to half carry his friend, nearly fa pain, toward the door. Velmeran watched them until they were gone, then saw that Lenna was staring at him.

"Do not be afraid of me," he said. "I might not hesitate to use violence, but only against those who ask for it."

"You broke his damned wrist," Lenna muttered in open awe. "You took hold of it and it snapped. Sergei, you've got to get out of here. Treck won't take it well, not at all. He'll kill you when he finds you."

"Would you explain what this is all about?" Velmeran said firmly. "Why is a murderer like Treck Lesries and his misfits allowed to walk around free?"

"Oh, Lesries is a Unioner," she explained. "Commando-trained in their military, trained to kill. Union supposedly gave him permission to settle here, but he's still Union. On detached duty, as we see it, here to stir up all the trouble he can. Our treaty says that we can't touch him, and every time we file a complaint they say we have no evidence. Him and his lackeys earn their bread and beer by poaching; they sell langie pelts on the black market. Several times a year we find a ranger dead, his neck broken, and nothing left of his herd but skinned carcasses. That's his trick. He breaks your neck with one swift kick. He's done that to about five of our boys here in town."

Velmeran frowned. "What is this business about your being his girl? You seem to think otherwise."

Lenna nearly spat in anger. "He thinks he's a stud! He names certain girls to be his own, and if anyone goes near them he breaks their neck. He's not touched me yet, but he will come for me eventually. What happens then, I don't know."

"What do you mean?"

She frowned regretfully. "My brother, Iyan, he's port police, and he hates Lesries with a passion. If Lesries does touch me, Iyan will go after him. Either he'll kill him and get himself into trouble, or get himself killed. But first I'll see what my Trader's strength and a few of my brother's tricks can do against that kicking idiot."

"You have nothing to worry about now," Velmeran assured her gently. "I will take care of Lesries before I leave."

Lenna stared at him. "Sergei, this isn't your problem."

"It is now," he said. "Lenna, I am not a Trader like you now. I have fought the Union all my life. I have killed before, I will again. And I can certainly handle this Unioner. Getting rid of him is one loose end I can tie up while I am waiting for more important matters."

"You mean to kill him?" she asked.

"He means to kill me. Besides, if he is pretending to be half Starwolf, I owe it to him. Most of my friends are Starwolves. How did he come up with that, anyway?"

"He's a heavy worlder," Lenna explained. "Growing up in two and a half G's left him as strong as a bull langie."

Velmeran laughed. "Charming fellow! I believe that we should just wander around until your friend does make his appearance. Then we will really celebrate."

6

Velmeran forgot all about the matter of Treck Lesries after the first hour. As the Kanians already suspected, Lesries was no doubt a Union agent, not so much a spy or subversive as an embarrassment and a nuisance. He was a wolf in the fold, and the Kanians were unable to protect themselves from him for fear of creating an incident with the Union. The only "safe" way to remove this annoyance was for him to provoke a fatal incident with a Starwolf . . . and Velmeran was the perfect bait for that trap, a Starwolf in sheep's clothing.

He was still unsure of just where he stood with Lenna Makayen. She was quietly but obviously in awe of him for how easily he had dealt with Lesries's henchmen and his apparent disdain for their leader; he suspected that, in spite of her initial interest in him, she had also dismissed him as the skinny little off-worlder he appeared to be. Whether she was conscious of it or not, she did see him as the key to getting what she had always wanted. Either she was mercenary enough to try to seduce him, or else she was trying to force herself to love him because she thought she should.

Later that night, after they had taken in several hours of music at a Ranger pub, Lenna suggested that they should spend the night together at the port inn. Velmeran skillfully maneu-vered his way out of that one, explaining that he had to report back to his ship for the night. Lenna arranged to meet him for late breakfast at the same restaurant; she had downed enough of the local beer to know that she would not be able to drag out very early. Velmeran desperately needed a few hours to himself. For one thing, he needed to eat; he had been dining on portions suitable for a human his size, which was hardly adequate. He did need to check on the members of his pack. And he simply needed a rest from Lenna's dauntless exuberance.

By morning Velmeran clearly sensed that this would be his last full day of port leave. He arrived at the appointed meeting place well ahead of time to give himself an early start on that late breakfast, in the hope that two breakfasts and one lunch would be enough to last him until night. He had just finished when he became aware that trouble had arrived.

"I got your message, little one," someone said behind him, someone who lacked the thick native accent. Velmeran rose calmly and turned to face his enemy. The first thing the Kel-vessa saw was a chest and shoulders at least twice as broad as his own. Lesries had the hard looks to match his reputation, with a high, hooked nose and small, penetrating eyes made all the harder by a perpetual squint.

Treck, seeing his own adversary more clearly, laughed scorn-fully. "You are a little fellow, aren't you? No matter. You know who I am?"

"I know what you are not," Velmeran answered calmly.

"And what's that?"

"You are not half Starwolf, since there is no such thing. And you are not going to leave this place alive."

Treck laughed again. "My brave little man! And what are you that you think that you can take me?"

"More than I seem, I assure you."

"Prove it, then!"

Whatever Lesries thought of his tiny adversary, he still did not intend to fight fair. He struck with a lightning swiftness meant to catch his enemy off guard, launching himself with remarkable grace to deliver a fatal kick to the base of the neck. His martial cry of attack turned to one of surprise when he felt himself plucked out of the air. He found himself suspended like a doll, two hands holding his wrists while two more held his ankles.

"Oh, shit!" he muttered in quiet despair as he realized his mistake. It was his last conscious thought.

Iyan Makayen stepped aside as medics hurried out of the room with the body, then turned back to survey the damage. He had seen some very strange things in his short career, but this was surely the strangest. It was inconceivable that this tiny off-worlder had thrown Treck Lesries across the length of the room, through an inner wall of the restaurant, across a second room, and halfway through the outer wall. And Lesries might well have gone through that second wall, except that it had a solid brick outer facing. Heavy wooden studs were scattered like matchsticks, and a fine, white powder from shattered plasterboard covered everything.

Den Ohlera, proprietor of the pub and owner of these shattered walls, also stared in disbelief, but it was the disbelief of an almost childlike delight. "A bull langie couldn't have knocked him harder. Look at the hole he left! Just as neat as neat."

"You'll have a bit of a mess to tidy up, that's for sure," Makayen said.

"Oh, I don't know," Ohlera speculated. "Thought I might leave that one hole. Give the gang something to talk about, how that little off-worlder damn near pitched Treck Lesries into orbit. A regular conversation piece, as they say. He was bad for business in life, the way folks would scatter when he walked in. In death, he might be uncommonly good for business."

"What about the damages, all the same?" Makayen asked.

"Oh, he made good on that right away," the proprietor said, displaying a piece of jewelry worth at least twice the costs of repairs. "Surely you'll not be arresting him for this. If you do, I'll be the first to hire him a lawyer."

"And I'll be the second," Makayen agreed. "I don't expect I'll have to, as long as he can give me fair answers to a couple of questions."

They returned to the adjoining room, where Velmeran was sitting at a table with a cold drink, looking unconcerned.

"Let me get right to the point," Makayen began unceremoniously. "Last night my sister came home half drunk and worried about some off-worlder she had met. A Trader by the name of Sergei Rachmaninoff. She said that he had run afoul of Treck

Lesries, and Lesries was looking to kill him. Would you be that person?"

"I might."

"Well, I thought that odd from the start, since there is no independent freighter on the ground or in system at the moment. No ship of any kind, for that matter, except the Methryn. So I ran a computer check on the name Sergei Rachmaninoff, and it told me something quite amazing."

Velmeran shrugged. "It is hard to be original on short notice."

Makayen nodded thoughtfully. "I figured as much. Well now, if you can give me an honest accounting of who you are, where you might be from and what you're doing here, I'll call it good and trouble you no more."

"My name is Velmeran, Commander-designate of the Methryn," he said, drawing aside his cape to reveal his lower arms—and the guns he wore. "I am trying to enjoy port leave."

"Bless me, I've something cooking in the kitchen!" Den Ohlera exclaimed and ran from the room.

"Well, you can see why I would want to take a vacation from that name . . . and the reputation that goes with it," Velmeran said, amused.

"I suppose I can," Makayen agreed. "I was a little peeved at you, I must admit, for doing what I could never allow myself to do. You were waiting for him to come, weren't you? Why did you do it?"

"Well, for any number of good reasons. Because he was a Union agent, for one. Because the Union cannot retaliate for his death if a Starwolf was responsible. To give Lenna something in exchange for the one thing she wants most and I cannot give her. And to keep you from having to sacrifice your career, your freedom, and possibly even your life trying to handle the matter yourself."

"Then I owe you a lot, I suppose," Makayen said. "And taking care of Treck Lesries for her makes up for your deception. But it will still break her heart when you go, for she's expecting you to take her with you."

"Yes, I know. This much, however, I can do. The Traders are a race apart, and they take care of their own. I can put the word out that someone with the training to be an apprentice in helm and navigation wants a place on a ship. Someone will come for her."

"Fair enough," Makayen agreed. "I think she's a fool, but I can also see that she'll never be happy here. Now be on, before I arrest you for possession of illegal arms."

Velmeran smiled as he smoothed his cape into place. "Is there such a thing?"

"Sure, and that's what we call it," the Kanian replied. "For that matter, those jack-snappers you wear probably qualify . . . not that I would try not take them from you. Just promise me that you'll try not to kill anyone else this visit."

"Except Unioners," Velmeran said on the way out.

"It's open season on them!"

Velmeran had only just stepped outside the small café when he saw Lenna racing toward him down the narrow street of the Mall. He hurried to intercept her, although he suspected that she already knew something about his morning's activities. She stopped just short of him and walked around him in a slow circle, inspecting him for damage.

"I saw the medics taking someone away just now," she said. "I was afraid that Lesries had caught up with you."

"He did," Velmeran explained. "That was his body they were hauling off."

"His body, did you say?" Lenna demanded, turning momentarily white in that curious way she had. "You killed him, did you now? And why the hell didn't you wait for me? You sat in that pub until he came for you, didn't you?"

"Sure, and I did," he replied lightly. "I did not want you to be there when it happened."

"Spare me not your barbarity, Mr. Rachmaninoff!" she exclaimed in exasperation as they started down the street. "I hope they plant him fast, so that I can have the pleasure of dancing on his grave."

The *Challenger* left starflight reluctantly, her vast bulk refusing to lose momentum. The moment she dropped to sublight speeds she sent out her riders, a hundred destroyers and twenty battleships she carried in bays hidden within her outer hull. They quickly fanned out ahead, forming a protective cone about the larger ships. A fleet of stingship carriers followed close behind, and then the supply convoy with spare engines and cannons transported in long racks. A planetary invasion force brought up the rear, then regular carriers and five battleships with a score of destroyer escorts. Two separate forces, one to deal with the rebellious planet they had come to tame, and the other to deal with the Starwolves who would come to protect it.

The Challenger's bridge was a scene of organized confusion. It now seemed that Maeken Kea was the only Captain of this ship. Commander Trace clearly deferred to her in the operation of the ship, staying completely out of her chair and, for the most part, off the bridge as well. That did not mean, however, that she was not under his orders, and she waited now for him to tell her what he expected.

"All secure, Captain?" Trace asked suddenly over com, obviously still in his cabin. She bent over the unit in her console to answer.

"All secure, Commander. She fought us a little coming out of starflight, but I understand that you've see that before. What are your orders?"

"My orders?" Trace asked. "I brought you along to give the orders. What do you think we should do?"

Maeken Kea sat back in her chair a moment to consider that. "Actually, there are not just a great many options. First, we send in the invasion force immediately, standard procedure, and get that out of the way. It seems to me that this ship will fight best alone. Send the convoy into hiding and give it all our fighting ships for protection, since it is the weak link in our defenses. When the Starwolves realize that they cannot fight us directly, they will go after the convoy to rob us of our advantage in damage control."

"Interesting," Trace commented. "I had always thought to keep the convoy close, but you're right. What next?"

"Well, a Fortress is no good in a chase, so we have to get the Starwolves to come to us. I would park it in a very wide orbit over the planet. With any luck they will see it, take it to be a large armored battle station like I almost did, and come strolling over to take a look. That way we might get them well within our range before the fighting starts. Then we move the stingship carriers halfway between us and the convoy so that they can move quickly to support either position at need."

"Carry on as you see fit. You are in complete command."

"Does that include the invasion force?" she asked.

"Fleet Captain Margis is responsive to your orders. But he has done this before, so he knows what he is doing and you can trust him to handle things at his end."

"Very good, sir," Maeken said, although Trace had already closed the line. She shrugged and looked up. "Marenna Challenger?"

"Yes, Captain?" the machine responded promptly.

"Get me Captain Margis."

The response came momentarily. "Margis here."

"I've been busy with this monster of a ship, so I haven't had a chance to look at what you're up against. What do you think?"

"This is going to be a tough nut to crack," Margis explained. "They've got quite a horde of fighters, and if they're smart they'll make us come inside the planetary defense shield to fight. They have the fighters and the defenses to make it hard to get at their defensive installations. We will take it slow and careful."

"That's fine," Maeken answered. "Keep your communications closed so that nothing gives us away. We're going to be parked a little way out pretending to be a battle station, and no one is to know otherwise. I certainly don't want the locals tipping us off to the Starwolves. Proceed when ready."

"We're ready now, so we might as well go straight in," Margis said. "I'll keep you informed of our situation. Out."

"Out." Maeken glanced up. "Marenna?"

"Yes, Captain?"

"Find us a likely place to hide this convoy, will you?"

"Word does have a way of getting around," Lenna Makayen offered helpfully as Velmeran stared dejectedly at the pitcher of beer in front of him. He had been receiving "presents" all afternoon, rewards from various members of the grateful population of Kanis for his brave act of pesticide. He had no use for any of it; Lenna stood to do well by his notoriety.

"You have no place for me in your ship. I've guessed that already," Lenna said, returning to their original subject as she reached for his empty glass, set it beside her own, and filled up both.

"So? I have connections with the regular Traders. All I have to do is put in a good word for you, and someone will come for you soon. Or advise you where to meet them."

"I'd rather go with you."

He smiled. "Once you step on board your own ship, it will be a long time before you think of me again."

"You'll not be an easy one to forget," Lenna said, reaching across the table to catch the end of one of his braids. The thick, soft tufts of fine hair fascinated her. "You come from some-where outside Union space, don't you?"

"No, I was born in this very sector," he said. "Why do you ask?"

"Because you're the most curious little fellow I've ever seen. You look like the people I grew up with, only they didn't wear their hair in braids. And they didn't speak with an accent."

"Everyone has their own dialect."

"Sure, but I know the Trader's dialect," she insisted. "Yours isn't a dialect. It's the accent of someone who knows Terran very well but speaks something else at home. For one thing, you don't contract."

"Just because I don't doesn't mean I can't."

"You know what I mean," Lenna said, frowning. "There's something about you that is as alien as can be in something that's still human."

"What? Oh, come on!" Velmeran declared, rising swiftly and pulling her with him. "I learned last night that when you begin to wax philosophical, it means that you are getting drunk."

They paused outside the door of the pub, looking up and down the street. Velmeran was unaware that there was anything different about this night compared to the last, but there were more people out and about the narrow streets. And he thought from their manner and dress that they were looking for enter-tainment rather than just shopping.

"You realize that there is nowhere we can go tonight that people aren't going to make a fuss over you," Lenna said after a moment. They started down the street to their right.

"Why?" Velmeran asked. "Are they that glad to be rid of Lesries?"

"Everyone hated Lesries, that's a fact, and everyone is glad he's gone. But you, now. You're a hero. It's you they're cele-brating."

"Me?" he asked, confused. "I only paid back a murderer."

"And so you did, " Lenna agreed. "That's what people ad-mire you for. You saw what needed to be done and you did it, simple and quick. You're a little like Treck in that. Sure, he was a murderer and a first-rate bastard, but he took what he wanted and never gave a damn what anyone else thought about it. He was completely independent and never afraid of a thing, and neither are you. You've got to admire that in a man, because most of us don't have it."

Velmeran did his best to understand, but he was defeated by that curious sense of panic of a mind struggling with an impossible concept. To Kelvessan, the concepts of good and evil were nearly absolute. Their own laws of society were instinctive and inviolate, without the need of the enforcement of police and courts. For humans, he realized, the laws of nature were instinctive, laws that held that the self is all-important and each took what he wanted. The laws of society had to be learned and accepted, but were always in danger of being lost beneath older, more basic standards. He could understand that much, but that was the limit of his comprehension. He could not begin to understand why humans actually cherished that lawlessness in themselves.

He noticed that Lenna was staring at him very intently and shrugged. "Perhaps, but I still do not care for all the notoriety. I certainly do not want the reputation of being a killer."

"You said it to me yourself. 'I've killed before and will again,' or something like that."

"Well, it's not as if I go around killing people all the time."

He stopped short, as if listening for something. In the next instant he spun around, his guns already in his hands, and fired two rapid shots through the sparse crowd of astonished people behind him. The bolts entered the short alley they had just passed and exploded through the middle of an open door, cracking the opaque glass of its window and leaving two smoking holes. Velmeran stood for a moment staring at the door. Everyone, over a dozen people in all, turned and looked as well, then scattered. He glanced back at Lenna, who was regarding him skeptically.

"As you were saying, Mr. Rachmaninoff?" she asked coolly.

"Oh, you are a . . . here!" He thrust a gun into her hands. "Take this and stand guard."

"I have one of my own," Lenna said, holding up a big Union service pistol, powerful enough to dent Starwolf armor. He stared in mild surprise, wondering where she had kept the thing hidden.

He shrugged and turned toward the door, opening it cautiously. A young man, clearly an off-worlder, lay on the floor inside, panting in his pain. One bolt had discharged against his sternum, shattering his rib cage. The other had passed completely through his chest, just under his right shoulder. There was nothing remarkable about him, just a sandy-haired boy in his early twenties. A very businesslike gun in his right hand was the only thing to indicate his profession. Velmeran confiscated the gun, handing it to Lenna.

"Who . . . ?" she asked as she accepted the gun hesitantly.

"Kuari assassin," he replied simply.

Lenna understood what he meant. The Kuari were an odd, barbaric religious sect occupying three frontier worlds, a small empire in themselves since not even the Union wanted them. The assassins were the elite of their priesthood, their purpose to earn the favor of their death-god with the innocent lives they took. The more lives they took, the greater their prestige and power in the death-god's spirit guard, but they themselves had to meet an honorable death to win their place. The Assassin's sect did not, for any reason, accept a pact on a Starwolf, but older assassins would sometimes cross a Starwolf to win the honorable death they needed.

"Do you hear me?" Velmeran demanded.

"I hear you, Lord," the boy answered, gasping in pain.

"Have you killed before, boy?"

"I have, Lord," he said, smiling grimly with pride. "I have assured myself some small place in the spirit guard, if you will give me honorable death."

"That remains to be said," Velmeran said. "I have two claims upon you. I have beaten you fairly, and I am your only hope for honorable death. The police will be here in a moment. Your injuries are not so great that they cannot steal you back from death. If you desire honorable death, then you must give me something in return."

"I hear you, Lord," the boy answered. "What would you know?"

"Do you know who I am?"

"Yes, Lord."

"And what led you to attempt the foolhardy?"

"My lord, a pact was offered. An agent of your enemy came half a year ago, offering impossible riches for your death. He knew that the pact would be refused, but the reward was very tempting. And the honor."

"And so you came hunting?" Velmeran asked.

"No, Lord," the boy insisted. "I was here when your ship arrived, hunting by pact the chief of the Trade Association. When your ship came, I watched the port for you. I knew that I could never kill you while you wore your armor. But when you came from the tailor's shop dressed as you are, I began to hope that I could do the impossible if I was very careful. But not careful enough, it would seem."

"Sergei," Lenna interrupted softly. "My brother's coming and he's in a hurry."

"The police?" the young assassin asked fearfully. "Lord, I have answered truthfully. What else would you know?"

"Nothing else." Velmeran placed his hand on the assassin's throat, and the sound of snapping bone filled the small, dark room. Lenna drew back fearfully. She had never before seen death, certainly not given so casually and received so eagerly.

Velmeran rose and indicated for her to precede him out the broken door. He stepped outside just as Iyan arrived, stepping through the small crowd that had gathered at a cautious distance.

"You again?" he asked wearily.

"It was a Kuari assassin," Lenna told him, still pale and shaken from what she had witnessed.

Iyan rolled his eyes and muttered some colorful local obscenity before looking at Velmeran. "And you shot him?"

"Self-protection," the Starwolf offered calmly.

Makayen frowned and shook his head slowly, like a superior reluctantly conferring a deserved punishment. "What am I going to do with you?"

Velmeran regarded him questioningly. "You are not going to do anything except mind your own business. Under no circumstances are you to presume any authority over a Starwolf."

Makayen drew back in alarm, suddenly aware that he was indeed asking for trouble. But Lenna, predictably, would not let the matter rest.

"Oh, come off it, Iyan," she said indignantly. "That assassin was here to get Allon Makvenna. Said so himself. So you should be glad he got distracted with our friend here."

"Then I suppose he deserves our heartfelt gratitude," her brother said sarcastically.

"Sure, and I suppose you'd have been happier if he had gone ahead and shot old man Makvenna?" She demanded in return.

"Then you'd have a nice crime to solve, and everything would be as it should be."

Iyan opened his mouth to protest, then noticed the Starwolf watching them both in a mildly amused manner, like a tolerant parent watching two children. He closed his mouth and smiled. "You'll have to excuse me, but it's my sister I'm arguing with, not you. And I'm a terrible one for wanting the last word."

"If you will forgo the last word, I will gladly forget the entire matter. And you," Velmeran turned abruptly to Lenna, "will please shut up and come with me."

"Just be careful!" Iyan called after then as they made their way through the small crowd that had gathered at a respectable distance. The medics had just arrived, effectively breaking up the congregation.

Lenna cringed. "Damn! He had the last word after all."

Now that they were beyond the small crowd, Velmeran quietly returned his guns to his belt and folded his lower arms behind his cape, retreating into his assumed role. Lenna, observing him, tucked her own gun back inside her jacket. Then the delayed shock caught up with her. She wavered, pale and shaken, and paused to lean against a heavy wooden post.

"Great Spirit of Space, you shot him," she muttered uncertainly. "You shot him and you broke his neck."

"A moment later he would have been shooting at us," Velmeran said gently, as if that was supposed to have been reassuring. To a Starwolf it would have been, but somehow Lenna did not quite see it that way. She stared at him in disbelief.

"I don't even want to think about that!" she declared, and closed her eyes as she trembled at the thought. She blinked and looked at him again. "You. You have no regrets."

"Of course I regret," he insisted. "I regret every life that is lost, whether I had any part in it or not. But that is the way life is, and I do what I have to do."

"Sergei, he was only a boy."

"So am I. But he would have shot me in the back and been pleased with himself for doing so. At least I am not pleased with myself for what I did." He paused, frowning. "Lenna, you know what I am. I make a career of shooting warships and freighters, and most of the time I do not think that there are lives—innocent lives—on those ships. Later, when I do think about it, I regret what I have done. I have killed twice today, and for once I have the reassurance of knowing that the lives I took were not innocent. Do you understand what I am saying?"

Lenna shrugged without looking up. In truth, not a word of what he said made a bit of sense to her, although she could tell that it sounded perfectly reasonable to him. Just as her thoughts had earlier been alien to him, now his own thoughts were alien to her. But he was alien, she reminded herself, a member of a race designed for war, with their own thoughts and emotions that kept the peace between their conscience and their duty as warriors. Even if she could not follow his exact reasoning, she did understand the greater intent of what he was trying to tell her. At least he did have firm, logical reasons for his actions, even if his reasons were outside her comprehension. And she could trust him.

"Sorry about that," she said, needlessly straightening her clothes. "You've been brought up to it, I suppose. But I've never seen anything like that before, and it hit me all of a sudden. I'm fine now, though. Are you ready to go on?"

"You do not object to my company?" Velmeran asked.

"And why should I, now?" she asked in return. "I knew that you were something different from the start, and I was beginning to catch on near the end. I would have caught on sooner, I think, if I hadn't been so busy making you out what I wanted you to be."

"I never meant to deceive you," he said dejectedly. "I just thought . . ."

"So did I," Lenna agreed, and looked at him in desperation. "Sergei, you cannot leave me. I . . ."

Velmeran silenced her quickly. "Do not say that. You know that it is not the truth, however hard you try to convince yourself of it. You do not love me, and I certainly do not love you. You are a friend, a casual acquaintance I have met on port leave. And that is all."

"You already have someone of your own, don't you?" she demanded, almost accusingly.

"Yes, I do have a mate. Her name is Consherra. She is the Methryn's helm and first officer, and she has a temper nearly as sharp and quick as your own. And she also has all the love I have to give."

Lenna made a rude noise. "Sure, and that's all the happiness that you could want. But where does that leave me?"

Velmeran took her chin in his hand, his irresistible strength forcing her to look up at him. "Tomorrow morning I will be gone, I am sure of that now. But I have made you a promise, that I will find you a ship as soon as I can. Trust me?"

Lenna smiled reluctantly. "It's hard not to. But I'd rather be a Starwolf."

7

Ten packs of Starwolf fighters were closing quickly on their target, the Union invasion force above Tryalna. Behind them cruised the vast, menacing shape of their carrier, three kilometers of sleek, powerful fighting ship. And the Union forces appeared to be waiting for them. Their handful of warships pulled back instantly, not in retreat but to assume a battle formation.

Schayressa Kalvyn did not like what she saw. Something about that quick defense made her suspect that the Unioners had been waiting for her. Surely they should have expected Starwolves to come sooner or later. But it seemed almost that their attack on Tryalna had been a ruse, that their real objective was to fight her. And that simply made no sense. Something else that was not normal was that armored battle station that sat parked in remote orbit. It was far larger than anything she had ever seen, heavy with armor and cannons, and that made her very uneasy. At least it was slow enough to be harmless.

"Is anything wrong?" Commander Tryn asked. He could always tell when Schayressa was worried by the furtive movements of her camera pod.

"I do not like it," she answered. "Too many things simply are not quite as they should be."

"Is it that battle station?" Tryn asked.

"What do you think?" the ship asked in return. "That thing is five times larger than any mobile battle station I have ever seen. What are they doing with something like that?"

"They mean to hold on to Tryalna whatever the cost. If this

world goes free, five more will revolt in the coming month. Their entire forced sterility program will face a major setback."

"Which is why we have to make sure that Tryalna stays free," Schayressa agreed. "Still, I do not like that machine. I am going to check it out."

She changed course abruptly to intercept the thing. She would not willingly call it a ship. At twenty-five kilometers in length and wider than she was long, it was by far the largest machine she had ever seen moving under its own power. She had seen mobile stations before, but nothing this big. It was certainly the first thing she had seen in a long time that made her feel dainty. Her intention was to come close enough for a thorough scan, then proceed to blow it to bits.

"We are going to full battle alert," she announced over intership com. "Everyone to your stations. Stand by your monitors and manual controls. We will be coming into firing range in less than a minute."

"Does it worry you that much?" Tryan asked.

Schayressa brought her camera pod around to the upper bridge. "I can see from here that it has the shields and cannons of a planetary defense system. There is certainly going to be a fight."

"Bad?"

"Well, I am going to prime my conversion cannon, just in case."

Commander Tryn stared at her in surprise. "If it worries you that much, then leave it alone. Break off."

"I cannot," she answered. "If that thing is a mobile planetary defense system, it might take half the wolf fleet to crack that nut once they get it into operation."

"Then we have no choice," the Commander agreed reluctantly. He had been a first-rate fighter for most of his three hundred and ten years, a fearsome pilot and pack leader and the best strategist in the fleet . . . at least until Velmeran had come along. But he did not like unknowns, and he thoroughly disliked anything that made his ship nervous.

Schayressa banked sharply as she came into good scanning range, dropping down nearly to the plodding crawl of her target as she began a careful scan. What she saw surprised and frightened her. But still she held on, probing every bolt and circuit of that ship. For it was indeed a ship, a fighting ship the likes of which she had never seen.

"Commander!" Keldryn, the helm, warned suddenly.

"I see it," Schayressa answered. Her power sensors leaped off the scale as the immense ship engaged its drives and threw up its shields. Schayressa brought up her own battle shields and targeted her largest cannons.

In the next instant she was under fire. A steady barrage of bolts centered on the Starwolf carrier with deadly accuracy, deflecting off the battle shields with a sound like hailstones ringing against the hull. Occasional shots penetrated the shields to skip off the gentle curve of the armored hull, sounding like strikes even though the bolts deflected harmlessly. Then one shot hit at just the right attitude, biting into the thick armor. The achronic carrier beam discharged its full load of raw energy and superheated metal exploded. It was a minute tear against the vast, featureless expanse of the armored upper hull, but it was only the first of many scores.

Schayressa Kalvyn fought back fiercely. Her own cannons were more accurate and slightly more powerful, but she had only ten against thousands. And yet her shots were deflected harmlessly by the hull of the giant warship. One of her shots struck an unarmored section of a turret and the entire upper portion of the gun exploded. Clued by that, she set her targeting computers to concentrate on the Fortress's guns, the only part of the ship she seemed able to damage.

"Tryn, I cannot fight this thing," she said, and paused a moment as a bolt struck almost directly overhead. "They are trying to hit my bridge, and they seem to have a fair idea where it is. And I cannot hurt them in return. That entire ship is covered by quartzite panels baked by a very firm shield."

"Break off!" he told her.

"Not yet," she said. "If nothing else. I have will work against this thing, I am going to give it my coversion cannon. I have already called back my packs to support me . . . damnation!"

"What?" Tryn asked, perplexed.

"Stingships! Wave upon wave of stingships. There must be a thousand in all, with battleships and destroyers closing from every direction. *Val traron,* have we wandered into a trap!"

Another explosion rocked the entire ship. Tryn glanced around apprehensively, well aware that something major had been hit. "What was that?"

"One of my forward engines," Schayressa replied absently. "Prepare for firing. Keldryn, stand ready to take the helm."

Schayressa ceased firing as she readied her conversion cannon, opening the armored portal in the flattened hexagonal tube beneath her shock bumper. In the conversion chamber at the base of that tube, over half a kilometer back from the Kalvyn's tapered nose, hundreds of liters of distilled water were being converted rapidly into energy, temporarily confined within heavy containment fields. Special field-projecting antennas dropped down to either side of the cannon's muzzle, which glowed with the white-hot energy contained at its core.

In the final seconds before firing, Schayressa centered the cannon by aiming herself at her target. At the same time the Fortress ceased firing and cut all acceleration as if calmly awaiting certain destruction. Then, even as the Kalvyn fired, the Challenger merged the full power of all her generators into the formation of a single defensive shield so powerful that it enveloped the entire ship in a solid white sphere. That devastating blast of raw energy from the conversion cannon struck the shield dead center . . . and was deflected harmlessly.

From the Kalvyn's point of view, that was not immediately apparent. For three full seconds she poured the power of a star against that glowing white shell. Seconds more passed as the glowing clouds of red, yellow, and blue dissipated and nothing could be seen. Then the Fortress emerged from that fiery mass, unharmed. The vast warship seemed to pause a moment to look around, then turned every gun it could on the Starwolf carrier.

"Val traron de altrys caldarson!" Schayressa muttered in her surprise as bolts rang against her hull. After a moment she looked at her Commander. "Tryn, I am beaten. I am getting out of here as fast as I can."

Engaging her star drive momentarily, she jumped past the Fortress and out of range in a matter of seconds. Coasting at just sublight, she made a slow retreat out of the system to give her fighters a chance to overtake her, still engaged with the hundreds of stingships that had already altered their course to follow. It was humiliating for a Starwolf carrier, beaten and battered, to turn and run, unprecedented in recent memory.

"All fighters close to five hundred kilometers and remain on defensive alert," she began her instructions. "Damage control and engineering, begin immediately repairs. Engineering, take a look at that damaged engine. All nonactive personnel will remain at standby until further notice."

"How bad is it?" Tryn asked.

Schayressa brought her camera pod back to the upper bridge. "Not so bad, really. Aside from the wrecked engine, I have no mechanical damage. I just need acres and acres of new plating."

"So? Are you thinking about going back to fight that thing?"

"Oh, I can fight again," she assured him. "But I am not going to until I figure out how . . . Hello?"

Commander Tryn glanced up at her. "What is it?"

"A message coming in," she explained, looking bemused. "Sector Commander Donalt Trace wants to talk to us."

"Oh?" The Commander sat back in his chair, pondering that. "Surely he has more on his mind than just gloating."

"It cannot hurt to listen to what he has to say," Keldryn offered. Like all good second-in commands, she was certain that the upper bridge needed her advice to function best.

"Very well, put him on," Tryn agreed. "Do you have a picture?"

"Audio only."

"Good. I do not have to look at him."

"Commander?" a voice asked over the static of an open channel. The Union did not have good achronic communications.

"This is Commander Tryn of the Kalvyn."

"Yes, this is Commander Donalt Trace on board the Fortress Marenna Challenger. So, what do you think of my new ship?"

"Very impressive," Tryn agreed, very noncommmital in his reply. He meant to learn all he could while not giving away any information . . . not even an opinion. "You are the Captain of this ship?"

"Me? No! I designed the Fortress, but Maeken Kea is the Captain of the Challenger," Trace continued. "You know, I was hoping that it would be the Methryn that would come blundering into the trap you sprung. Still, it might be better this way. I knew that the first ship to run up against my Fortress would turn tail and run until it knew what it was fighting. The second time around will be a fight to the death. Now you, of course, are thinking that you are going to find a way to defeat my Fortress, while I know you cannot. We shall see who is right."

"I suppose we shall."

"Better yet, why not send for Velmeran and the Methryn," Trace suggested. "He is the best you have. This is the best I have. Why not just have it out, and settle that question once and for all?"

"This is the Kalvyn's sector, not the Methryn's," Tryn said to avoid a direct reply.

"Perhaps, but Velmeran has often fought where he is needed," Trace reminded him. "Still, whatever you think best. My Fortress has already given you a minor mauling. I would just as well finish you off now and deal with Velmeran next. He should come running in a hurry when he hears that my Fortress destroyed one of his own carriers."

"As you said earlier, we shall see," Tryn replied.

"Yes, so we shall," Commander Trace agreed. With that the channel went abruptly dead.

Tryn looked up at Schayressa's camera pod. "Well, what do you make of that? He seems very sure of himself."

"He might have reason to be," the ship answered. "I have been reviewing the scan of his 'Fortress' . . . a very apt name, I might add. It has a defense for everything we could throw against it. The only way to beat it is by superior strategy."

"Superior strategy?" Tryn sat for a moment, musing on that. He looked up at Keldryn, waiting patiently at his side. "You go and take a look at our damage and report back to me. Schayressa, park yourself outside this system and do what you can with your damage. Send out two or three drones to scout out what they can. I want to know where those warships and stingships came from, and what else they might have in hiding. And warm up the achronic."

"The Methryn?"

Tryn shrugged. "If he wants Velmeran so badly, I suppose that we should send him Velmeran."

The weather at the port of Kallenes had turned bad during the night. A wet mixture of hail and sleet was driven by a fitful gale, whipping down out of the mountains now hidden behind a blank wall of mist and clouds. Dawn came late and warmed only to a dim twilight. The port field was transformed into a glacial expanse of damp, heavy snow that had gathered in crusty banks on the backs of the black wolf fighters and transports huddled like langies against the winter blast in the near corner of the field.

The Mall that morning was cold, damp, and dark, the skylights covered over with snow so that the dim lighting gave the appearance of late night. To add to that, no one was about the narrow streets that morning except those who had no choice, and a few dozen Starwolves who had the place entirely to themselves. One of the few travelers about the Mall that morning was Velmeran, waiting impatiently for the tailor to open his shop so that he could collect his armor.

After two days in regular clothes, the heavy, restrictive suit was actually a welcome comfort. He had never felt so vulnerable as he had these past two days without it. It had been a confused, violent port leave, he reflected as he untied his braids and brushed out his long, thick hair. Still, he did not regret a moment of it.

The Feldennye tailor packaged up his new clothes and he left with the bundle under one of his lower arms. Although he had not expected it, still he was not surprised to find Lenna waiting for him outside, pacing against the cold. She glanced up expectantly as he opened the door, and he could tell by her astonishment that she did not recognize him.

"Sergei?" she asked hesitantly, drawing back a fearful step.

"Sure now, and you were expecting Pack Leader Velmeran?" he asked, affecting the local dialect to reassure her teasingly. She still did not know who he really was, assuming the name he had given her to be his own, and he preferred matters that way. "You are out early this morning, considering that you put away my complimentary drinks as well as your own last night. Come to see me off?"

"You've been called away, then?" Lenna asked, frowning, as she stared at the ground.

"There has been trouble, barely an hour past, and I must go," he explained simply. "The rest of the pilots will be recalled to the ship before the morning is over. I must go back immediately."

"And you are needed so badly that they could not spare you a few minutes more?"

Now Velmeran frowned, wondering if he could spare her that much. "Perhaps we could walk—slowly—to the port together. That would be a few minutes."

"And all I'm going to get, it seems," Lenna muttered as they started off together.

"If you were human, then I would love you," Lenna mused quietly as they walked. "And I do regret that you didn't take me to bed last night. Just between friends, and I had thought that we were friends enough for that."

"I have a mate, Consherra the Terrible, and I love only her," he reminded her. "But I will not forget my promise. I will find a ship for you. Do you believe me?"

"Of course I believe you," Lenna insisted, although that thought no longer filled her with the excitement it once had. There was now only one ship for her, and that was the Methryn. "You'll be coming back? I'll see you again?"

Velmeran shook his head. "I doubt that we will ever meet again. You will be gone long before I ever make it back to this place. Valthyrra Methryn will be going home for her overhaul after this, and that means half a standard year in airdock."

"Well, I'll miss you," Lenna said. "Friends we may be and nothing more, but you're certainly the most interesting friend I've ever had."

"Thank you," Velmeran replied, smiling. "You are a little strange yourself."

Lenna laughed. "I didn't mean it quite that way, but you have it right after all. At least now I know what we have in common. Is this it?"

The Starwolves had landed their ships in the corner of the field less than a hundred meters from the door where they now stood. Velmeran pushed open the door and stepped out into the dim light and swirling snow. Here, in the corner of the building, the storm did not seem so bad. But they had not gone ten steps when a violent blast of wind struck with hurricane force. Velmeran, anchored by the weight of his armor and his great strength, hardly noticed, but Lenna had to hold his arm to keep from being blown away.

"Perhaps you should stay here," he told her. "You are not dressed to go out in a storm like this, not all the way out to the fighters and back."

"This is good-bye, then?" she asked. "So, take care of yourself, Mr. Rachmaninoff."

"*Val lerrasson vyen de dras schyrrassalon,*" Velmeran said, then turned and walked away into the storm. Lenna stood for a long moment looking as if she might call to him or run after him. But his black form disappeared quickly into the blowing snow, and he was gone.

After a moment more she turned and hurried back inside. Not because of the cold, but because she had resolved to go through with her plan and time was of the essence. Using the shelter of the Mall as much as she could, she cut diagonally across its length to that section of town where she shared a wood-frame house with her brother. He was not there, and she hurried to take advantage of his absence.

Fortunately she had what she needed in her own meager wardrobe, one of the three good sets of clothes she kept for special occasions. One suit was in most ways identical to the one Velmeran had worn, the pants a dark brown with a shirt of a somewhat lighter shade. The cape was a slightly darker brown, a size too large to accommodate her length so that it hung too loose and full from the shoulders. But that, she reflected, was all the better. The boots and belt were leather dyed to match the cape.

Once dressed, Lenna looked at herself appraisingly in the mirror. She was fortunate that she reflected her mother's space-faring race rather than her father's pale, stocky folk. She was just a little taller than most Starwolves, but she had the same wiry build, long of limb and small of body. Her eyes were large, if not quite large enough, and her small nose was not quite small enough. But proper use of makeup corrected most of her shortcomings, and her artistic skills were equal to the task. At least her skin was the same medium tan, her eyes dark, and her hair the same curious wood-brown.

She combed the front portion of her hair down over her face and carefully cut and trimmed until she had the typical long, heavy bangs of a Kelvessa. Satisfied that she had her hair right, she divided its length into two parts and tied it into the thick, loose braids that Velmeran had worn.

Finished, she returned to the mirror to admire the results. Obviously she could not pass herself off as a Starwolf, but she did make a passable Starwolf pretending to be human. It was a disguise that would not work long, but it should be enough to get her into a transport and aboard the Methryn. Once on the ship, she could surely keep herself hidden until they were under way.

Realizing suddenly that she had spent a full hour on her disguise, she hurried to collect a few things she meant to take with her, mostly extra clothes. She added to this her helm and navigation manuals and all the Union credits she had, over eight thousand in all. She was still packing when she heard her brother enter.

"It's me," he called. "Bit of an accident down at the warehouses, and I got my pants thoroughly soaked helping to clear boxes."

At that moment he passed by the door of her room on the way to his own, then paused and backed up to stand in the doorway. He did not need to ask what she was planning; that was obvious enough. He also knew better than to try to talk her out of it, although he did make a token effort.

"Do you really think they're going to permit that, now?" he asked. "They'll throw you out the nearest airlock when they find you."

"As that may be," Lenna agreed. "But I'd rather take an hour of heaven than stay planet-bound a moment longer. I was born up there, and it may be that I'll die up there soon enough. But you worry for nothing. They'll not do a thing to hurt me."

"You're sure of that, now? You've only met the one, and he threw Lesries through a wall and then shot another to pieces and broke his fool neck. Some friend you've got there, Lenna Makayen, to go betting your life on his mercy." He paused a moment to regard her closely. "Well, I can see for myself that you're resolved all the same. Be off with you, then, but hurry. This last hour you couldn't tell the howling wind from their little ships going up."

Lenna stared at him in disbelief. "You'll not stop me?"

"I thought I made that plain."

Lenna returned to her hurried packing. "There's a fair number of things in the studio I've been saving. You can sell them to the next buyer to come through. Remember that there will be some money coming in on those limited-edition representations. Keep it."

"How do I explain your disappearance?" Iyan asked. "'Lenna? Oh, she ran off to join the Starwolves'?"

"Don't be silly," she said as she tied the bundle together. "Say I went back to the Traders. That's where I'm likely to end up, so it will likely be the truth in the long run. Tell the Trade Association to replace me with that kid they've had me training."

"He's ready?"

"Good enough."

"And will I be seeing you again?"

She paused and sighed heavily. "How can I say at this time? Don't count on it. But if I don't go out the door now, you'll be seeing me again soon."

"On your way, then," Iyan said as he stepped back to allow her out the door. "You be careful, now. What you have in mind is dangerous enough. But then, you know who you've taken up with."

The problem, of course, was that she did not. She knew that the Methryn was the abode of such legendary figures as Velmeran, Mayelna, and Valthyrra Methryn herself, but she also had Sergei to protect her from them. In her own overactive imagination, Velmeran was a towering, dashingly handsome hulk with sophisticated wit and daredevil nerve, while Sergei was gentle and pensive.

Her clothing, adequate for a Starwolf, was by no means sufficient to keep her warm in this weather, and the large bundle under her right arm was a wearisome burden. She crossed the Mall and left through the door where she had parted from Velmeran an hour earlier. She could not see five meters ahead for the snow and mist, and she had no way of knowing if Starwolf transports were still parked out there, or even for certain where they might be. The Kelvessa sensed the secondary generators idling in the ships, but she knew only the direction in which she had seen Velmeran go. Dressed as she was, in this wind and bitter cold, she would not survive long if she became lost.

Lenna had gone perhaps three-quarters of the distance when she heard the dull, bone-shaking roar of a transport heading straight up. Seconds later the curtain of snow parted before her, revealing the right side of a transport buried up to its hull in a drift. She ran up to the airlock door just behind the forward cabin and pounded on it with a numbed fist. The door opened immediately, and a startled Starwolf in black armor stared down at her.

"Are you going up soon?" she called over the wind.

"Right now, in fact. They just called down to say that everyone was accounted for. Another minute and you would have been left behind."

He reached down for her bundle. Although it was nearly a third of her weight, she did her best to lift it up with the contemptuous ease a Starwolf would have displayed. By the time that she had climbed aboard, the pilot had gone to stow her package. A lucky guess showed her which button closed the airlock. She collapsed in one of the four seats behind the forward cabin, too cold to be properly frightened.

"Did you miss the call?" the pilot asked as he returned.

"I was not in armor, and I did not have a radio," she explained, hoping that was a valid excuse. She slipped into the curious Starwolf accent with amazing ease.

"That must be the best disguise that I have ever seen," he said as he passed. "You look almost human."

"Thanks," Lenna muttered. The truth was that she was fearful that melting snow caught in her hair was threatening her makeup.

The pilot took his seat in the forward cabin and she heard him strapping in, so she did the same. Moments later she felt the transport lift straight up on its field drive. Then she was flattened into her seat by at least twenty-five G's as the little ship climbed steeply. Her space-bred ancestry allowed her to endure this with little discomfort; no true human could have remained conscious under that unrelenting stress. Some would not have survived.

It did not last more than five minutes, presumably all the time it took to get this ship into orbit. She released her straps and searched the rear cabin until she found a small mirror. Quickly reassured that her disguise had not suffered, she went to the forward cabin for a look out its wide windows.

The first thing she saw was the Methryn, no more than twice its own length away and completely filling the forward view. She had seen pictures of the carriers and knew their specifics, but nothing could accurately convey the true size, power, and majesty of these vast ships. The transport overtook the larger ship rapidly, passing beneath its broad belly, making for the small bay that stood open near the front, a pocket of intense light against the blackness.

"Who are you, anyway?" the pilot asked as he maneuvered into position.

"Consherra." She offered the name of the only female Starwolf she knew, the one that Velmeran had named his mate.

"Consherra!" the pilot exclaimed incredulously. "Well, you are late. I had thought that you had not gone down in the first place."

Handling arms reached down from the bay to pull the transport in, and the thick bay doors swung shut beneath it. This was not one of the two immense holding bays, of course, and it had looked insignificant against the bulk of the ship. But it was larger than any warehouse in port Kallenes, as Lenna could see now.

"We are home," the pilot announced as he hastily closed

down all the systems aboard the transport. "Half a moment and I will have it open. I suppose that you want to go straight to the bridge."

Lenna nodded absently. She was too busy thinking ahead to what she should do next to truly appreciate that she was actually aboard the Methryn, and the only uninvited guest the ship had seen in her eighteen thousand years.

8

Lenna stared as she stepped down out of the transport. The smooth inner panels of the bay doors had folded shut to form the featureless deck on which she now stood, still cold with exposure to space. The walls of each side of the bay were filled with racks of two different sizes, the smaller holding transports such as she had just ridden while the other held capture ships and a large type of transport. They were lifted into place by rectractable handling arms such as the set that held her own transport a meter above the deck while five crewmembers in white armor trimmed in black hurried to service it.

"Here!" a voice called from behind. She turned quickly, and the pilot tossed her bundle into her arms. The weight nearly knocked her over backward, and she strained to get it under control before the Starwolves noticed that she was not as strong as themselves.

"Are you going up to the bridge?" the pilot asked as he leaped down beside her. He started toward a shelflike area at one side of the bay, and she thought it best to join him until she could slip away.

"If we are getting under way soon, I should be there," she answered, recalling Consherra's duty as helm.

"We will be getting under way immediately. They were waiting for me."

"I should be in my armor, but no time now," she said with a touch of regret. In fact, she was wondering if she could hide out easier if she could get herself into a suit or armor, letting the lower arms hang free. She had not yet considered that the Starwolves spoke a language of their own.

"Have you heard what the trouble is?" the pilot asked as she stopped before the lift door to press the call button. "I was wondering what Velmeran had to say."

"Oh, I have not seen Velmeran since I left on port leave," she answered quickly, and it seemed to her a very good answer. She did not even know if Velmeran had left the ship. She certainly had not seen any Starwolves she had thought might be Velmeran.

The transport pilot, however, found that a very astonishing answer. Kelvesan, with their insatiable curiosities, were natural if benevolent gossips. They were also remarkably gullible. If Velmeran and Consherra were avoiding each other's company during port leave . . .

The lift snapped open and they quickly stepped inside, the pilot setting the controls for his own destination and then on to the bridge. The doors snapped shut and the lift started off with its customary lurch, causing Lenna to stagger. This lift was the fastest she had ever known.

"Valthyrra does need that overhaul," the pilot observed, smiling.

Lenna only nodded. She had good luck with this particular Starwolf, but she was beginning to think that she had been with him too long. Sooner or later he was going to ask her something and she was going to say the wrong thing. Or, worse yet, the real Consherra was going to be standing on the other side when that door opened. She did not know that he was sharing her game by speaking Terran to her.

Then it seemed that the lift began to pick up speed like a fighter going into battle. As the stress increased she moved slowly backward until she was leaning against the rear wall of the lift. Still the force continued to build, until she released her bundle to concentrate on fighting the crushing pressure. Flying alone and empty, she had occasionally pushed her freight shuttle to G's as high as this, but she had always been supported by a cushioned seat. The Starwolf might have been immune to those stresses, standing idly by the door. But he was aware of her distress, and was regading her closely.

"Are you well?" he asked. "The Methryn is accelerating to starflight, but we are pulling no more than thirty G's."

Thirty? Only her Trader heritage kept her conscious during this, unprotected and penned against a metal wall. The pilot suddenly realized what the problem was. He stepped over to her and lifted up her cape, and discovered exactly what he expected not to find. He checked her quickly for weapons, retrieved her bundle, and returned to the lift controls. Pressing a button, he leaned slightly forward to the speaker.

"Attention, bridge!" he said sharply. "Cut acceleration. I repeat, cut acceleration immediately. Class Two intruder alert. Intruder has been apprehended on lift five."

He looked over at Lenna, who smiled weakly. The next moment she collapsed to the floor as the stress of acceleration disappeared.

"This is Valthyrra Methryn," came the reply momentarily. "Do you consider the intruder to be under control and not dangerous?"

"No problem here," he replied. "I suspect this to be a stowaway rather than a spy or saboteur."

"Very good, I am bringing you straight up to the bridge."

Velmeran knew that something was wrong when he felt the Methryn cut acceleration and he was on his way to the bridge immediately, so that he was there within a minute of Lenna's arrival. He was starting up the steps to the upper bridge when he looked up and saw Lenna, pale and shaken, seated at the Commander's console while Mayelna, Consherra, and Valthyrra's camera pod faced her from three sides. Realizing exactly what had happened, he turned and retreated quickly the way he had come.

"Just a moment, Velmeran," Mayelna called after him.

He paused and reluctantly returned to the upper bridge. Ignoring Lenna, who was staring at him in complete astonishment, he smiled sheepishly and shrugged. "She followed me home, Mom. Can I keep her?"

"Ah, so you are the mysterious young Starwolf who inspired this lady to attempt the foolhardy," Mayelna said.

"You . . . you are Velmeran?" Lenna asked incredulously, even paler than before. "*The* Velmeran?"

"Of course he is," Mayelna answered irritably. "Who did you think he was?"

"Well, he said that his name was Sergei Rachmaninoff," she explained.

Valthyrra nearly popped her lenses. "Sure, and I'm Fanny Mendelssohn!"

Mayelna glanced up at her impatiently before turning back to the girl. "Were you not aware that he was a Starwolf?"

"No, not until he killed the assassin. I knew that something was odd about him from the start, but I was too busy wanting him to be a Trader who would get me off-world."

"Velmeran told me—briefly—of his exploits, although I suspect that he deemphasized certain points where you were concerned. Did you really believe that he would want you?"

"Oh, no!" Lenna insisted. "I'm not following after him now. He has been a good friend, but I cannot pretend to love him, and he has told me often enough that he has a mate of his own. I just wanted to see this ship."

"You surely knew that you could not avoid detection for long."

"I never meant to. I just thought that if I could get on board, you would have to keep me."

"Oh?" Mayelna looked mildly surprised. "And do you have any idea what we should do with you?"

"Well, there seems to be a number of options," the girl replied. "At the best, you might let me go along for the ride until you find a good place to leave me—preferably a Trader. At the worst, you'll pitch me out the nearest airlock. But the way you're building to speed, I know that you're not going to take me back where you found me."

Mayelna actually chuckled. "You think you know us very well."

"No, Commander," Lenna said. "I know your reputation, and I believe it. But I also know that it's an act. You're Starwolves and I'm of Trader stock, and that makes us first cousins at least. But that's all that I can say in my defense. I knew that I was asking for trouble."

Mayelna regarded her, not unkindly, for a moment, then turned to Velmeran. *"Vel aveyssa fvayralkon tras ayressan?"*

Velmeran shrugged. *"Val fvayralkon aveyr. Aveyssa von len tresdon, schayrkonarran, dverron aveyssa von thryverdaison aval, val laeron, faern leivayrdhay lreykon."*

Mayelna considered that a moment before looking at Valthyrra, who nodded her camera in agreement. Consherra, for once, seemed to have no opinion to offer. At that moment the Methryn made a smooth transition into starflight.

"Well, it seems that you are going along for the ride," Mayelna said at last. "Unfortunately, you picked a very bad time. We are in something of a hurry and we need to make the best time we possibly can, so you will have to sit there and take a few very high G's. Consider that your punishment. After that, Consherra will show you to your cabin and indicate the areas of the ship you may visit. The Methryn really is not a warehouse of secrets, so any place you are told not to get is for your safety. Remember also that the deck plan of this ship looks like an explosion in a kite-string factory."

"Thank you, Commander." Lenna sighed in relief.

"Just behave yourself, if it is . . . humanly possible. Velmeran. Valthyrra. Shall we take a little walk?"

"Walk?" Valthyrra asked. "Walk? Who can walk?"

Mayelna sighed. "Just send one of your evil eyes to my cabin."

Velmeran and the Commander descended the steps together, leaving Lenna to stare in helpless astonishment. She felt a disturbing sense of unreality as she sat pinned in her seat, gasping for breath under the burden of crushing forces while everyone else walked about in complete ease. The Starwolves had solved the problem of moving about under acceleration by adjusting the ship's artificial gravity one step ahead of the G's of acceleration, which would otherwise throw all loose objects toward the back of the ship.

"How did she get on board, anyway?" Velmeran asked as they made their way from the bridge.

"How else?" Mayelna asked in return. "She presented herself at a transport and asked to be brought to the ship. She looks enough like us that she looks remarkably like a Kelvessa pretending to be human. She told the pilot that she was Consherra—"

"Consherra?" Velmeran interrupted.

"Well, yes. I suspect that was the only name she knew to give. She probably learned just enough general information from you to give the right answers to a few questions. And there was a good measure of the old Kelvessan gullibility. The transport pilot just assumed that no one but a Starwolf would want aboard a Starwolf ship."

"Gullibility?" Velmeran asked. "Such as how you not only pardoned her but gave her the run of the ship?"

"Blarney, they used to call it," Mayelna mused. "There must

have been more Irish settlers on that world than Scottish. Only an Irishman can use the plain truth like she does the way other men lie. We have a protective instinct, and she seems to have a talent for making the most of it. I seem to recall that you threw someone through a wall to protect her."

"I did it because he was a Union agent sent to harass the Kanians, and because he pretended to be half Kelvessan," Velmeran said defensively.

"And then I should pardon someone who pretends to be a real Starwolf?" Mayelna asked.

"It is a simple matter of intent. How did she give herself away?"

"G's." She shrugged and turned the corner, only to find herself face-to-face with one of Valthyrra's remotes. She drew back.

"Hello," Valthyrra said. "What is taking you so long?"

"We were talking," Mayelna said curtly, and turned back to Velmeran. "Where did you get that ridiculous idea of dressing up as a human, anyway?"

"That was your suggestion," he reminded her.

"Was it?" She paused a moment to reflect. "Well, even good ideas can go wrong. As that may be, stowaways are the least of our worries now."

Mayelna herded the two ahead of her, down the side corridor and into her own cabin. The door shut behind them, and it did not open again for several hours.

Lenna sank into the Commander's seat like melting butter after half an unrelenting hour of acceleration. Her system was, in fact, designed for this type of stress, but it had been too long. Flying freight had not been enough to prepare her for this. Consherra was there immediately with a drink, a pill, and something to eat.

"Take this," Consherra insisted, offering the pill and the drink. "Our medic Dyenlerra wants to find out if it will kill you."

Lenna paused in the act of taking the pill to look at it closely. "Is this Starwolf medicine?"

"No, strictly for human consumption," Consherra assured her. "You might be our first uninvited guest, but we pluck humans out of wrecks all the time. I also have bread and cheese."

Lenna accepted the light meal and leaned back in the seat as she waited for her strength to return. Consherra had remained at her side nearly the entire time. Lenna could see now that she had been lucky to get away with pretending to be this girl for as long as she had.

"If that was holding back, what kind of G's do you people normally take?" Lenna asked.

"In normal cruising, about the same," Consherra explained. "When we are in a real hurry, we still hold off at about forty-five. That is about all we can take and still be able to move about easily. Emergency accelerations are something quite different. The most I have ever known was about one hundred and forty, and I was flying at the time."

"Do you fly this ship often?" Lenna asked, rising unsteadily to peer over the front of the Commander's console at the helm station on the middle bridge. "Are those manual controls retracted under the central monitor?"

"Of course. You can fly this ship like an overgrown fighter. Valthyrra flies herself for the most part, although I get to set runs from time to time. But I hardly ever touch the manual controls. I really spend most of my time assisting Mayelna and Velmeran in running this ship, not flying it."

Lenna frowned. "I think that I would prefer a Trader, if you'll pardon my saying so. I'm more interested in flying than giving orders."

"I can understand that. How are you feeling?"

"Fairly good, actually," she said, rising and stretching her arms. "I am getting a bit cold, though. I've done some serious sweating this morning, and not all of it from the G's. You do keep this place a bit cool."

"Did you bring a change of clothes?"

"I did come prepared for a wee bit of a stay," Lenna remarked guardedly.

Consherra smiled. "If you are able, I will show you to your cabin now. You can change and rest a bit there. I will come for you again when it is time for you to eat, and then I will show you about the ship . . . before you take a notion to wander off on your own."

Lenna was shown to a cabin that she considered luxurious by the standards of space travel. There was carpeting on the floor and real wood paneling on portions of the wall, with a small kitchen and a regular bathroom. Her first thought was for a shower, for she was eager for the feel of hot water on sore joints and muscles as well as to rid herself of the heavy layer of makeup. Valthyrra had prepared the room for her, turning the thermostat up as high as it would go. But she had no desire to be wet and naked in an environment that was now only slightly uncomfortable, and she had some doubts about what the Starwolves would call hot water. But she did find that she could get water hot enough to suit her, and letting it run with the door partly open steamed the small bathroom to a bearable level. She did wonder what a shower was like in high G's. Apparently that was taken into consideration; the door shut and locked so tightly that the shower needed special ventilation.

She really did not care to rest afterward, testimony to her ability to recover quickly from such stresses, not to mention the fact that she was entirely too excited. It was thrilling to think that she was alone in a ship full of Starwolves—a community of Starwolves, as it were, and all her very own. It was as well that she did not need to rest, for Consherra returned for her soon after she was dressed.

"You do not look quite so Kelvessan as you did before," she said, pausing just inside the door to regard the girl closely.

"Makeup," Lenna explained. "I know how to use it. It might be that my eyes no longer seem quite as large."

"That must be it," Consherra agreed, although she did not sound entirely certain. "I am glad that you have returned to native costume. It is something of a treat, having an alien visitor on board. I especially want to show you to the little ones. They have never seen a human before."

"These clothes were made for Kanis, where it's mostly as cold as it is here," Lenna said. She had been looking at the Kelvessa nearly as intently. Consherra had been in armor before, but now she wore white pants and tunic that formed the quasi-uniform of a Starwolf officer. In a way she looked far more alien now, since these clothes did not mask but emphasized her alien features. More than anything, that second set of arms, which did not appear so out of place with the heavy armor, now stood out prominently.

The first thing Lenna learned was that there was no division of night and day on a Starwolf carrier, since Kelvessan did not sleep. As a result the meals were not divided into breakfast, lunch, and the like, just three dinners a day. Unfortunately, the dining hall was mostly empty; the last meal was only just over, having been delayed until the Methryn was in starflight.

After that the tour began in earnest. Lenna saw everything of importance from the cannons retracted into the shock bumper in the nose of the ship to the fighter bays in the rear, with everything, including the cavernous holding bays and the Methryn's immense generators, in between. Her favorite part, predictably, were the fighter bays, where every fighter had been brought down to the decks to final servicing.

Lenna's tour ended in the Methryn's school complex. When she was told that the first level consisted of ages from three months to three years, she had envisioned infants. That was hardly the case. Young Kelvessan, even at only three months, were perfect miniatures of the adults, long-limbed, wiry, and strong, well able to walk, run, and talk. They were also, in Lenna's opinion, irresistibly cute.

There were only twenty-one students in this age group, fewer than she had expected. She calculated that to be about one hundred and thirty children out of a population of two thousand, a very small percentage, although, because of their long life expectancy, it did represent a very modest population growth. In this first level the young were taught reading, writing, and simple mathematics, and an introduction to Terran, their second language. By the time they "graduated" at the age of eighteen, every Kelvessan had a surprisingly broad and extensive education, and they had yet to receive special training in their chosen fields.

Consherra left Lenna with the students, explaining that she did have duties of her own to attend to, and departed with the instructions for where she could be found during the next meal period. She managed to get lost navigating the corridors on her own. But it was a simple matter to find a lift, and she set the section and level coordinates that Consherra had given her.

"Late again, I see," she remarked as she seated herself at the large table where Consherra and Velmeran were seated with at least a dozen Kelvessan she did not know.

"Treg, you were going back for more," Velmeran said. "Will you take Lenna up and help her find something to eat?"

"Right away, Captain," Tregloran answered promptly.

"Do you have children's plates?" Lenna asked as she hurried after him. "I'll be getting fat like this."

Consherra smiled and shook her head slowly. "If she could

take a few more G's, I would be tempted to keep her. She is entertaining."

"Sure, and it must be her odd way of speaking," Velmeran agreed. "I cannot imagine what the Traders are going to do with her."

"The Kanians are of Irish descent, are they not?" Baress asked.

"Mainly, but with a great many Scots thrown in," he explained. "Makayen—McCain—is a Scottish name, unless I am mistaken. Of course, Lenna would not know a Scotsman if he bit her on the leg."

Consherra laughed in mischievous delight. It was hard to say if she found his odd choice of terms amusing, or if she simply liked the idea of anyone biting Lenna Makayen on the leg.

"Of course, she told me once that her Kanian accent is a pure act, and I have heard her drop it," Velmeran continued. "I suspect that she is just using it to beguile us."

"There is no question of that," Consherra agreed. "When she is talking about ships, she acquires a definite Trader's accent. And she uses their terms. She calls a transport a 'lift,' and a launch a 'roundabout.' And she really knows her business, too. I quizzed her about navigation for some time, and not only does she know it, but she actually understands what she is doing."

"Well, for a human, that is something new," Baress remarked.

"You know what I mean," Consherra snapped. "Most human navigators learn their formulas by rote, but they have only a vague understanding of the actual mathematics involved."

"The Traders are not a degenerate race," Baressa pointed out. "And their mathematical ability is very strong. Lenna may sound like a Kanian, perhaps because it suits her. Do none of your know your genetics? Traders are nearly a separate species from true humans. The offspring of a Trader and a human is what is known by the vulgar term of a mule, a sterile, invariably female offspring that is essentially a smaller, stronger version of a true Trader. If they know, they might not want her back."

"She seems amorous enough to me," Velmeran remarked.

"Sterile hardly means sexless."

"Well, at least we have a replacement for Consherra," Velmeran remarked, then looked up. "Sherry, could you teach her to fly this ship?"

Consherra was plainly astonished. "Lenna? *Varth!* She has only two hands, Meran."

"A distressing handicap, I do admit," Velmeran agreed blandly. "But then, humans have done quite well in spite of it. I did not mean to put her on direct manuals in battle."

Consherra considered that for a moment and shrugged. "How should I know? I have always said that the Methryn is, for her size, a remarkably easy ship to fly."

They glanced up as Tregloran and Lenna returned, each balancing a plate. She seemed to be adjusting very well to life among the Starwolves, although "making herself at home" was probably the best way to describe it. But then, for all Velmeran knew, she had already forgotten that she was not a Starwolf.

He quickly introduced the members of his pack, forgetting that humans did not have a memory like a disk drive. And yet, Lenna never forgot the name of a single Kelvessa she was introduced to. The problem lay in identifying names with the proper owner, since she could not easily tell most Starwolves apart.

"And then there are the members of my special tactics team," he continued. "Baress and Tregloran are subsets of both groups. They are about tied as the best pilots on this ship."

"Second best," Baress corrected him, pointing to the one who actually deserved that honor.

"Trel and Marlena are the pilots of our modified transport. This is senior pack leader Baressa, and the quiet old gentleman at the end is Keth. He gets our students ready to fly with the packs."

Lenna stared for a moment, since this was the first old Starwolf she had met. Or at least the first she was aware of as being old, since there was nothing about elderly Starwolves to indicate the fact. As she looked closer, she could detect the tiniest creases about his eyes, such as she had also noticed on Mayelna. And both had a few black hairs among their brown; they apparently did not get gray.

"Did you teach Velmeran to fly?" she asked hesitantly.

"No, indeed," Keth replied. "In fact, I flew in his pack for a short time before I retired. I could no longer take the high G's."

"I know how that is," Lenna muttered.

"In fact, Velmeran's first grand adventure was to rescue me when I was captured," the older Kelvessa continued. "If Valthyrra and the Commander were here, you would see gathered at this table all the people that Union High Command hates most. The Methryn's Magnificent Maniacs."

"Which reminds me," Lenna said turning to Velmeran. "Where have you been all day?"

Velmeran shrugged. "Making battle talk."

"The whole time?"

"Yes, actually," he said, frowning with consternation. "Life was easier when we were secure in the belief that the Union could not throw anything at us that we cannot handle. Don has found himself a really first-rate toy this time. I hardly know what to make of it."

"That sounds ominous," Tregloran remarked. "And we are going to fight it?"

"If it is at all possible, then we must. And if we do fight, this is going to be our most difficult one yet."

"Great Stars, I would not miss this one for anything!" Lenna was practically shaking with excitement.

Velmeran regarded her blandly. "If you see this fight at all, it will be from a distance. You will be transferred to the Kalvyn with the rest of the nonessential personnel."

"Nonessential?" she demanded indignantly.

"That seems like an adequate description for a stowaway."

Lenna let the matter drop, seeing perhaps that there was no argument she could make that would keep her on this ship. Or perhaps she simply had ideas of her own.

9

After half an hour of cautious deceleration, the Methryn left starflight as gently as if her hull was porcelain and likely to break. Although she was still moving fast in terms of ordinary ships, her gentle approach was so unlike the sudden, darting movements of Starwolf carriers as to be remarkable. The system that was her destination lay well ahead; she had stopped short for a final meeting with the Kalvyn before going into battle. Valthyrra quickly cast about for her sister ship and altered her course in a long, lazy turn.

"Methryn?" a voice called out questioningly over com. "Valthyrra Methryn? Is that you sliding in?"

"Why, so it is," she answered. "Who were you expecting, Schayressa?"

"Well, the last time I saw anything move that way, it was one of our own freighters with her hold so packed that she could barely move," the Kalvyn answered. "Is there something wrong with you, Val? Have you hurt yourself?"

"You might describe my problem as a pain," Valthyrra said. "Actually, I have a passenger."

"A passenger?" Schayressa was incredulous. "A paying passenger? Great Spirit of space, Valthyrra, this is hardly the time for you to consider converting yourself to a luxury liner. Starwolf Express! A human passenger?"

"A stowaway, to tell the truth."

"A stowaway? On a Starwolf carrier? I have never heard of such a thing. What did you keep it for?"

"To give to you," Valthyrra snapped.

"Oh. I had to ask."

"If you will hold your diodes for a moment, I am trying to get myself slowed down. Do you have any idea how hard it is to move our ancient bulks like we were hauling breakables?"

"Tell me about it," Schayressa answered. "I lost a forward engine, and that means cutting the corresponding engine to maintain balance. Suddenly I have half the deceleration power I used to. I hate the thought of trying to put myself into airdock for repairs."

"You could be towed in," Valthyrra suggested.

"Towed? That would give me nervous fits. Have you ever been towed?"

Mayelna glanced up, then returned to her monitor, shaking her head slowly. *"Aval den tras etrenon.* They are all crazy."

"What?" Velmeran asked, glancing up from where he had been watching the monitors over Consherra's shoulder.

Mayelna regarded him blandly. "Someday, my boy, all this will be yours. One aging, know-it-all, gossiping starship."

Valthyrra rotated her camera pod at the end of its boom, as if looking over her shoulder. "All the world is a stage, and everyone is a critic."

Everyone looked up expectantly as Lenna Makayen entered the left wing of the bridge, staggering under the strain of G's that would have left most humans unconscious. Traders had developed remarkable strength and resilience from thousands of years of such conditions; Iyan Makayen had always been embarrassed by the fact that his rangy half sister was considerably stronger than himself.

"The last time I saw her walk like that was near the end of that first night in Kanis," Velmeran remarked. He hurried to her assistance, half carrying her up the steps. "You should have stayed in your room."

"And miss all the fun?" Lenna demanded, and bowed her head respectfully to the Commander. *"Val edesson,* Mayelna."

"Val treron," Mayelna corrected her; Lenna still had her days and nights reversed. "That, I suppose is your way of informing me that I am in your seat?"

"Sure, I'll not be asking you for your seat," Lenna insisted, spreading her accent thickly. "If it's all the same, I would be happy with Conshera's seat."

"Varth! Schon il vessa!" Valthyrra exclaimed softly, calling their attention to the main viewscreen. Just then she jerked herself to a sudden stop with a final blast of reverse thrust, disturbing no one except Lenna. She executed an interesting forward flip and would have broken her neck except that she landed on Consherra, who was coming up the steps at that moment, and they tumbled all the way down to the main bridge. For a moment they provided a more interesting diversion than anything that could have been happening outside, and everyone stared in speechless astonishment, then calmly applauded the acrobatics.

Lenna picked herself up, bruised and swearing, and turned to the main viewscreen. The Kalvyn sat motionless perhaps seven kilometers away, and turned almost directly toward them so that her forward hull was in plain view. Cannon blast had ripped round and oval craters intermixed with long, narrow tears in the thick armor.

"Are you finished staring yet?" Schayressa asked in mild irritation as the silence continued, unaware that most of the time had been taken up with Lenna's amazing distraction.

"I suspect that I will look much the same before this is over," Valthyrra replied.

"Perhaps, but you will have something to show for it. All I

was able to do was run," the other ship pointed out. "If you will open a bay, the Commander and I are on the way over."

Valthyrra laughed softly. "So soon? You are anxious to see me blast that monster. We will be down to meet you."

"Bring that passenger of yours as well, if you can trust it," Schayressa added. "When dealing with humans and the deceptions of humans, we might profit from the opinion of a human."

Valthyrra glanced at Lenna, who was checking herself for broken bones. The Trader girl was learning Tresdyland at an astonishing pace, but she could hardly follow a conversation after three days. Lenna would not believe her good fortune when she discovered what she was going to do now.

The delegation from the Kalvyn stepped off the right bridge lift, where Mayelna, Velmeran, and Consherra were waiting to meet them, their unexpected guest standing to one side. And everyone stopped short to stare in disbelief. Even Lenna could see clearly that Velmeran was almost a exact duplicate of Commander Tryn, nearly three hundred years his senior. Everyone was amazed. Everyone, that was, but Mayelna, the only one who had known both Velmeran and Tryn before this meeting. Tryn was himself as surprised as anyone.

"Hello, Mayelna," Tryn said at last, turning to her. There was a curious look of both fear and satisfaction in his eyes. "It has been a long time."

"Eighteen years," she agreed, then turned to her son. "You know Velmeran, I suppose. He runs this ship now, although he still keeps me around to handle the trivialities."

"Do you remember me?" Tryn asked. "I met you once, a long time ago."

"I had forgotten," Velmeran replied uncertainly.

"Well, I do recall this girl," Tryn continued briskly. "Consherra, if I remember correctly. I know that you are the Helm."

Consherra smiled and nodded. "Yes, I do remember you. Velmeran is my mate now."

"Is that so?" Tryn replied to that rather odd admission, then glanced over at Lenna. "Your passenger, I suppose?"

"Hello," Lenna said in one of her rare self-conscious moments.

"Lenna Makayen, our artist in residence and expert Starwolf impersonator," Mayelna said.

"Well, I can see how she could get away with it," Tryn said, smiling reassuringly in the mistaken belief that Lenna was shy. If he had not been distracted by other thoughts, he would have realized that shy people did not sneak aboard Starwolf carriers. He glanced around quickly. "Oh, this is our Helm Keldryn and our Commander-designate Denlayk."

"Hello," the pair said in unison.

Mayelna frowned, deciding that matters had deteriorated from bad to ridiculous and that she had better put a quick end to this before the conversation drifted into areas she had no wish to explore. "I suppose that we should get down to the business that brought us here. Valthyrra is waiting."

They retreated quickly to the third and smallest of the council rooms behind the bridge. Valthyrra was indeed waiting, the camera on its short boom above the oval table glaring as they took their seats.

"Were you aware that Daelyn has been made Commander-designate of the Karvand?" Mayelna asked suddenly. "The Karvand fought with us at Vannkarn, and again a few months later."

"I had heard that she had been made Commander-designate," Tryn replied. "And Velmeran's raid into Vannkarn is a matter of legend. But then, everything Velmeran does assumes legendary proportions."

"Then I suppose that we have the making of another here," she said, and turned to Velmeran. "Tryn is Daelyn's father."

"Is that a fact?" Velmeran answered guardedly.

Valthyrra, who had missed the previous conversation out in the hall, glanced about in complete mystification. Her gaze passed over Commander Tryn and she did a quick double take, then looked at Velmeran and back again. Several of the others, observing her, were trying not to laugh.

"Ah . . . if we could get on with the business at hand," she began uncertainly, her camera pod rotating around to center on the Kalvyn's probe, seated astride the arms of the chair beside Lenna. "If you will begin."

"Yes, we will start with an analysis of this machine that Donalt Trace has built himself," Schayressa said, and employed a video link with Valthyrra to project her intricate scans of the Challenger on the large viewscreen beside the table. Using this to illustrate her explanations, she began a very careful accounting of the Fortress and how its various systems functioned . . . and why it was so invulnerable.

Lenna, watching from the edge of the discussion, noticed that Schayressa was directing her explanation at Velmeran, and that there was some unspoken consent among everyone present that he was very much in command. As she watched, he seemed to grow in character, evolving from the little boy she had met in Kallenes to become the person that legend argued he must be. Perhaps not the daring, devil-may-care hero of her romanticized image but the capable and responsible Commander-designate that his fellow Starwolves trusted and respected.

Schayressa concluded with a step-by-step analysis of her battle with the Challenger, the complex nature of the trap that she had wandered into, and how the Union Commander had quickly and effectively blocked her every move.

"Meran, what do you think?" Mayelna asked as Velmeran sat in thoughtful silence for a long moment.

"Somehow that does not sound to me like the Donald Trace I knew two years ago," he explained. "Weapons design is his strength, but his idea of strategy is a strong, straightforward drive that either succeeds or fails in its initial thrust. Such subtlety and refinement of strategy simply is not his style."

Tryn and Schayressa stared at him in amazement.

"Well, you do know your business," Tryn remarked. "Trace talked to us the moment it was over. He said that he was 'just along for the ride,' to use his own words, that a Maeken Kea is the Captain of this ship."

Velmeran looked up at Valthyrra. "Maeken Kea?"

"A prominent fleet commander of this sector," she explained. "She outmaneuvered a Starwolf attack force some time ago and actually forced them to withdraw. That probably impressed Don a great deal."

Velmeran sat back in his chair, both sets of arms crossed, and sat for a long time in silent contemplation. "The problem with this Fortress, even if it did not have quartzite shielding, is that it is simply too big to make a run at the thing and expect to destroy it with regular cannons. Either we find a way to take it apart piece by piece without getting blasted in the process, or we find a way to get past its heavy shielding. What about simultaneous firing of conversion cannons from several ships?"

"That would work, but it would take a simultaneous firing of seven ships to overload that ship," Schayressa replied. "But there is some hope for sequential firing. The Fortress can only maintain that shield for a few seconds. Two strikes at full power would bring it down, and a third strike would penetrate the quartzite shielding and destroy the ship. But you need three carriers for that."

"Will a shielded fighter or missile penetrate that outer shield?"

"Oh, certainly. But you need a good, strong shield of your own to guard against being fried by the backwash of energy your ship is going to pick up by induction. But you have to have a thirty-five-megaton explosion directly against the hull to crack the quartzite shielding."

"Then we are back to the starting point on that problem," Velmeran said. "We really have no choice. We sit here and wait for another carrier to show up and help us with sequential firing."

"Two more," Schayressa corrected him. "I fried the conversion generator in my cannon when I fired it earlier, and nothing short of airdock repairs is going to make it operate again. I anticipated this and sent out the call for additional ships. The Karvand will be here in thirty-six hours, and the frighter Lesdryn twelve hours behind her. The freighters have the same forward battery and conversion cannon, even if they lack our armor."

"Is this the only way to fight it?" Mayelna asked.

"No, not the only way." Velmeran said, "We could probably go in and take it apart piece by piece. But lives would be lost and the Methryn would be half wrecked in the process. That is too high a price when we can deal with this matter easily in just two days."

"I would rather not get my nose shot up if there is an easier way," Valthyrra agreed.

"There still remains the problem of Tryalna," Velmeran continued. "If we cannot go through that beast, at least our fighters can go around it. I would like . . ."

His voice died away into silence as he sat tensely, as if staring at something that no one else could see. He had the same unfocused look of a camera pod while the ship's attention was elsewhere. For that matter, Valthyrra and Schayressa had the same distant look.

"What is it?" Tryn asked softly, afraid to disturb his concentration.

"The Challenger is moving toward Tryalna," Velmeran answered. "Perhaps it means to turn its big cannons on planetary targets."

Everyone paused to listen, although only Velmeran and Consherra had the superior senses to detect the droning of the Fortress's powerful engines from this distance. Lenna sat looking about in complete bewilderment.

"Valthyrra, can you rush in to distract that ship before it moves into range?" Mayelna asked.

"Too late," Schayressa said. "The Challenger carries an arsenal of nuclear weapons on missiles with crystal engines."

Even as she spoke, the Challenger launched a single missile. Driven by a small but powerful engine, it accelerated rapidly for several seconds, then shut down and flipped itself over to prepare for detonation.

"Fifteen seconds to target," Valthyrra reported. "The only way we could have stopped it would have been to have had fighters waiting in orbit."

"What target?" Mayelna demanded.

No one answered. The missile decelerated for several seconds, then flipped itself back over and began to orient on its designated target. It hurtled into the atmosphere at impossible speeds, protected by an atmospheric shield that parted a narrow channel of fiery air just ahead of its nose, serving to slow it further.

"Detonation," Valthyrra announced. "The target was the spaceport of a major industrial center. Since that was a relatively small warhead, the damage was restricted largely to the port itself . . . which was apparently evacuated at the time. Actual damage was minimal, and I suspect that there was very little loss of life."

"But why?" Lenna demanded, pale and shaken.

"That seems obvious enough," Velmeran answered bitterly. "Donalt Trace knows that I am here, and he will do whatever it takes to make me fight him. He will do it again and again until I do. He knows that I must."

"There does not seem to be any choice," Valthyrra agreed. "Any thoughts on the subject?"

Velmeran did indeed look very thoughtful. "The Fortress's shields are dependent upon the tremendous energy generated by its power network. And the more generators we take off the grid, the weaker its combined power for shielding becomes. In theory, we can eventually weaken it to the point that it becomes vulnerable to our attack. Is that not so?"

"Indeed, it seems the only option we have," Valthyrra replied. "If we do weaken it to such a point, which I calculate to be nine hundred and fifty-two guns remaining of its initial two thousand two hundred, then a single shot of my conversion cannon will short out its defensive shield."

"That means that you have to shoot out twelve hundred and forty-eight," Consherra observed. "Why so many?"

"Because most of the power for the shields comes from the larger generators in the engines and the ship itself, which are invulnerable to attack. My calculations are based on the assumption that no engines are shot out. Needless to say, you get more points for shooting out an engine."

"And when you do shoot out a gun or an engine, you want it to stay that way," Velmeran continued. "We have to take out that support convoy so that the Fortress cannot repair itself. And we have to get rid of those stingships so that we will be free to concentrate on the Fortress."

"Needless to say, you can have our packs to assist you," Tryn said. "And the bay crew and support personnel that goes with them. Is there anything else the Kalvyn can do?"

"Yes, you can set yourselves up near Tryalna to prevent retaliation from the invasion force and to intercept anything else that Donalt Trace might throw at it. He might not be so careful about his next target."

"That leaves the Fortress itself," Schayressa pointed out.

"I have one thought on that," he said. "We still have to take it apart a piece at a time, but I know something that might make that easier. All we have to do is to get it to follow the Methryn into the debris ring of the fourth planet."

There was a moment of silence as everyone tried to figure out what he could have in mind with such a plan. The ring of the fourth planet was well known, not for its beauty but as a curiosity. Most rings were thin disks of very small particles. But this planet possessed instead a thick band of heavy debris, large pieces of solid rock ranging in size from boulders to pieces as massive as small moons. A powerful static charge caused the pieces of rock to repel each other, maintaining a thickness of several hundred kilometers. Starwolf fighters often negotiated the ring as a game, but they were the only regular visitors.

"I am assuming that both our carriers and the Challenger have debris shields capable of clearing a path through the ring?" Velmeran asked.

"Yes, of course," Valthyrra answered. "Do you think . . ."

Velmeran shrugged. "For all its hundreds of cannons, the Fortress would be very limited in range and accuracy trying to shoot through that mess. It would be slowed down to a crawl, and its scanners would be hopelessly confused by the static."

"And the same would be true for me as well," Valthyrra pointed out.

"No doubt. But our fighters can negotiate the ring with no problem and they can use the debris to shield their attacks. The Fortress is more vulnerable to attack there than in open space."

"That is true, of course," Valthyrra agreed. "But Donalt Trace may not be stupid enough to follow us into a trap."

"He might be persuaded."

The council of war ended soon. They had to move quickly, before Donalt Trace grew impatient and launched another warhead to prod them along, and there was still much to do. Those members of the Methryn's crew who had no part to serve in actual battle were sent to the Kalvyn. Lenna accepted her order to join them with unusual grace. Perhaps she had enough of heavy G's to understand why it was necessary.

Schayressa had known that the Methryn would need her own packs, as well as the bay crew members and service personnel to assist them. She also meant to send over her entire engineering and damage-control crew to help keep the Methryn in working order. Since very little of a carrier's crew was designated as nonessential, Valthyrra found herself with eight hundred more crewmembers than she had to begin with; the Kalvyn, who was not going into battle, was the one to send away most of her crew. Denlayk and Keldryn were sent back to the Kalvyn to supervise the transfer of personnel, and Schayressa removed her presence to her own ship as soon as the discussion was over.

As soon as Velmeran declared their business concluded, Mayelna rose and hurried purposefully from the room as if she was needed somewhere else and was late already. Noting her hasty escape, Tryn ran after her.

"Mayelna, wait!" he called after her. She turned and waited for him a short distance down the corridor that led to her cabin.

"It has been a long time," Tryn began questioningly, as if that was a substitute for what he actually wished to say.

Velmeran and Consherra paused at the door of the council room, already aware of something. Lenna, ignorant of what was said because she did not speak Tresdyland, hurried off on business of her own.

"Yes, it has been a long time," Mayelna agreed after a moment's pause. "Eighteen years, as you said. And we did not see that much of each other even then. We have never been able to see each other as often as we would wish. You have your ship and your responsibilities, and I have mine. And the paths of our ships cross only once in a great while."

Tryn nodded slowly. "And when we part this time, will it be another eighteen years before we meet again? Our years are passing quickly now. We were not old the last time we were together, but now we are. Will one of us be gone before chance brings us back together again?"

"Tryn, there is no way that either of us could know," Mayelna replied "I cannot leave the Methryn to be with you. The way things have been these past two years, my responsibility to this ship is greater than ever. And I will not even ask you to leave the Kalvyn to be with me."

"No, that is not possible," he agreed regretfully.

"Then the only answer is that we must continue as we have, taking the time that is given to us, and hope that chance will be kinder to us in days to come," Mayelna said, and smiled. "This much I can promise you. By the time we are finished here, we are going to have a matching pair of ships that are going to spend at least half a year in the repair docks together, longer than all the time that we have had together in all the years since we first met and loved. Then, when the time comes to part, we will treat it as our last, knowing that it may well be. And if we do meet again in years to come, then that will be chance's gift to us."

As if on cue, Valthyrra drifted around the corner at that moment when her name was mentioned, moving silently up behind Velmeran and Consherra. Having grown impatient with waiting in Mayelna's office, she had sent her probe to investigate. Consherra reached out with one hand to hold her back.

"I often think of joining you here," Tryn continued after a

moment. "I always meant to. But then I went up to the bridge to stay, and there was no longer any question. And yet it was never because I did not love you enough. I hope you understand that."

"I understand completely," she assured him. "The same was true for me. Anyone else may change from ship to ship but not us. I am needed here. I could not have loved you more, but not even that was enough to break the bonds of responsibility that tie me to this ship."

"And so there was never any hope for us?" Tryn asked.

"No, there never was," Mayelna said, shaking her head sadly. "Perhaps it was foolish of us to even allow this to begin."

Tryn reached out gently, almost cautiously, to take up her hand in his. Their reunion was one of reconciliation from the start, as if they must first apologize to each other and themselves for allowing the years to slip away while they remained apart.

"No, it was never foolish," he insisted. "I have often felt frustrated by the circumstances of our union, but I have never regretted it. My only regret is that I cannot have you with me always."

Maylena smiled, and it seemed to Velmeran that he had never seen his mother so happy. They took each other in their arms and kissed their reconciliation complete. With the shadows of the past laid aside, they could now look to what was and what may yet be.

"Mayelna, there is one thing that I must know," Tryn said gently. "Is Velmeran my son?"

Mayelna stood silent for a long moment staring into his eyes as he held her tightly into his arms. Velmeran took a few hesitant steps in their direction, waiting for her reply. Consherra and Valthyrra remained where they were, forgotten for the moment, as they watched expectantly.

"Do you even need to ask?" Mayelna answered evasively. "Looking at the two of you together, can there be any doubt?"

"No, Mayelna. I want to hear you say it," Tryn insisted. "You would never tell me before, and I have never pressed you. I cannot imagine that you would not want to admit that Velmeran is my son. Is there some reason that he should not know that I am his father?"

"No, of course not," she said, turning away. "Is it really that important to you?"

"Yes, it is. I will not be parted from you again without hearing you say it. Please, tell me."

She turned to him slowly, seeing the desire and need to know reflected in his eyes. Then she saw Velmeran, waiting quietly a few steps away, silently begging her to say it was true. Tears came suddenly to her eyes, and yet she smiled warmly. "Of course he is."

For a moment Tryn and Velmeran stared at each other. Then Tryn turned to his son, smiling in warmth and reassurance as he held out a hand invitingly, and Velmeran hurried to join them. The three embraced quickly, in silence, then walked together down the empty hall to Mayelna's cabin. Valthyrra, staring intently at the small group, began to drift after them. Consherra caught her by the base of the probe's long neck and hauled her back.

"Not this time," she hissed. "For once keep your nose out of it."

"But she does not know that for a fact," Valthyrra protested, turning her camera pod to look up at her captor.

"What does it matter?" Consherra demanded quietly. "They have what they believe, and what they want to believe. And that is all the truth they need."

Valthyrra considered that, and her camera pod nodded in silent agreement as she turned for a final glimpse of the three. She wished them all the happiness they might find.

10

The transfer of crewmembers between the Methryn and the Kalvyn proceeded quickly and was completed in only two hours. Valthyrra shed all the weight she had to spare, such as over a hundred tons of refined ores and other raw materials in her holds. For the same reason, she did not send out her distillation ship to collect pieces of drifting ice to replenish the supply of water she carried as fuel. Her tanks were only a quarter full, but she considered that more than adequate. Converted to pure energy, a little water actually went a very long way, even when feeding a carrier's big engines.

Velmeran hoped to buy himself an extra hour or two by having the Methryn move forward in steps, edging cautiously into system and then pausing for final preparations. An important question in his mind was whether or not Trace knew that sequential firing of conversion cannons would destroy his ship. If so, he knew that he had to fight and defeat the Methryn before more carriers showed up. The other question was why he had not used the same tactic to force the Kalvyn back into battle and destroy her while he had the chance, before the Methryn had time to arrive.

And so the Methryn began her leisurely run into system. There were twenty packs, nearly two hundred fighters, standing free on her decks in the landing and storage bays as large accessory cannons were being mounted to the undersides of their hulls. Other work was progressing as well, including the erection of a slender tripod on wandlike legs a hundred meters above her upper hull.

The Methryn's bridge, as large as it was, needed to be twice as big to accommodate all the people who had business there. So it seemed to Mayelna, who seemed to have some trouble trying to follow six other conversations at the same time. At that moment Velmeran marched onto the bridge from the right lift corridor. He had been from the bridge to various parts of the ship and back again so many times that on his last visit, hardly ten minutes earlier, Valthyrra had teased him for simply riding the lift for fun.

"Is everything ready?" he asked as he approached Mayelna and Valthyrra, waiting at the base of the steps leading to the middle bridge.

"It will be," Valthyrra answered simply.

"The tower will be ready ahead of schedule," Mayelna added. "The construction crew reports that they will be finished and back inside by the end of the hour. Which is good, since we need to have them in well before we come deep enough into system for any activity to be scanned on our outer hull."

Valthyrra made some curious, noncommittal sound. She approved of Velmeran's plan completely. The tower was constructed of slender aluminum rods, light enough to escape detection by Union scanners even at close range. Valthyrra did not object to the tripod, but what went atop it.

"Speaking of scanning, Don has to know that we are moving into system by now," Velmeran said. "And he also has to know that we are stalling for time. Has he given any indication of a threatening gesture to hurry us on?"

"No, not yet," Valthyrra answered. "But then, we have been under way only the last three minutes. I will be keeping a very close watch."

Velmeran paused for a long moment, so obviously in the grips of a new idea that the others waited patiently for him to finish. Whatever it was, he did not need long to decide.

"Call me a lift, Valthyrra," he said as he turned and hurried away. "I have to talk to someone."

"And they are off!" Valthyrra remarked softly. "It is Mayelna's Folly ahead by a length, followed by Out of Time, with Lost Patience a close third."

"Do you ever stop?" Mayelna asked as she started up the steps to her own station.

"Never. Keth is calling for you."

"Very well." Mayelna sat down heavily and rolled the seat to its forward position, then leaned over the intership com. "Yes, what is it, Keth?"

"Commander, I wish to report that I have discovered an intruder."

Mayelna looked up at Valthyrra, who only stared back in return. She turned back to the com. "I understand. Send her up to the bridge."

"Should I provide escort?"

"No, she knows the way."

"But what if she escapes?"

Mayelna frowned. "I should be so lucky."

The unexpected but relatively minor problem of the intruder was forgotten within minutes. The Kalvyn was now ready to move herself into position, where she would be ready either to assist the Methryn or, according to plan, move in to stand watch over Tryalna. She would have liked to have consulted with Velmeran a final time, but he had not yet returned. Mayelna and Valthyrra did their best to advise her.

"As I see it, you should go ahead as planned," Mayelna said, watching the scanner images on the main console at her own station. "Velmeran is certainly busy over here, but as far as I can tell he has no intention of changing his original plan."

"Very well, then," Schayressa replied. "I will pace myself with your attack so that I do not get ahead of you. Be careful."

"We will keep that forever in mind," Mayelna assured her, and glanced up at the figure in black armor waiting patiently at the top of the steps.

"Yes, what is it?" she asked absently. The Starwolf was no one she recognized, but she assumed this tall girl to be a pack leader from the Kalvyn. Then she did a double take and nearly jumped out of her seat. "Heavenly days! Lenna Makayen!"

Valthyrra spun her camera pod around so fast that something inside the hinge made an odd noise.

"Just me," Lenna said, grinning sheepishly. She carried the heavy armor with no problem, in spite of the fact that it weighed fully as much as she did. "You are the trusting sort."

"I knew you would come," Mayelna told her. "My problem is not keeping you, but getting rid of you. I must compliment you on your disguise."

"I'm back in makeup," she said, obviously pleased with herself. "All I have to do, it seems, is make my eyes look bigger. And hide my ears. All the Starwolves on this ship have pointed ears poking through their hair, but no one seems to notice that I have none."

"I see what you mean," Mayelna observed. "Then what gave you away this time?"

Lenna shrugged helplessly. "I just overlooked the fact that when you walk around a Starwolf ship looking like a Starwolf, the other Starwolves expect you to speak Starwolf."

"Tresdyland," Mayelna corrected her.

"Anyway, I thought it safe enough to go down and use the simulator. I never thought that Keth would still be lurking about. I expected him to have gone to the Kalvyn with his students like he was supposed to."

"Yes, some people do that," the commander remarked dryly. "Where did you get that suit?"

"Oh, it's Velmeran's, to be sure." Lenna beat her head forward to look at the armor. "He's the tallest Starwolf on this ship, so I thought his suit might fit me. And I knew that he had an old suit standing on a rack in his cabin."

"And the lower arms?"

"Empty, of course. So what do you propose to do with me? If it's all the same to you, I would as well remain in the simulator. It is in a heavily protected part of the ship. And the artificial gravity simulates the G's in a fighter, so that I'm increasing my tolerance for accelerations. I can hold the controls through a fifty-G turn now. You show me an ordinary human who can do that."

Mayelna regarded her speculatively. "Just what is your fascination for the simulator?"

"It's not a matter of fascination, Commander. Velmeran and I both know what he's going to have to do to destroy that big ship, and he's going to need my help. I'll need to be good enough to fly with him, and I haven't so long to practice."

Mayelna frowned thoughtfully. "I think I know what you have in mind, and you may be right. Very well, then. Lenna Makayen, you are now a Starwolf. Valthyrra, how long will it take to make her a suit?"

"The better part of a day," the ship replied. "For now, it would take only fifteen minutes to pull the lower arms off that suit and set some plugs in the holes."

"All right," Mayelna agreed, and turned back to Lenna. "You are now a pilot on board this ship. It is impossible for you to fly with the regular packs, but I am assigning you to Velmeran's special tactics team. First, you will go immediately to have that suit modified. Keth will meet you there, and take you to the fighter assigned to you. That will give you perhaps two hours of practice in a real ship, with emphasis on launching and landing. Is that agreeable?"

"Very," Lenna replied, trying vainly to hide a triumphant smile.

"This solves a couple of problems," Mayelna continued. "It is not safe to send you away . . . safe for either you or us. If the Union learned that you had been aboard a Starwolf carrier, they would take you apart for any information you might have. Also, I suspect that Velmeran's special tactics team will prosper from having a human spy. And to keep you busy between missions, I am also going to assign you to Consherra as an assistant helm. Now, is there anything special you might need?"

Lenna thought for a moment. "For now, I will probably need a Union officer's uniform of intermediate rank. I will certainly need other disguises in the future, including a suit with four arms for when I need to be a real Starwolf. Could we possibly mechanize the lower arms?"

"It can be done," Valthyrra agreed.

"Consherra told me that you are an experienced pilot," Mayelna said. "We will be giving you a cabin on the pilot's level, and do what we can about giving you a little more heat. And just what do you find so amusing?"

"It's my father, Commander," Lenna explained, grinning broadly. "He didn't even want me to be a Trader. If he was still around, he would blow a gasket if he knew that I was a Starwolf. But I wonder if Velmeran is going to be agreeable to all these plans."

"He anticipated this, and it was his idea. He had already discussed it with me," Mayelna said with a sly grin. "Get on with you, now. We have work to do, and so do you."

"Yes, Commander!" Lenna turned quickly and almost ran down the steps. Smiling with amusement, Mayelna thought that this might not be such a bad idea. After all, it was not every day that a problem became a potential asset.

Three hours later, the Methryn was ready to begin her attack run. Originally, Velmeran was to lead the fighters against the Challenger's support fleets, but he had decided at the last moment to remain aboard the Methryn. It was the carrier, after all, that would be doing the actual fighting in this battle; the packs were going out just to provide a diversion.

Still, Velmeran thought it best to encourage Donalt Trace to believe that he was away with his pack. The packs were divided into two groups. A smaller, under Baressa, would go after the supply ships orbiting the fifth planet. The larger group, which was to have been his, was to attack the fleet of warships stationed at the seventh planet. Baress was given command of both Velmeran's pack and this attack force, and Lenna Makayen was elected to fly replacement in the pack. Although she could never equal real Starwolves in either skill or endurance, she could run a good bluff.

"All packs away," Valthyrra reported. "Both assault forces have formed under their leaders and are ready to advance."

"You may relay to them their order to advance," Velmeran responded as he stood leaning over the front console of the Commander's station, watching the forward viewscreen. "Close and secure the landing bays and ready your primary and secondary batteries."

"Yes, Captain," Valthyrra answered with martial formality.

Velmeran turned quickly as he became aware that Mayelna was standing behind him.

"This is your first time to fight from the bridge," she began. "It seems to me that you should be sitting at the Commander's station. It has all the monitors and controls you need to keep an eye on everything."

"But . . . that is your place," he protested.

"That seat is for the Commander of this ship," Mayelna insisted. "I will assist you in every way I can, but just now you are the Commander."

"Oh, no. I could not," Velmeran objected as she physically pulled him over to the seat, retracted back on its runners. "I do not feel up to that seat just yet."

"Nonsense. It fits you just fine, I am sure." Mayelna managed to force him into the seat and activated the control to roll it forward. "You see, it fits just fine."

"I feel like a pretender to the throne."

"Heir apparent, I believe they used to say," Mayelna corrected him, smiling. "You know, it has been just about twenty years since you used to come up to the bridge and sit in my seat. I never suspected that you were trying it on for size. But you have certainly grown into it. I am glad that I am here to see it."

Velmeran smiled shyly, glancing down, well aware of her deep sincerity. Then he noticed Valthyrra's camera pod hovering not two meters away.

"What are you waiting for? Begin your attack run," he ordered sharply. "This is where you get your lumps."

"Here she comes now," Maeken Kea warned, looking up from the monitors of her own console.

Donalt Trace turned sharply from the forward viewscreen to

look at her. "Is she? They were taking so long, I was beginning to think that they must be up to something."

"That remains to be seen," Maeken remarked. "There is something about the way she just jumped up and started a run straight at us that makes me think she knows exactly how to handle us. Marenna Challenger?"

"Yes, Captain?"

"Turn your forward battery to meet that ship, then shield your engines," she ordered sharply. "Give full power to your hull shields. Open fire as soon as the Methryn comes into range."

"Yes, Captain."

Maeken sat back for a long moment, staring in silence at the Methryn's projected path on the central monitor of her console. Donalt Trace became curious about what she could be thinking, and slowly walked over to stand looking unobtrusively over her shoulder. He thought he understood. The Methryn was moving fast, and projected to pass at one-half light speed. And she would pass only two thousand kilometers to one side. That was not very far, not at that speed, and much nearer than he would have expected.

"Do you know what they are up to?" he asked at last.

"Perhaps," Maeken mused. "They might be thinking—with some justification—that their weapons track better than our own. Or rather, that they can move too fast for our weapons to track. By moving fast enough, they can sneak through an attack run with little risk of serious damage."

"For all the good it does them," Trace remarked contemptuously. "A few seconds of cannonfire each run will get them nowhere."

"True, but it does waste time for more ships to arrive," Maeken pointed out. "Or, if she is carrying nuclear or conversion missiles, this is exactly the type of run she would make. And where is the Kalvyn? We hurt her, but she is still perfectly capable of a stiff fight."

Commander Trace did not reply; there was hardly any need. If Velmeran knew that help was coming, he needed only to keep the Challenger occupied until a number of carriers converged on the vast warship. And if the Methryn was carrying a score of high-energy warheads, this battle would be a short one. The quartzite shielding could turn such an explosion, but not a sustained barrage. Quartzite shielding was incredibly brittle; the smallest crack would spread in seconds to peel the shell off the entire ship. And the heavy outer shield was useless against missiles.

"Stand by," Maeken warned the bridge crew. "Marenna Challenger, remember to fire as soon as possible. The Methryn is going to be moving into your bolts."

"Yes, Captain," the ship responded. "I calculate approximately seven seconds of effective firing time on the Methryn's approach, with only about three as she passes. Beginning the count in five seconds from . . . now."

It was as if the entire ship snapped to attention as console after console on the Challenger's vast bridge leaped into life. Five separate scanning and tracking systems identified the target for hundreds of cannons, and each cannon locked on, not on the Methryn herself but where she would be. A moment later those same consoles hummed with frantic activity as over half the Challenger's guns opened fire, shooting well ahead of their fast-moving target so that their bolts would be there in time to intercept the Methryn.

The two ships closed to range and, for two full seconds, exchanged a fierce barrage of fire. Then the Methryn was rocked by an explosion so intense that, for a moment, she actually disappeared from scan in the violent backwash of energy. The Challenger ceased fire immediately. Then the Methryn shot past, still and lifeless, her original course deflected slightly by the force of that explosion. She was tumbling already, her bow dipping as she began to roll end over end.

"We got her?" Commander Trace asked in the stunned silence that enveloped the entire bridge.

"I think . . . ," Maeken answered hesitantly in her disbelief.

"An apparent hit on the Methryn's main generators amidship," Marenna Challenger reported with her usual calm detachment. "I scan only emergency power in effect. The Methryn is drifting out of control."

"Open fire!" Maeken snapped impatiently.

"The Methryn is out of my range."

"Then follow her! Chase her down! Pursue at your best speed until you have her back in range," Maeken ordered, repeating herself, in what was becoming a habit, to be certain that she was understood. She turned to Donalt Trace. "Hold on, Commander."

Trace hurried to a spare seat at the rear of the bridge. Union ships did not increase their gravity to counter acceleration, since ordinary humans could not endure the extra stress. Instead they cut gravity and counted on everyone being in a seat. The Challenger swung her blunt nose around and began to accelerate, and she had a surprising amount of jump for her size. Even so, the Methryn, drifting at one-half light, was leaving her far behind.

"How long?" Trace asked.

"Marenna is pushing herself to the limit," Maeken reported. "Even so, we're looking at seven minutes to match her speed and another nine to overtake her. I have already ordered the stingships to intercept her packs and keep them clear. Surveillance just reported that the Kalvyn is coming after us in a hurry, but we will overtake the Methryn first."

"We have to disable the Methryn completely in time to meet the Kalvyn," Commander Trace said. "Only missiles will catch her now. Give her a pair."

"The Methryn has no shields," Maeken informed him.

"I want that ship as intact as possible," Trace ordered. "Set the missiles to explode close enough to give her a good, stiff jolt."

"Right." Maeken quickly relayed the order. The Challenger needed only an instant to ready and fire the two missiles, which shot away on flaring star drives.

"Two missiles are away," the ship reported. "Estimated impact in three minutes, eleven seconds. The Methryn has restored directional control."

"What?" Maeken demanded, and checked her own scanner monitors. The Methryn's power levels remained practically nonexistent, although she had apparently found the power for field-drive steering. She had ceased her slow tumble and now flew straight and level, although she continued to drift. That meant that the Methryn was repairing herself, recircuiting auxiliary power back into her main systems. The missiles had already covered a third of the distance to their target; Maeken silently urged them on, hoping that they would disable the Methryn somewhat more permanently before she recovered any more control.

Seconds passed, and the two missiles gained steadily on their target. At fifteen seconds to detonation, they armed their warheads and moved into position so that one would pass below the carrier and one above, only a kilometer separating them, catching the Starwolf ship in the worst of the concussion between the two. That was hardly enough to destroy the Methryn, even without hull shields, mostly because space was a very poor conductor of energy, but it should slow down the repairs. But the situation resolved itself quickly. The Methryn caught both missiles just two seconds short of their target with a couple of precise shots from her rear cannons.

Maeken Kea muttered a favorite oath of her home world. "Well, that answers that. Now we have to catch her ourselves."

That still seemed likely enough, as long as the Methryn did not save herself. The chase continued, and the Challenger gained steadily. Then, just as the larger ship had closed half the distance between them, the Methryn turned her bow nearly forty degrees and engaged her main drives. It seemed that she was certain to escape, but after only seven seconds her power failed again to leave her drifting. And yet the thrust, as short as it had been, threw her well out of the Challenger's reach. The Fortress adjusted her course on her own initiative; she was not yet ready to give up the chase.

"Damn them!" Maeken declared. "I should have guessed."

"What is it?" Trace demanded, mystified.

"They found their escape," she explained. "Apparently their damage is such that they can never outrun us. But they do mean to duck into the ring of the fifth planet for repairs."

"Can we stop them?"

Maeken bent over her terminal to do some hasty calculations. Donalt Trace was impressed; very few people had the mechanical ability to perform their own trajectory mechanics. After a moment she sat back and frowned.

"Well, this is certainly going to be close," she remarked at last. "Assuming that the Methryn has to shed all her speed before she can enter the ring, she should be coming into our range at almost the same instant she loses herself in the debris. We have just over twenty-one minutes to try to catch her."

The race continued. After a few minutes the Challenger matched the Methryn's speed, and the task of closing on her prey began again. After eighteen minutes more of running, the Fortress was now nearing seven-eighths the speed of light. One of the brighter stars ahead suddenly began to expand rapidly, quickly becoming a large world banded by yellow and reddish-orange clouds and framed by an immense ring. Rings were common enough, but this one was unique in that it was not banded and segmented but consisted of a single disk that was a noticeable brown in color, with a grainy texture that betrayed the large size of its components. Moments later the Methryn herself became visible at the limit of the highly magnified image.

The Methryn was braking sharply now as she prepared to match speed with the mass of the ring, rising quickly below the ship. The Challenger cut her own acceleration but continued to drift at near light speed. But the race was lost already, if by mere seconds. The Methryn braked hard a final time before disappearing both visually and from scan. A moment later the Challenger fired a quick volley at the region where she thought the carrier to be for the few seconds that she remained within range, already braking with her forward engines as she shot past the large planet. She began a slow circle that would bring her back to the same area of the ring by the time she could cut her speed to orbital velocity.

"Now what?" Trace demanded, gasping for breath as he was held against the straps of his seat by a five-G deceleration.

Maeken spent a long moment studying her monitors before reporting. "The Kalvyn is holding her distance, apparently too damaged herself to fight us alone. On the other hand, the packs have destroyed our stingships and are coming in a hurry."

"And your recommendation?"

Maeken frowned, but made her decision quickly. "Finding the Methryn in that place will be a real chore. Both ships can navigate the ring, but it will keep our speed limited to little more than orbital velocity of the ring itself And cut the range of our cannons. Neither ship will have effective scan. The Star-wolves can keep us preoccupied with their fighters, but we have the undamaged ship. But she is leaving a trail for us to follow, And if she loses power again we'll have her. And if we do not go after her now, before help arrives, she will get away. I say that we should go in after her now."

"So do I," Commander Trace agreed.

Maeken Kea gave the order for the Challenger to follow the Methryn into the ring. It was as Velmeran had foreseen. Donalt Trace could not resist the prize under any circumstance. But Maeken Kea was also tempted, beyond her better judgment.

Maeken Kea was unaware that she was chasing an intact, undamaged Starwolf carrier into a trap.

<h1 style="text-align:center">11</h1>

A large part of Velmeran's success lay in his talent for conceiving and executing plans that his human opponents did not expect. Lenna Makayen, expressing it from the human point of view, declared it was the sort of thing that no one in their right mind would consider the first time she heard it. Velmeran thereby reasoned that it was also the sort of thing no one would expect and somehow saw a compliment in that remark. Either he knew a few things about humans that they did not themselves suspect, or else he was, as Lenna implied, not entirely in his right mind. Whatever the case, it had certainly worked.

The execution of the plan had been simple enough. Valthyrra had made her run at a speed and heading that had put her in the general direction of the fifth planet, requiring only one course correction. The large explosion in her engine rooms had been in reality a quarter-megaton conversion device rigged from the salvaged generator of a fighter, and placed atop the tripod erected a hundred meters above her hull. The Fortress's scanners were not accurate enough to detect the light structure or determine the fact that the explosion had actually been safely outside the Methryn's shields. Marenna Challenger had assumed from misleading evidence that her main generators had been hit, and Maeken Kea had seen no reason to question that.

The rest had proceeded simply enough, although it had required careful timing. Valthyrra had simply shut down her engines to set herself adrift, idling her main generators, then gave herself a very slow nose-over roll. Everything, from her high initial attack speed to her one course correction and short bursts of power, had been carefully calculated to keep her just outside the Challenger's reach.

If Maeken Kea had been at all suspicious, she would have easily seen that there were entirely too many convenient coincidences. But those suspicious coincidences had instead become enticing lures. After one piece of incredibly good luck followed by a string of near misses, neither Maeken Kea nor Donalt Trace could resist the urge to continue the chase. As prey, the disabled Methryn was simply too tempting to refuse.

Velmeran knew that the Challenger would attempt to follow the Methryn's trail through the ring. The powerful static charge of the ring caused its relatively large fragments to repel each other enough for Starwolf fighters to slip through with ease; the larger ships would simply force a path with their debris shields, a path that could be easily followed for several hours before gravitational and static forces caused them to close again. Velmeran actually pointed out the Methryn's corridor to the Challenger by having the returning fighters duck almost beneath the larger ship's nose to fly down the open path.

"How long until the fighters come in?" Velmeran asked, removing himself at last from the Commander's station.

"The first packs should be in about two minutes from now," Valthyrra replied. "Baress and Baressa will be leading their packs in first. Do you want me to send them here as soon as possible?"

"Send me those two, and the rest of my special tactics team," he decided. "What is the Challenger doing?"

"Casting about for the opening I left in the ring," the ship replied. "She obviously means to follow."

Velmeran spent the next few minutes reviewing the careful scan of that area of the ring that Valthyrra had made during her approach. She calculated that the giant Fortress would not be able to make better than two thousand kilometers per hour—relative, of course, to the speed of the ring itself. Within the ring, its floating mass of boulders and moonlets appeared as a motionless landscape to any ship sharing the same orbit . . . that is, traveling in the same general speed and direction. Actually, the Methryn could go little faster herself, since speed was determined by how fast rocks could be shoved away from an oncoming ship.

They had entered the ring near its outer edge, and had been working their way steadily inward ever since. Because of the low speed, they could expect to confine their chase to a relatively small area. At this rate, it would take nearly two full days just to pass completely through the ring and reach the outer atmosphere of the planet below. They were in fact spiraling slowly inward, moving "downstream" with its motion.

The crewmembers he had requested, and some he had not, arrived on the bridge within minutes. Baress and Baressa arrived with Trel and Marlena, the other two official members of the special tactics team, and Tregloran, who had been an unofficial member for over a year. Lenna Makayen, none the worse for her first turn as a combat pilot, quietly brought up the rear.

"How did it go?" Velmeran asked as they approached.

"Quite well," Baress replied. "We did not get a scratch. And at this point, the only stingships they have left are any the Challenger herself might be carrying."

"I got three!" Lenna proclaimed proudly. Since she had not had time to remove her makeup, Velmeran had recognized her by the fact that the black armor she wore had only one set of arms.

"Three what?" he asked. "Ours, or theirs?"

"Stingships, of course," she said indignantly. "Like shooting fish in a barrel."

Velmeran glanced at Baress, who shrugged helplessly. "I got only three myself. Valthyrra cut down the phasing of her engines so that we would always know where she was. And, to tell the truth, we were flying in such close quarters that you could not tell her from the regular pilots."

Velmeran regarded the girl for a moment and shrugged. "That should not be surprising, I suppose. Just tell me when your ears begin to point. How did the attack transports work out?"

"It was a simple matter of overkill, shooting at stingships," Trel replied. "They were designed for bigger game."

Valthyrra steered her camera pod in behind Velmeran. "I thought you would like to know that the Challenger has indeed entered the ring and is following my corridor at such an alarming pace that I have had to increase my own speed. I have a probe following her at a discreet distance."

"Then we really are in business," Velmeran muttered to himself, and turned back to Valthyrra. "How soon can the packs go out again?"

"Back out?" the ship asked in desperation. "I only just finished getting them all in. But you can head out immediately, if you must."

"That might seem a little extreme. We need to make it look

like we had to take stock of what we have and hold an emergency conference on the subject first. We will start putting fighters back into space in exactly one hour. Right, Lenna?"

"Right, Captain."

"I will lead twelve packs after the warships," Velmeran continued. "Baressa, you will take twelve packs after the supply convoy."

"What about me?" Lenna demanded.

"You will . . . ," Velmeran began sternly, but paused when he saw her look of determination, ". . . need all the practice you can get. I do not have a pack for you to fly with this time."

"She can go with us," Trel offered. "We should be easy to keep track of, since she has to depend upon scan entirely to know who she is with."

"Good enough," Velmeran agreed. "Lenna, if you can hold your own against stingships, you can certainly handle the warships."

"And if you do not come back, I am only out a fighter," Valthyrra teased.

Donalt Trace arrived on the bridge at a run, only to find that no one was at the Captain's station. He paused just long enough for a quick look around, and found Maeken Kea bending over the shoulder of the officer at the main communication console. She turned to meet him just as he arrived.

"The support fleet and the convoy are both under attack," she explained quickly.

"Is there anything we can do?" Commander Trace asked.

"It is already over, as far as I can tell," Maeken answered. "That fool of a fleet commander thought that he could handle the problem himself; he didn't call for help until he realized that he had lost. The last ship went silent only a moment ago. We cannot scan accurately from inside the ring, but the answer is plain enough. We have no support fleet, and we can no longer repair this ship."

"We have no damage now, do we?"

"No, nor could the support fleet do us much good inside the ring," she answered. "Stingships could not begin to navigate this mess, although it seems that Starwolves can."

"Do you consider this a major setback?" Trace asked as they turned toward the Captain's station.

"No, a relatively minor one, under the circumstances." Maeken had to run every few steps to match his long-legged stride. She wondered if he had really come to value her judgment so much that he would agree to retreat on her recommendation. She decided to test that. "As I see it, we can risk another twenty-four hours to try to fish the Methryn out of the ring. I am only guessing that we will be fairly safe until then, but any time after that we're likely to be up to our necks in carriers. We can only hope that the Methryn will either have to shut down for repairs or else simply break down again, and we have to overtake her during that time."

"And we have no idea how fast she's moving. She might be gaining on us, or we might be gaining on her." Trace started to seat himself in the Captain's chair, but remembered and quickly stepped aside. "You are right, I suppose. But what good does it do him to go after those targets?"

"It's just what I would have done," Maeken said. "At least he now has his problems limited to just one big one. And now we have to ask what he intends to do about that problem."

Velmeran was contemplating that very question during his return to the Methryn. As far as he could tell, he had only three options. He could either lead his packs against the Challenger and see what their cannons could do against her guns, take the Methryn in for a real battle, or else go immediately to his reserve plan. He did not doubt that he would have to resort to that third plan, but he preferred to try something simpler and more direct first.

The truth was that Velmeran had no idea just how effective a fighter would be, but he had little hope that this was the answer to his problem. That depended more than anything on how fast and accurate the Challenger was at tracking a target as small as a twenty-meter fighter. To destroy a cannon, the pilots were required to put a bolt through the small opening in the turret for its tracking lenses, a task complicated by the fact that they had to align their entire ship to fire their own cannons. That might prove impossible even for Starwolves, between dodging rocks and enemy fire. Still, he thought it was worth a try.

Velmeran allowed another hour's rest before the next attack. Kelvessan, because of the tremendous demands of hypermetabolism, had surprisingly little endurance, but they also recovered very quickly. That was Lenna Makayen's peculiar advantage over her fellow pilots. But when she did tire, she was much slower to recover. That was part of the reason why she did not protest when Velmeran told her that she would not take part in this attack. She really did know what she could and could not do; she could easily navigate the ring, something no true human would attempt, but not fight there.

The problem of endurance was also very much on Velmeran's mind. He knew that his pilots were only good for about ten or twenty minutes of this kind of work. If this attack did show reasonable promise, it would take hours of picking away at the Challenger's guns and engines to leave the ship vulnerable to the Methryn's conversion cannon. He would have to divide his twenty packs into four groups of five each, each group attacking for fifteen minutes and then resting at a safe distance for forty-five.

"There simply are no easy answers," Valthyrra had concluded when he had discussed his ideas with her. "The question, of course, is do we really have to defeat this thing as long as we can keep it here?"

"I have not forgotten that," Velmeran said. "But this Maeken Kea is smarter than anyone I have fought before, and she is going to be hard to fool. I am sure that she expects me to put up a stiff fight, even if she also expects to win. It seems to me that there is little difference between doing my best and doing enough to keep her satisfied, so I might as well try to win."

"And what if you do too good, and she decides that it is time to leave?" Valthyrra asked.

Velmeran smiled. "The Challenger is as penned inside this ring as they believe we are. She cannot open the shields on her engines to run without leaving them vulnerable to our attack. But I actually want them to run at the end. We certainly cannot use the conversion cannon here. We would blast away half the ring and ourselves with it."

Valthyrra's cameras had a decidedly shocked expression. "Funny I had not thought of that."

"Then I suppose that I might as well get on with what I can do," Velmeran said, already on his way down the steps from the upper bridge. "Call the pilots to their ships and have the capture ships stand by."

Velmeran collected the packs just above the ring and back-tracked along the Methryn's path until he was sure that he was behind the Challenger. Returning to the ring, they quickly found the five-kilometer-wide corridor left by the Fortress's passage. Velmeran sent two groups of six packs each into the ring to either side, then waited with the remaining eight packs until they were in place. When all was ready, he took his group down the length of the corridor in a high-speed run.

They came upon the Fortress suddenly, taking out the exposed engines quickly before the giant ship had time to react, then skimmed just meters over the surface of her hull and catching as many targets as they could as retractable turrets began to emerge from their protective sockets. This move was less effective than it might have been, since Velmeran had expected the cannons to be extended and ready for battle. As it was, the first wave of fighters was nearly past before any targets became available, and none was destroyed. The fighters separated immediately, disappearing into the ring before the Challenger's forward battery could orient on them.

At that instant the other two groups of fighters attacked from either side. These fighters did not rush in but, paralleling the Fortress, used the cover of the ring as they darted back and forth on evasive paths, dipping in every few seconds for a shot volley of bolts before retreating. Their advantage was that the Challenger's scanners could not identify and lock on individual targets, but had to direct its cannons at each ship as it appeared momentarily from the confusing background of static-laden debris. On the other hand, the Fortress had the advantage of just over eleven guns for each fighter.

These odds impressed themselves upon Velmeran very quickly, as if he had not been aware of it before. In the first half-minute the Challenger lost one cannon, and he lost one fighter. A bolt seared completely through the right wing of the ship, sending it tumbling through the ring to bounce off several large rocks, although never actually hitting because of its inner shields. After a third such impact the pilot regained some control, and a capture ship snapped up the fighter only seconds later.

Just over a minute into the attack the Methryn's corridor turned sharply and began to head at a steep angle inward, and the Challenger began to accelerate quickly as she fell toward the planet. It was Velmeran's hope that the vast ship would have to open her forward engines for short blasts of braking thrust rather than risk accelerating beyond her limit. Although there was an alternative that would spare her engines that risk.

Unfortunately, it seemed that Maeken Kea knew exactly what

to do. For half a minute the Challenger began to gain speed, then turned abruptly to her right, looping around until she was heading back out. Within another minute she pulled to a stop, braking with field drive aided by the pull of gravity and the resistance of the material of the ring itself pushing against her shields. She corrected her course a final time and settled into a stationary orbit, motionless in respect to the movement of the ring, and turned her full attention to the attacking fighters.

Coming to a stop in the ring not only solved the Challenger's problem of drift, it had the unfortunate effect of increasing her advantage tremendously. When she had been in motion, her scanners had been overturned with trying to distinguish real targets from countless metallic rocks shooting past; now they only directed the guns at anything that moved. Three ships were clipped in as many minutes, while the raiders destroyed only nine more guns. The odds remained in the Challenger's favor, since Velmeran would run out of ships before she ran out of cannons.

Velmeran was just about to order a retreat when he saw a fighter just about a kilometer ahead take a bad hit that sent it tumbling end over end away from the Fortress. He accelerated and moved to intercept the stricken fighter, for a quick scan showed him that it was drifting without the protection of any shields and unlikely to survive a major impact. He was momentarily unaware of another ship following his own.

"Captain?" Tregloran asked uncertainly, identifying the pilot of the damaged ship.

"Hold on a moment, Treg," Velmeran said as he dived in beside the tumbling fighter and used his auxiliary cannon to blast a small boulder in its path. "Who is behind me?"

"Steena?"

"Help keep the path cleared," he ordered. "Baressa?"

"Here, Commander."

"Order a very hasty retreat and collect the packs just above the ring," he instructed quickly. "Treg, can you get your ship under control?"

"I am trying to get auxiliary power," the younger pilot replied. "The main generator is cycling back into itself, and building slowly to an overload."

"Forget it, then," Velmeran said, and paused as he and Steena concentrated their fire on a larger rock. The boulder shattered at the last moment, and the fighter rolled through the opening as its pieces flew apart. "Treg, can you eject?"

"Sorry, Captain. The canopy locks are jammed by hydraulic back pressure, and I cannot get the leverage to force it. All I can hope for is auxiliary power."

"Be quick about it, then," Velmeran said. "You are about to come up on a group of very large rocks."

That was something of an understatement. The larger pieces of debris, moonlets of several hundred meters to several kilometers across, tended to gather in small groups, drawn together by their own feeble gravity but never touching because of their tremendous static charge. If Tregloran's ship was on a collision course with one of these massive rocks, nothing short of the Methryn would get it out of the way. And there were no capture ships free.

Two massive rocks, hundreds of meters across, emerged out of the background haze and grew quickly in size as the stricken fighter hurtled toward a deadly meeting. Tregloran remained blissfully unaware of the situation. He was busy at the keyboard of his on-board computer trying to force a reluctant auxiliary generator to start while trying to keep a damaged generator from exploding.

Velmeran had been watching the matter closely, however. It soon became apparent that the damaged fighter would catch the outer edge of the second, smaller rock, less than a kilometer behind the first. A small moonlet, six kilometers across, stood unavoidably ten kilometers behind that. Velmeran cautiously moved backward and to one side, using the inner shield of his ship to deflect Tregloran's slightly.

Tregloran suddenly found enough power to halt the tumble of his fighter, and for the first time he became aware of the trouble he was in. He passed within a hundred meters of the larger rock, and barely two seconds later skimmed over the surface of the second with only five meters to spare. Velmeran, who continued to push from that side of his ship, barely cleared the surface. Tregloran put all the steering control of his own ship into turning away from the moonlet directly in his path.

The damaged fighter was sluggish and unresponsive. Velmeran never gave up, all but carrying the wrecked ship on the back of his own, even in the final seconds when it was obvious they had failed. But at the last instant Tregloran gained much more control and cleared the surface of the small moon through a pass between two ragged projections.

"Captain, can you lead me back to the corridor?" he asked immediately. "My main generator is going to explode at any moment."

"You do that and I will back up along my corridor to intercept you," Valthyrra insisted. "Can you hold out for another three minutes?"

"I am sure of it," Tregloran said. "I am holding it by sheer will right now, and it is going to explode seconds after I let go of it."

"Long enough for us to pry you loose and throw it overboard," Valthyrra asserted. "Just pop your wings and slip in on the deck, gears up so that we can get to you."

Tregloran's ship had no drive power, just steering. The power lines of his main generator were burning now, as much as they could in the absence of air, leaving a trail of hot gasses and glowing particles behind the fighter. The Methryn, moving quickly up her own corridor, intercepted them as they reached it and began to accelerate forward to match the speed to that of the fighters approaching from behind.

Tregloran tripped the explosive bolts in the wings of his fighter as he moved behind the Methryn's tail, and small, gas-filled pistons inside the downswept wings lifted them into a level position. Valthyrra matched his speed carefully so that he entered the bay at hardly more than a very fast run. Velmeran and Steena accelerated now, passing through the bay and out the forward door. Tregloran allowed his own fighter to travel half the length of the bay before lowering it gently to the deck, leaving a trail of sparks and thick smoke as it slid to a stop only five meters from the forward door.

Benthoran and an assistant were there immediately, and at the same time a pair of handling arms moved in from overhead to seize the damaged fighter. Flames and sparks shot out of every opening in the shattered hull as burning power lines exploded under the stress of a generator building quickly to an overload. The two crewmembers ripped loose the locked canopy and threw it aside, while Valthyrra gently lifted the fighter barely a centimeter from the floor and began to move it slowly toward the open door. While Benthoran helped the nervous pilot free himself from his ship, other crewmembers aimed a frigid blast of carbon dioxide into the fighter's engine compartment to cool the faulty generator and delay its explosion.

At the last moment Benthoran bodily lifted Tregloran out of the cockpit and threw him to safety, then leaped over the fighter's wing just before it swept him through the containment fields into open space. Valthyrra carried the ship free of the deck, as far out as her handling arms would reach, and gave it a firm push downward. Then she thrust herself forward, barely clearing the fighter before it exploded.

Benthoran walked over to where Tregloran's motionless form lay on the deck, under the attentions of three crewmembers who had removed his helmet. "Are you all right?"

Tregloran glanced up at him. "Just glad to be here."

"I can imagine." Benthoran laughed softly, then gestured impatiently to one side of the bay. "Clear this wreckage from the deck. We have to land the damaged fighters before the packs can come in."

"Damnation!" Maeken Kea muttered as she fell back into her seat, then immediately pushed herself back up again. "Marenna, give me a report. Are they really gone?"

"They appear to be," the ship responded noncommittally. "All fighters have disappeared from scan."

That did not mean much; inside this orbital rock quarry, everything disappeared from scan within a few kilometers. But Maeken Kea did not have long to decide. After a moment she launched herself from her seat and began to pace the edge of the central bridge. "Return to the Methryn's corridor and follow her. Damage report."

"I have lost two complete engine clusters, fourteen engines in all, although the loss will not seriously affect my speed even in starflight. I have also lost seventeen cannons."

"Keep the units that still have functional generators so that we can have their power on the grid, and pitch the rest overboard," Donalt Trace said as he joined her. "It occurred to me during the design of this machine that they would shoot up through the damaged units to get at the interior of the ship, so the module sockets have the same quartzite shielding."

"Eject the malfunctioning units," Maeken told the ship.

"Yes, Captain."

Maeken Kea resumed her nervous pacing for a moment, then hurried back to her seat to consult the monitors on her console.

Trace smiled privately. Except when penned to her seat by accelerations, Maeken fought her battles with a display of physical rage and strength equal to her amazing mental agility.

"Well done, Captain," he said, moving to one side of her chair.

Maeken glanced up at him. "Whatever for? Velmeran called the shots. Brilliant moves, but he left an answer for every problem. This was just to see how well his fighters work against this ship. Now he knows better."

"Will he be back?"

Maeken frowned. "I really suspect that he is just trying to slow us down until the Methryn can be repaired . . . which indicates that we must be gaining on her. This attack bought him a little time, but not all that much. He has to come back. I just wonder what he plans to do next."

12

Velmeran called a meeting in the Methryn's smallest council room the moment he returned to the ship, and for as soon as the requested members could arrive. This was no problem for most, although Lenna had been trying to sneak in her required eight hours of an activity that Kelvessan did not need, and she had only just started the third. And Dyenlerra had caught Tregloran before he was able to escape; only a direct request from Velmeran was able to get him out of the medical section.

"Well, I would not exactly call it an exercise in futility," Velmeran began suddenly. He had been sitting at the table, deep in his own thoughts, waiting for the others to arrive. Lenna had just sat down at the table, propped her chin in one hand, and appeared to go to sleep. He regarded her briefly and continued. "I did have my first good look at the Challenger and I know what she can do. Obviously the Methryn cannot fight her, and the packs are not much good either. I guess that I will have to do it myself. Damage report."

When Valthyrra did not respond, he reached over and gave her camera pod a sharp rap. She turned to look at him. "Damage report. What was the final score? I left before the game was over."

"You did not miss a thing," Valthyrra answered. "We have six wrecked fighters and two injured pilots . . . slightly injured, but they will not be flying again for a few days. You trimmed the Challanger of seventeen guns and fourteen engines. Ordinarily I would say that you came out slightly ahead."

"No, not this time," Velmeran agreed. "Don designed his ship entirely too well, and Maeken Kea is every bit as smart as I was afraid she would be. Not only did my plan to force them to expose their engines fail, but she used it against me."

"As you were afraid she might, as I recall," Mayelna pointed out.

"Recognizing your mistakes before you make them is hardly an asset, not when you go ahead and make them." He looked up as Tregloran entered and quietly took an empty place at the table. "Ah, here he is at last, the Kelvessan cannonball. Explain to me one thing. Did you keep your main generator from overloading by keeping the power lines open with a rather surprising exercise of your newly acquired talent?"

"Why, Treg! I never knew you had it in you," Consherra exclaimed. She was the self-appointed trainer of psychic talents to the Methryn's handful of mutant Kelvessan. Tregloran looked insulted.

"And why not?" he demanded indignantly.

"And why not?" Valthyrra repeated that question. "It is hardly surprising, when you consider that nearly all the Dvonnan Kelvessan that we have identified so far have been fairly closely related."

Everyone, except for the apparently dozing Lenna, regarded her questioningly. As the implications of that became evident, Velmeran and Tregloran turned to look at each other.

"No, not you two." Valthyrra laughed. "I have been able to put together a vague history of the Dvonnan Kelvessan by lengthy consultation with the other ships. There seems to be two distinct clans of mutants that arose separately at about the same time some ninety years ago—although I suspect that some link between them has yet to be found—originating from a single parent who was not Dvonna Kelvessa himself."

"Both male?" Velmeran asked.

"That is not surprising," the ship explained. "It is our system of taking duty mates that has contributed to the mutation. As I said, these clan progenitors are nearly but not quite mutant themselves, but remarkable people and very desirable duty mates, and their unions were often with females like Mayelna and Baressa who are themselves near-mutant, and whose union produced true mutants. Commander Fverran of the Schaylden originated the larger group that gave us Baress and Tregloran, while the smaller but somewhat more talented clan descended through Commander Tryn gave us Velmeran and his sisters Daelyn and Consherra."

"Me?" she asked. "Where do I come in?"

"Do you remember your father?"

"My father? I barely remember my mother."

"Well, I remember that both the Kalvyn and I were at Home Base several months before you were born."

"Yes, but . . . ," Consherra faltered, aware that everyone was staring at her. Even Lenna opened one eye. She frowned, then gave the camera a hard stare. "Do you know this for a fact, or are you just supposing?"

"Call it an educated guess. Although I could not help but notice that Tryn did remember you." She turned her camera pod to look at Velmeran. "The two of you should produce some amazing offspring."

Lenna blinked sleepily. "Oh hell, we're just one big, happy family! How does that work out, anyway?"

"We do not have the problem you must be thinking of," Mayelna answered, obviously amused with the whole affair. "Close inbreeding can be advantageous for us, as long as we do not make a habit of it."

"Well, it's strictly your affair," Lenna said as she again propped her head in her bed, closed her eyes and, to the mystification of all present, appeared to go to sleep. They were still staring when she opened her eyes a final time. "I should point out, however, that you are straying from the subject."

Velmeran started and stared accusingly at Valthyrra. Everyone present knew from experience that she could not only change the subject but lead it on a merry chase before someone remembered what they were supposed to be talking about. Valthyrra recognized that stare and looked away quickly.

"Now, it seems to me that we were discussing the problem of

one very large ship," he began, sitting back in his chair. "I have now either tried or rejected every idea I can think of—"

"Just how certain are you of that?" Consherra insisted suddenly, although she was not talking to Velmeran but to Valthyrra. "Have you actually discussed the matter with Commander Tryn?"

There was a long moment of silence as everyone, including Lenna, regarded her with a mixture of surprise and mystification.

"No, I did not," Valthyrra answered. "It is a possibility, but some other crewmember of the Kalvyn, one of Tryn's offspring, could have easily been your father."

"That is true, of course," Consherra agreed softly, then noticed that Velmeran was watching her with an expression of forced patience. "Sorry."

"I quite forgot what I was saying."

"You have tried everything," Lenna reminded him.

"Ah, yes." He shrugged. "The answer is simple. If—"

"But how can that be?" Consherra interrupted again. "You said that the Dvonnan Kelvessan have been around for about ninety years, and I am going on seventy. I doubt that Commander Tryn had any children old enough to have been my father."

"Mutant children, perhaps," Valthyrra answered. "He could have had nonmutant children from earlier matings who share his ability to sire mutants."

"Oh." Consherra was utterly disappointed, to everyone's surprise.

"As you were saying," Mayelna prompted.

Velmeran looked up and hastily closed his mouth, which was hanging open. "Yes, I was . . ."

"But you obviously think so," Consherra insisted.

"Yes, I do," Valthyrra answered. "Are you not aware of how much you look and act like Velmeran? If you were just a bit taller, you could almost pass for Daelyn."

Consherra considered that, felt her small nose, and shrugged. "I guess so. And he did remember me."

"But is that any real trick in a race that has selective recall?" Lenna asked. "And besides that, you all look alike to me."

"Actually, you do have a point," Consherra admitted with disappointment.

"Tral de lessan!" Velmeran exploded. "So you happen to be my half sister. Is that so bad?"

"Bad?" Consherra regarded him in complete surprise. "Nothing could make me happier."

The entire group sat in silence for a long, expectant moment as Velmeran glanced from one to the other. At last he sighed heavily and sat back in his chair. "Now, if . . ."

"You will ask Tryn and Schayressa about it, though?"

"As soon as this is over," Valthyrra promised, then turned to look at Velmeran, who sat with his arms crossed, staring at the ceiling. "Well, what are you waiting for?"

"I am going inside the Challenger and reprogram her so that she cannot shield effectively," he said quickly, and waited. This time there was no question that he had everyone's complete attention—everyone except Lenna, who was so impressed that she again propped up her head and closed her eyes. Valthyrra was speechless, and Consherra appeared likely to explode as soon as she could collect her wits and find her tongue. And yet Mayelna, the source of many past arguments, was not in the least bit surprised.

"There is no way to destroy the Challenger from the outside," he continued. "We have proven that. The only solution is to do something from the inside so that she can no longer assemble her complete power grid. Consherra, that is your department. What would you do if you had access to the Challenger's primary programming?"

Consherra was caught off guard by that question; whether he intended that particular result, it had the effect of putting out her fuse before she reached an explosive level. She was about the most gifted programmer in the fleet, with access to the secrets of Valthyrra's construction. Certainly no one in the Union knew as much about advanced sentient systems.

"Well, there are any number of bugs you can throw into the system," she answered uncertainly. "Under the circumstances, the best would be to insert a loop that throws power sources back out of the grid as others come on line."

"But to do anything effective, you have to get free access to the Challenger's basic programming," Valthyrra protested. "You know yourself the types of safeguards they are going to have on that system. It probably takes hours to get inside even when you know the codes and passes."

"True," Velmeran agreed. "But what if you could bypass the

guards and go directly into the system? I can get instant control of the Challenger."

"Nice trick! How do you think..." Valthyrra's voice faded suddenly, and her lenses assumed a distant stare. Then, as everyone watched expectantly, she began to recite.

> "There once was an entrepreneur
> Auditioning girls for his tour.
>   One girl showed her stuff
>   But it wasn't enough.
> So he promptly proceeded to ... to ..."

She seemed almost to blink, then turned her camera pod to look at Velmeran. "And so you get control of the Challenger. What then?"

"Then I order her to open her programming from the inside," he explained.

"Simple enough," Valthyrra agreed. "I should be ashamed of myself for always underestimating you."

"So you should."

"Where did you come up with that, anyway?"

"Lenna."

"Yes, I recognize the material." She turned to Mayelna. "Yes, he really can do it."

"I have already learned from experience that he can and will do what he says," Mayelna replied. "So, you create a diversion, land on the Challenger's hull, and enter through a convenient airlock. I suppose that you can force one without being detected?"

"Easily," he assured her.

"Then you juggle her programming and get back out again?"

"Preferably in a hurry," Velmeran added. "We will have to arrange our timing so that Valthyrra will attack as soon as possible after the tampering. That way, even if they know what we did, they would not have time to correct the damage."

"Wait a moment," Consherra interrupted. "You can bet that Marenna Challenger has the ability to review her own programming. That is how our own ships develop personalities; they are continually altering and expanding their personalities."

"Yes, but there must be a way to hide the alteration," Velmeran insisted.

"Of course. You can insert the alteration in an invisible loop.

The information inside such a loop instructs her to be blind to the loop itself while incorporating the alterations into the master program. It is by no means foolproof. Once she realizes that she cannot raise the grid as she should, she will go back in to look for the problem. Still, there will be an interval between the time she recognizes the trouble and is able to correct it. That will be Valthyrra's one chance to destroy her."

Velmeran nodded. "I knew that. I was hoping that you would be able to insert an invisible loop that she would find particularly difficult to detect and delete."

"Well, yes, I could," Consherra agreed. Then she realized what he had in mind. "Now, wait a minute! That is not my line of work."

"We all have to start somewhere," Velmeran said.

"But how do you plan to get me there?" she protested weakly.

"You can fly yourself there, like the rest of us. You keep a fighter of your own, and you have practiced with me often enough for me to know that you happen to be a very good pilot. I also know that you flew with the packs for several years before you transferred to helm."

"Yes, but I am needed here." Consherra seized upon that thought as an excuse.

Valthyrra regarded her closely. "Just who do you think is flying this ship right now? Your value is as second-in-command, not as an emergency flight computer, and just now your knowledge of sentient computer systems makes you invaluable to this mission."

There was a long moment of silence, during which there was an abrupt shift in viewpoints in this argument. Velmeran, who had been considering the requirements of this expedition only as its leader, suddenly remembered his earlier prophecy was likely to be the cause of his own death. He had forgotten that prediction mostly because it had ceased to be valid. But now it was back. Someone in this room, himself included, would not survive the assault on the Challenger, but he had no idea who. At least he could be certain of Consherra's safety.

"Actually, Consherra is right," he said quickly. "There is no reason for her to go. I can modify the Challenger's programming as easily as she could."

"Oh, of course," Valthyrra agreed, supporting him enthusiastically for some reason of her own. "I doubt that her abilities would make that much difference."

Consherra, however, had been considering the matter herself, and she had realized that this might be her only opportunity to accompany Velmeran on one of his special tactics missions. "Now wait just a moment. No one can hide that loop as well as I can, and the success of the mission depends on it."

That was followed by a moment of complete silence. This abrupt and complete reversal of positions left everyone speechless with confusion and surprise. Even Lenna appeared to be fully awake for the first time.

"Meran, I have to share the risks like everyone else on this ship," she continued. "It happens that there is a task to be done that I can do better than anyone else."

Velmeran frowned and looked up at Valthyrra. Her camera pod made a helpless shrugging motion. "She is right, as much as I hate to admit it."

Velmeran knew that himself, although he found it almost impossible to agree. He shivered imperceptibly at the memory, more vivid than it had been these past two years, of the horror of waiting for Dveyella to die while he had been unable to help her. At last he nodded slowly, then looked over at Baress. "Will you come with us?"

"I would be delighted."

"What about me, Captain?" Tregloran asked anxiously.

"Oh, I had something in mind when I asked you here," Velmeran said, smiling. "I need for you, Trel, and Marlena to stay with the ships and guard our way out. Our suit communication will not penetrate the quartzite shielding on the hull, so I need a good telepath on the outside to relay any messages."

"And me," Lenna added with determination.

"You?" Velmeran looked at her questioningly. "Just what do you think you can do for us?"

"Any number of things," she declared. "For one thing, I can put on a Union junior officer's uniform and walk around that big ship just about anywhere I want to go. That's why you hired me, remember. I'm your spy. And saboteur."

Velmeran considered that for a moment and nodded thoughtfully; he knew exactly what she had in mind. "I believe you might just be useful after all. If you are not previously occupied—and able to stay awake—I would be honored if you would accompany us."

Lenna smiled mischievously. "I already knew that you would be needing me."

"And I knew when I called you here that you were planning to go," Velmeran added. "So this is where we stand. Baress, Consherra, and I will go inside the fortress to do the program tampering. Lenna will go along to do whatever she can. I have been looking at Schayressa's scan, so I know where we can enter. It involves a walk—in straight-line distances—of just over five kilometers. Since our direct communication will be cut off, we had better make arrangements now. As soon as we go in, Valthyrra will allow the Challenger to pass and fall in some distance behind. We can use transports in formation to clear a corridor that resembles her own. At our signal she will close for the attack, forcing the Challenger out of the ring and into open space."

"And just how do I force her out?" Valthyrra asked.

"She is going to go willingly," he assured her. "When she sees an undamaged Methryn coming at her from behind, she is going to run to open space where she can fight more effectively."

The camera pod nodded thoughtfully. "You are probably right. But how do you land seven fighters on her hull undetected?"

"In a mass of general confusion. To put it simply, we need a diversion."

"Oh? What kind of a diversion?"

"Oh, I had something in mind," Velmeran said as he leaned back in his chair. "If nothing else works, we can always throw rocks."

"Are you sure that you feel up to it?" Velmeran asked, pausing at the door as he followed the others out.

Valthyrra regarded him quizzically. "Do I feel up to it?"

"Well, you are getting a little old."

"Old?" She lifted her camera pod threateningly. "I, for one, do not consider eighteen thousand to be old at all, not compared to how long I expect to last. Nor do I believe that Donalt Trace or any other two-armed primate can build a better machine than I am, and I intend to prove it."

"Just checking," Velmeran said, and disappeared out the door.

"I like that!" Valthyrra remarked to herself as she stared for a moment, then turned to Mayelna. "Surely he has no complaint about my performance."

Mayelna stared in disbelief. "Are you serious? He was just playing with you. When were you ever not ready for a fight?"

"I guess so," she agreed weakly, then turned to Consherra. "And what of yourself? What could possibly possess you to insist upon going?"

"As I recall, you and Velmeran did all the insisting," Consherra replied defensively. "Then, once you convinced me of the necessity, you abruptly changed your minds."

"I had momentarily forgotten one important matter," the ship reminded her. "As you seem to have forgotten altogether. How can you possibly go? Can you still fit inside your armor?"

Consherra glanced apprehensively at Mayelna, and could tell by the Commander's expression that she was well aware of what the ship was implying. She had the sudden urge to tamper with Valthyrra's programming; this was embarrassing enough as it was.

"Yes, I can still fit inside my armor," she insisted, turning back to the glaring camera pod. "I am still just a month along, with five months yet to go. This is something I must do."

"And what about the safety of your child?" Valthyrra countered.

"I am aware of the risk, and I accept it," Consherra replied firmly. "You know that little short of my own death will do my child any harm."

"Velmeran would not want you to take this risk."

Consherra drew herself up sternly. "Velmeran is my mate and the father of my child. I know that he would not approve, but the decision remains my own. Baressa is pregnant by the same father, and yet not even he questions her right to take part in this. In fact, he left her in command of the packs in his absence."

"Enough, Val," Mayelna interrupted when the ship was prepared to protest yet again. "She is right on two important points. She is needed, and it is her decision. Nor is Velmeran to be told of . . . her condition. He has enough to think about just now, and that would be too much of a distraction."

"Very well," Valthyrra agreed reluctantly.

Consherra turned to Mayelna and smiled self-consciously. "I am sorry, Commander."

"Sorry about what?" Mayelna demanded gently. "Dear girl, I can die happy now."

"But, commander . . ."

"No, girl, stop worrying about it," Mayelna said firmly. She began to rise but decided that she should not; this came as more of a surprise than she wanted anyone to know. "Listen, I know what this means to you, and I know how happy this is going to make him. That is all that really matters. If my approval is that important to you, then understand that I could not be more pleased. And you can bet that old chips-for-brains is excited, or she would not be so overprotective. Now, you go get ready."

"Yes, Commander," Consherra agreed eagerly, obviously pleased, although her cautious retreat from the room suggested that she was still afraid that she had done something wrong. She turned and hurried down the corridor.

"So, she got your little boy in trouble," Valthyrra remarked, amused. "I see the problem now. If you people did not have such a guilty conscience about neglecting your duty, I might have the crew I was built for."

Knowing that she had at least an hour, Lenna hurried to her cabin and hastily climbed into her armor. She had already set aside what she would need, putting the Union officer's uniform that Valthyrra had made for her in a pressure-resistant bag along with a modest supply of emergency makeup and her old Union service pistol. She preferred the more powerful Starwolf guns, but the aging jack-snapper was part of her disguise. Collecting her supplies, she went directly to the landing bay, where their fighters had just been brought out, and tucked the bag into the small storage compartment in her own ship. Then she climbed inside the cockpit, closed the canopy, and promptly fell asleep.

Such was her condition when the others arrived a little over an hour later. They halted in front of the first fighter while Velmeran mounted the steps of the boarding platform and rapped sharply on the closed canopy.

"Wake up, Lenna!" he ordered, although she could not have heard him inside the sealed cockpit.

After a moment the latches snapped open and the canopy rose slowly to reveal Lenna, yawning hugely. Velmeran reached in and lifted her easily from the seat, standing her on the edge of the platform. Still yawning, she led the way down the steps to join the others. Baress handed her a large rifle and a belt that held several small, thick metal disks. She looked at the items curiously.

"The Challenger is virtually uninhabited," Velmeran began. "She has about one regular crewmember to every cubic kilometer of interior space, and the Kalfethki are confined to a small area. Unfortunately, there are sixteen automatons to every cubic kilometer, and no handgun is going to dent their armor. That rifle has an armor-piercing carrier beam and enough of a charge to wreck the inside of any sentry, and it is also the only thing that can kill a Kalfethki quickly. The heat charges are just as effective against sentries, but you have to get one against the hull of the machine for it to do any good."

"I know how it works," Lenna assured him. "Tregloran explained it to me."

"He did?" Velmeran looked questioningly at Tregloran, who pretended ignorance.

All the various weapons were handed out to the members of the assault force, and they hurried to their ships to stow their equipment. Velmeran helped Consherra with her own, since she handled the weapons with such unease that they might have been fierce, alien creatures and likely to bite. Climbing into the cockpit, however, she betrayed her complete familiarity with the fighter.

"I will get you back safely," he assured her as he helped her fasten her straps.

She looked at him with open astonishment. "I am not concerned about myself. I know that you will be taking all the chances, so I want you to watch out for yourself. Just remember that the winning of this battle does not win the war. We need you alive for more important matters."

Velmeran smiled. "Now you sound like my mother."

"Oh?" she asked skeptically, and smiled. "When we come back, I have something to say that should convince you otherwise."

"Glad to hear it," he remarked, and kissed her quickly.

He left a crewmember to assist her in securing the cockpit, gathering the weapons he had left beneath the fighter and hurrying to his own ship. He knew that he was wasting too much time. Valthyrra had already begun her evasive maneuvers, and would soon be complaining that he was likely to ruin all their careful planning with his procrastination. The ship had long since ceased to be concerned for his safety, at least as far as he could tell. Mayelna did quite enough worrying for the two of them, so he was not surprised to find her waiting beside his fighter.

"I came to see you off," she said, almost apologetically. "I do not suppose that I need to remind you to be careful."

"That idea has already occurred to me," he assured her as he transferred his weapons to his lower hands and keyed the hidden latch to his fighter's cargo compartment. "Would it be pointless of me to ask you not to worry?"

"No way," she said. "How is Consherra?"

"Calm, confident, and nearly as eager to begin as Lenna is," Velmeran said, his voice echoing hollowly as he worked inside the compartment. "I wonder why this means so much to her."

"Well, she used to be quite a Starwolf when she was your age, when she still flew with the packs. That was a few years before you were even thought of, naturally. I think she wants to prove that she is also a very capable warrior, and not just a bridge officer." She paused a moment to watch him closely. "She has not forgotten that Dveyella was a warrior. And that, had she lived, she would be going out with you on all these missions."

"Consherra is comparing herself with a memory," Velmeran stated as he tightened the stowage straps around the gun. "And an increasingly dim memory."

"True, but the memory she is comparing herself against is her own, not yours. Perhaps it is more important for her to prove something to herself."

Velmeran seemed about to say something, but decided otherwise. She walked with him around the front of the fighter and up the steps of the boarding platform, holding his helmet as he climbed inside the cockpit. She obviously had something important in mind, some matter too important to wait. Velmeran seemed too distracted to notice. In truth, he had something equally important to say, if he could only find the words.

"Consherra means a great deal to you," Mayelna said at last, watching him fasten his straps. "You are aware, perhaps, that a male and female may share a special relationship. There most often comes a time in everyone's life when you meet someone, and both of you become aware that the two of you will be keeping company for a very long time to come. But you must also realize, when a male and female join as mates, they are also peforming a natural function and must be prepared for the results that nature intended. Do you understand what I am saying?"

Velmeran stared at her in utter amazement. With typical Kelvessan innocence, he completely misinterpreted her implications. "If this is the little talk we should have had fifteen years ago . . . well, we should have had it fifteen years ago. I am quite aware that Consherra and I are likely to have a child sooner or later. Considering her sexual instincts, it will probably be sooner."

"Soon enough," Mayelna agreed vaguely. "Would that please you?"

"I imagine that it would please me very much," Velmeran said as he fastened the last strap. He paused a moment, uncertain, and looked up at her. "Valthyrra will be going in for overhaul after this. I was wondering . . . perhaps . . . if you would like to retire then."

Mayelna stared in absolute astonishment and mystification. "Retire? Why would I want to retire at this time?"

Velmeran shrugged. "It makes about as much sense as what you were talking about."

"That may be so," Mayelna agreed, affording him a searching stare. "Are you ready to command this ship? I do not question your ability to do so; you have for the last two years. What I mean is, do you want to?"

Velmeran nodded slowly. "As you said, I have commanded here for two years now. I no longer have the time to run a regular pack as well as this ship and my special tactics team. Nor does my pack bring me the pleasure and sense of fulfillment it once did. I have outgrown it, you might say."

"So now you want my chair?" Mayelna asked, smiling with amusement.

Velmeran smiled shyly in return. "I would take nothing away from you. I just thought that—under the circumstances—you might want to take up residence on the Kalvyn."

Mayelna swallowed apprehensively and looked away quickly to hide the tears that rushed to her eyes. Nothing in all her long years had touched her as much as that simple offer. Nothing meant more to her. "Meran, what . . . what can I say?"

"You can say yes," he suggested hopefully.

"Are you going anytime soon?" Valthyrra demanded suddenly over com, her voice echoing dimly from the helmet

Mayelna held. She looked down at it, then reached out and set the helmet on his head.

"You go take care of business, Commander Velmeran," she said as she fastened the collar clips. "I will watch your ship until you come back."

13

Maeken Kea was still fastening her jacket when she arrived at the bridge. As a matter of fact, it was the only part of her uniform that she had on. In her years as the Commander of a warship, she had learned through experience to always wear something when she tried to catch a little sleep when battle was likely. But the Starwolves had a certain perversity on that score; they had been careful to attack while she was in the shower. She reasoned that, if she got only one thing on by the time she reached the bridge, the jacket was long enough to keep her decently covered—if just barely. She was correct, for the most part; she was blissfully unaware that the tail of the jacket was split in the same place her own tail was split.

Lieutenant Skerri saw her the moment she entered and pretended to notice nothing strange, although she could well imagine the stimulation to his postadolescent fantasies. She threw her pants in his direction and headed straight for her console.

"So what is it?" she demanded briskly as she bent over her monitor.

"Captain, the Methryn's corridor has turned straight out from the planet," Skerri reported. "It seemed suspicious to me, so I knew that you would jump on it."

"You bet your—"

"Collision imminent!" Marenna Challenger warned suddenly.

Maeken glanced anxiously at the main viewscreen, where the danger was immediately obvious. A rock of respectable size, a kilometer and more wide by half a kilometer high, was hurtling down the Methryn's corridor, moving fast and accelerating rapidly along a path designed to make the best use of the gravity of the large planet below. Numbers projected to one corner of the screen estimated time to impact and counted down sixteen to fifteen even as she watched. Maeken needed only an instant to decide.

"Arm missiles to launch!" she ordered briskly. "Detonation on impact. Fire one . . . and two. Hull shields to maximum—brace for impact."

"Condition réd—brace for impact." Marenna relayed the order to the entire ship as the first missile struck and exploded. The viewscreen dimmed automatically against the brilliant nuclear flash barely six kilometers ahead. The second explosion followed in the next instant. A fourth of the boulder was either vaporized or crushed by the concussion into gravel. The rest split into five sections that were still alarming in their proportions.

A second later the debris pelted the Challenger's forward hull. The quartzite shielding held, although the ship shuddered violently. Maeken remained standing through the impact only by holding on to the back of her seat.

"Shield your engines!" she yelled at Marenna even as the reverberations echoed through the ship's hull. She was only guessing what the Starwolves would do next, but it was a good guess. Four packs of fighters dived out of the ring in the next instant. Because Maeken had already given the order to shield, they got only six of the fourteen exposed engines.

"That tears it," Maeken muttered in disgust as she snatched her pants from Lieutenant Skerri's grasp. "Keep your eyes open."

Skerri did as he was told. As the Captain turned and began to pull on her pants, he did his best to watch closely while pretending to keep his eyes discreetly on the monitor. At forty-five, Maeken Kea was twice his age, on the far side of middle-aged by his own definition. He was all the more surprised to see a trim and shapely fanny.

"Do you see anything?" she asked.

"Captain, I . . . ," Skerri stammered guiltily, then understood what she meant. "All clear for the moment."

Maeken paused to glance at him over her shoulder. It did not do for junior officers to have any fascination for their seniors, but she could keep Skerri under control. Besides, he served her best for as long as she was able to keep him impressed, and she had the feeling that she had just impressed him in a way that neither of them had expected. She looked around for her boots and found that they must have been left in her cabin.

"Collision imminent!" Marenna warned again.

Maeken looked up at the viewscreen and saw absolutely nothing. At that instant the Challenger shuddered so violently that she left the deck. She struck the ceiling and was pinned there for a moment, hitting squarely in the middle of her back so hard that her vision dimmed. Then gravity returned and she was dropped sprawling to the deck. Skerri landed nearby and remained motionless. She began to pick herself up, cursing herself for not strapping in after that first attack but glad that she at least had her pants on. A second impact from the opposite direction flattened her to the deck. She was about to ask for a report when she saw Starwolf fighters on the main viewscreen.

"Do not return fire!" she ordered sharply as she rose to stand uncertainly. "Keep your power in the hull shields."

"Yes, Captain."

Maeken straightened her back experimentally, trusting that nothing hurt bad enough to actually be broken. Skerri remained motionless. She considered moving him but knew that she could not. He was a big, healthy boy, while she was technically a tall midget. She appreciated the fact that she was moving while he was not. Well, Mr. Skerri. Not so old after all, are we?

"Damage report!" She gasped in pain as she lowered herself into her seat.

"No damage to the ship," Marenna replied. "I believe that the better part of the crew is slightly incapacitated for the moment, and I will send automated sentries to investigate possible injuries to off-duty personnel."

"What happened?" she asked.

"There were two additional impacts," the ship explained. "Small corridors had been opened at right angles to our own. Boulders of approximately two hundred meters were accelerated along these corridors and struck the ship above and below the forward hull, the result of remarkably accurate timing. The impacts rocked the ship violently."

A slight understatement, Maeken reflected. She noticed that Lieutenant Skerri was sitting up and rubbing his head. At the moment that seemed to be a favorite activity of the Challenger's crew.

"With us again, Mr. Skerri?" she asked.

"I was never completely gone," he replied. "Just very close to it."

He rose and walked stiffly over to her console. Holding the supports of her seat, he quickly checked the scanner images. Starwolf fighters were swarming over the hull of the ship, skimming the gleaming black surface by as little as two meters. All to absolutely no effect.

"As long as we keep the guns retracted, they have absolutely no targets," Maeken explained. "Besides, it might be a trick. I want to keep that power to the hull shields in the event they throw something else at us."

"I see what you mean," Skerri agreed. "Tricky devils. These attacks are getting more sophisticated all the time."

Maeken nodded slowly; it was as fast as she could nod. "Perhaps I shouldn't say this, but I'm beginning to get scared. There seems to be no limit to how much Velmeran can think up and put together. We may reach a point where I will finally make a mistake."

Skerri frowned. "It is getting dirty."

"I'm glad you recognized something suspicious and got me to the bridge in time," she said, grinning mischievously. "At least they didn't catch you with your pants down."

Lieutenant Skerri laughed in spite of the pain.

The seventh and last fighter dropped quickly into the sheltered cove formed by three towering projections in the Challenger's hull. Watching from his own cockpit, Velmeran identified it as Lenna's. The little ship extended its landing gear and dropped down until its landing pads locked magnetically against the hull of the Fortress.

"All down and no problems," he reported over com. "You can break off the attack."

"Right, Captain," Baressa replied. "All packs break off. . . ."

Her voice was lost as he disconnected his suit from the fighter's com link and support system. He was surprised and delighted that the Challenger had held her fire on the way in; that was something he had anticipated but not expected. All he had hoped for was to create a state of complete confusion to hide the landing of the assault team.

After fully depressurizing the cockpit, he opened the canopy and cautiously climbed out. They had landed on the side of the Challenger and were in fact on a vertical portion of the hull, like spiders walking up the wall. But that hardly mattered, since there was no gravity on the outside of the ship. Electromagnetic inserts in their boots kept them on the surface of the ship, although the hold was feeble through the quartzite shielding.

The rest had gathered in front of the fighters, staring off across a flat expanse of open hull. Lenna arrived behind him; he could identify her easily by the fact that her armor had only one set of arms. Consherra was even more clearly identified by her white armor, an almost shocking contrast against an angular black landscape populated by black fighters and Starwolves in black armor.

"Out there?" Tregloran asked uncertainly. "We could waste half an hour looking for that airlock."

"You should have looked for it on the way in," Velmeran told him. "You might have landed on it."

He walked out eleven carefully paced steps and stopped at the edge of what now appeared to the others as a pit opening in the smooth surface of the hull. As they drew nearer, they could see that the rectangular depression was no more than ten centimeters deep, the lip designed to receive the hermetic seal of a docking tube. Inside that was the door itself, its two halves firmly sealed. They could also see now how he had found it so easily; the nose of his fighter was pointed directly toward it.

"So, wizard, you have found the hidden door," Baress remarked. "Do you know the secret word?"

"You have access to Velmeran's library," Consherra said accusingly. "How did you acquire that privilege? I was his mate for half a year before he opened his shelves to me."

"Needless to say, I found an easier method," Baress said dryly. "I asked. Perhaps you never thought of that."

"I lock the doors to keep the books on the shelves," Velmeran explained, interrupting his silent examination of the airlock. "Not to keep people out. A book serves no function unless it is read."

"Well, do you have any magic words?" Consherra asked impatiently.

"Certainly. *Quad erat faciendun, quantum placet. Allegro non troppo!*" he declared in a commanding voice, waving all four arms in elaborate gestures. "Open sesame!"

The doors snapped back instantly, revealing the brightly lit interior of the airlock. A second set of doors at the bottom were securely closed; the Union did not have the containment fields that Starwolves used on their own locks and bays.

"Quickly, now," Velmeran warned. "There are sensors on these doors that I am having to hold inactive."

"Right," Lenna agreed. Before anyone could stop her, she reached down to take hold of the edge of the lock and flipped herself inside. Gravity interfered halfway through her free-fall somersault and she fell heavily on her back on a wall that suddenly became a floor.

"Great stars!" She wheezed, and struggled to pick herself up. "Watch that first step."

Velmeran was the first to recover from his surprise. He turned and lowered himself cautiously into the airlock. Kneeling on the floor, he reached up to assist Consherra and Baress. Last of all, Tregloran passed their guns down to them.

"We have to get through this airlock before I let something slip," he said. "You remember what I told you. When the time comes, the three of you are to get away from here. If we are not back by then, we will not be coming back. Not to worry, though."

"Do I look worried?" Tregloran asked. "You can take on the lot of them, and bring this ship home for salvage. Especially now that you have Lenna to help you."

"I cannot tell you how reassuring that is," Velmeran remarked with droll sarcasm as he allowed the outer door to snap shut. He turned immediately to the control panel by the inner door and ran his upper right hand lightly over the surface, not quite touching, as if tracing hidden wiring. He quickly found what he was looking for, or so it seemed. Air began cycling into the lock, and a moment later the inner door snapped open.

Baress and Lenna were out the door immediately, rifles ready as they scouted the corridor in either direction, while Consherra stood with her rifle trained down the larger hall immediately ahead. Velmeran peered at them curiously.

"I could have told you nothing was there," he remarked. He turned to look at the door, and it obediently slid shut. "There. No indication that we ever came through."

"First things first," Lenna remarked as she set down her rifle. Taking her bundle of extra clothes, she headed for the suit room adjacent to the airlock. She immediately began stripping off her armor, hanging it on an empty suit rack in the wall beside the door, where it was less likely to be seen.

"Remember to avoid the sentries," Velmeran reminded them, having pulled off his helmet. "What one sees, they all know. It does us no good to destroy one before it has seen you, since its destruction will be noted and investigated. We need to conduct our business undetected, and leave the same way . . . if we can."

"Are those beasties able to identify legitimate crewmembers on sight?" Lenna asked.

"No. Visual identification is a complex function with a long history of accidents," Baress told her. "The uniform and the forged magnetic ident you carry will identify you as a legitimate crewmember."

"Just turn on the old Kanian charm," Velmeran added. "That should be enough to baffle even an automaton."

He glanced inside the little room to check on her progress, and found that she had just come out of her armor. It was his first sight of a naked human, and he did not care for another. The lack of a second set of arms made her look pitifully deformed.

"Since you will be on your own, remember to keep track of the time," he continued. "And give yourself enough time to get out. You have to be back inside your armor before you can leave."

"I'll keep that in mind," Lenna assured him absently as she struggled into her uniform.

"And above all, do not get yourself in more trouble than you can manage."

"Sure. All ready."

She emerged from the room, abruptly transformed into a stranger. She had put on her makeup in advance, hiding her Trader ancestry with a slightly different appearance to her slightly slanting eyes along with the hollow cheeks and wide, thin-lipped mouth of a native of the Lokuivea worlds, who still reflected their strong Polynesian and Amerindian background. Curiously enough, that might also explain any peculiarities in her speech.

"Ah, the girl of a thousand races," Baress said approvingly. "A true artist."

"That was my name at the bottom of the painting." Lenna retrieved her gun and joined the others. "Lead on, wizard."

The first task was to find a main corridor that would lead the

Starwolves to the forward portion of the ship, and where Lenna could find a lift to serve as the shortcut that she alone dared to use. There was a basic logic to the construction of this ship. In a sense the Fortress was a large ship inside a larger shell. The outer shell was the hull itself, its quartzite shielding and the vast sockets that held the guns and engines. Three hundred meters inside that was the inner hull that housed the mechanical workings of the ship itself as well as several cubic kilometers of crew quarters, storage bays, and machine shops.

The only inhabited regions in the outer hull were the rider bays and airlocks such as the one they had just entered. A single wide corridor extended tunnel-like to the interior portion of the ship, where a second airlock sealed it against emergency decompressions. Velmeran cycled this lock as he had the first, stepped boldly through the moment the inner doors opened, and found himself face-to-face with an automated sentry.

"Hello! Where did you come from?" he asked in mild surprise.

The sentry said nothing. The pair stood motionless as Velmeran stared into the glass eyes of the machine's cameras. Moments passed, and the apprehension of the others turned to complete mystification.

"Well, now, that is better," Velmeran said with disarming familiarity, as if he had just run across an old friend. "Do you have a name?"

The sentry appeared surprised. "I am called Ecs23-18."

"Oh, that is no name!" Velmeran declared. "What if we give you a real name? Bill, I think. Do you have any friends, Bill?"

"I have no friends. I am security automaton."

"We are your friends now, Bill. Would you like to work with us?"

"I would like that very much," Bill replied in his even, mechanical baritone, although it was easy to imagine tears welling up in his glazed lenses.

Velmeran took Lenna by the arm and pulled her forward. "This is Lenna Makayen. She is your very special friend. She has very important work to do. I want you to go with her, to help her and defend her. Will you do that?"

"I would like that very much," Bill agreed with a note of eagerness. "Lenna is my very special friend."

Velmeran turned to Leena, who was speechless. "Go on, girl.

Bill is totally obedient to our will now, and he will not turn on you. He can help you more than I can."

"Right, Captain," Lenna agreed, recovering from her shock. "You concentrate on your own business. I know what I need to do."

Velmeran nodded. "You have a very good idea, and I know that you can make it work."

She looked at him in surprise, then smiled. "Thank you, Captain. I'll not let you down."

Lenna hung the rifle by its strap and access hook on the towering automaton's humped back. "Can you take me to the nearest lift?"

By way of reply, Bill turned himself around and started down the corridor to their right at his even, lumbering gait. As slow and careful as he appeared to move, his long legs carried him at a pace that Lenna had to step quickly to match.

"There go two that I love, and the smallest not the least," Baress quoted.

Velmeran paused in putting on his helmet. "Is Professor Tolkien to be with us the entire mission?"

Baress shrugged. "I thought that we might have need of entertaining company now that Lenna is gone. What did you do to that machine, anyway?"

"Just a little judicious tampering with both the hardware and the software." He paused a moment to secure his helmet and switch on the outside audio pickups. The Starwolves could hear, if not as well, and yet converse freely without fear of being heard. "We have to hurry now."

"We should have asked Bill for directions," Consherra remarked as they started off in the direction the sentry had led Lenna.

"No need," he assured her. "All the major sections of the ship are located on a major corridor. Corridor three, level twenty-five ends at the auxiliary bridge. All we have to do is find corridor three on this level and go up five to level twenty-five, then follow that corridor forward all the way."

"And what about the sentries?" she asked.

"We will have no more trouble with sentries. I just needed a little practice at hearing them."

"Hearing them?" Baress asked incredulously. "You can sense the tiny generator in a sentry over the roar of this beast's engines?"

"Of course."

"If you say so," he said dubiously. "I only wish for half your talent. Still, it is as they say, do not meddle in the affairs of wizards, for they are subtle and quick to anger."

Velmeran glanced at him without pausing. "My mistake was obvious. I should have given Lenna access to my books, and given you my art supplies. Then neither of you would have understood what you had well enough to annoy me with it. Ah, here we are."

They emerged suddenly into a vast chamber, three levels high by nearly twice as wide and extending in either direction as far as even their sensitive eyes could see. Tubes of various sizes, from pencil-thin to large enough to walk inside, ran along the walls, ceiling, and floors, while several of the largest were suspended in frames in the center. Railed catwalks leaned out from the walls on various levels, and a raised platform wove a twisting path through the maze of pipes on the floor.

"This is your major corridor?" Consherra asked.

"Of course not," Velmeran replied. "We follow this forward to the next major transverse corridor, and that will take us directly to the major lateral corridor we need. Then we follow that forward until we find stairs leading up."

The Methryn sat in a natural pocket within the interior of the ring, her engines idle as she waited, and pivoted carefully until she was facing back the way she had come. Capture ships continued to arrive, every one both the Kalvyn and the Methryn possessed, and set to work plugging her corridor with boulders pushed aside in her passage. Transports of all sizes were gathering patiently in the main portion of the corridor five kilometers away.

"A report just came in," Valthyrra announced. "Tregloran says that the Challenger is moving again."

Mayelna nodded slowly without turning from the main viewscreen. "What about your mechanical self? That rock you pushed weighed a great deal more than you do."

"Oh, I can handle more stress than that," Valthyrra assured her. "That is part of the reason I have a shock bumper in my nose. However, I am reminded of something from ancient Terra, an animal called a seal that was trained to balance a ball on its nose."

"No seal ever had to balance its ball while running a path no wider than itself at four thousand kilometers per hour."

"I also doubt very much that seals ever threw rocks at battleships," she said dryly, then glanced at the viewscreen. "Only for him would I even consider doing such a thing."

Mayelna glanced up as well. The capture ships had completed their labor and were joining the transports in the main corridor. Seen from behind, their careful arrangement resembled the outline of a Starwolf carrier.

"All ready?" she asked.

"Just about," Valthyrra replied. "If the Challenger moves back up to her previous speed, she will be passing here in about ten minutes."

"Will this arrangement work?"

"Yes, it will work," the ship insisted. "But we are still taking a chance. All of those little ships will leave a very different energy-emission signature. For someone as intelligent as Maeken Kea seems to be, that might be too many hints as to our real tactics. Damn Donalt Trace anyway! The smartest thing he ever did was to admit that he is not smart enough to fight Velmeran. She also has the better ship."

"A better defensive weapon," Mayelna corrected her. "You make up for that in versatility. You also have the advantage of being a great deal smarter."

"I should hope so!" Valthyrra declared.

Mayelna smiled. "I just wish that you could fire as it passes."

"So do I," the ship agreed. Unfortunately, she needed half a minute to charge her conversion cannon, and the concentration of raw energy in her containment chamber would scream her presence throughout the system. "The decoy formation is ready to proceed."

"Send them on, then. They need to keep all the distance they can."

Five kilometers away, the decoy ships began to accelerate cautiously. The unique configuration of the formation allowed their overlapping shields to form a spearhead shape, gently pushing a passage through the ring that was identical in appearance to the Methryn's corridor.

Donalt Trace remained in his cabin, strapped in his bunk by acceleration belts, until he was reasonably certain that the attack was over. That was hardly an act of cowardice, but a practical consideration involving a couple of hard truths. He knew that he had very little to offer Maeken Kea, and there was no doubt that his reconstructed back would not endure being bounced around the corridors of the Challenger. And so it was a quarter of an hour after the last impact that he finally started for the bridge.

When the lift opened, he found two passengers already in the car. One was a cute if lanky Lokuivian girl in the uniform of a first lieutenant. The other was a sentry that took an abrupt step forward until the girl put a hand out to stop it. Trace naturally assumed that the machine thought it had reached its destination. He never knew how close he came to being killed by one of his own sentries.

"Bridge, Commander?" the girl asked, and he nodded as he took his place on the opposite side of the door. "The lift is set for there already."

"All secure, Lieutenant?" he asked.

"Yes, sir."

The lift pulled to a stop only a moment later and Trace was gone the moment the doors snapped open. Lenna Makayen rolled her eyes, sighed heavily, and gave herself an imaginary medal for acting. She would have liked to have let Bill shoot him, except that his disappearance would have thrown the entire ship into such a state of confusion that it would have been nearly impossible for the Starwolves to get away, much less complete the task at hand. With Bill at her side, she followed cautiously.

Commander Trace found the bridge in a state of organized confusion. Stunned and injured crewmembers sat in their chairs or on the steps leading to the central bridge. Lieutenant Skerri seemed the worst of the lot, and Maeken Kea, curiously enough, was wet and barefoot. Both were bent over the monitors at the Captain's console.

"Moving again?" he asked unnecessarily.

"This round seems to be over," Maeken replied. "Did you enjoy the ride, Commander?"

"It was interesting, to say the least. But what did they accomplish?"

"If nothing else, they bought more time. The final phase of repairing their generators has to be a shutdown of at least several minutes to tie in new power leads. They need to keep us off their tail."

"No doubt," Trace agreed, then paused to stare at her. "If you want to finish dressing, I suppose it might be safe for you to leave the ship in my care for a few minutes."

"I would like a dry uniform."

"And what about yourself, Mr. Skerri?" Trace asked of the junior officer. "You look like you need to visit the sick bay for a couple of aspirin."

"Yes, sir. I would appreciate that."

Lieutenant Skerri retreated gratefully from the bridge. His back ached fiercely, and his head hurt even more. All the same, he meant to return to the bridge as quickly as he could. His awe and respect for Commander Trace did not blind him to the fact that the old man was a mediocre battle commander at best. If he hurried, he might get back before Captain Kea left.

"Could you help me for a moment?"

Lieutenant Skerri stopped just short of the lift and peered at the small female figure dimly outlined in the darkened side corridor. "Yes, what is it?"

"Well, there seems to be a bit of trouble at hand, and I really need an officer of some standing to help me."

"I'm Lieutenant Captain Denas Skerri," he explained, trying to identify the crewmember.

"Sure, you can't get much higher than that," she agreed. "Tell me, do you happen to see that sentry standing behind you?"

He turned quickly and saw a sentry standing motionless in the shadows of the opposite corridor, not two meters from where he stood.

"Yes, I see him. What of it?"

"Well, it's a most peculiar thing. He said that if you don't do exactly as I tell you, he'll blow your damned head off."

"He does?" Skerri asked in complete mystification. Then the little wheels inside his head gave a convulsive jerk. "Hey, what is this?"

He turned abruptly back to the girl and found himself staring down the business end of a gun. "Actually, I'll shoot you myself if you don't do exactly as I say. Now, you just go ahead and call the lift. The three of us are going for a little ride."

The *Challenger* moved cautiously up the long corridor leading outward from the planet, laid by the Methryn to accelerate the massive rock toward her target. At the top of the run the

Methryn's corridor turned sharply and settled into a path that formed a more or less stable orbit. The Fortress accelerated to her best speed as she returned to the chase. She had only just achieved her maximum velocity when she shot past the Methryn, hidden in the ring a short distance to one side. Even at a relative speed of nearly a kilometer per second, it took her half a minute to pass.

"There she goes," Valthyrra announced as she brought up just enough power for her debris shields to deflect the rocks pushed aside by the Challenger.

Mayelna turned to look at her. "All I saw was a big, black shadow moving extremely fast. Are you ready?"

"Ready," the ship agreed. "I will begin powering up as soon as the Challenger is well out of range and follow five minutes behind until the time comes to move in."

14

Maeken Kea reviewed the scan data for the third time. Readings inside this highly charged nightmare were suspect to begin with. And it certainly seemed too good to be true, which meant to her that it probably was. She did not believe in luck. But the evidence remained, and she did not believe that static distortion could have altered the scanner reading so completely.

"It must be so," she agreed, although her reluctance was plain. "They are towing the Methryn."

"If the scan of energy emissions is at all accurate, that is the only explanation," Trace insisted.

"What convinces me is this additional evidence. Look at their orbital projections." She called up the data and a diagram on her monitor. "Their orbit is a slow spiral inward toward the planet, taking advantage of gravity to help maintain their speed. They're doing everything they can to keep that ship moving. The question is, did they break down or shut down?"

"Care to make an educated guess?"

Maeken shrugged. "It hardly matters either way. The important thing is that the Methryn is no longer moving under her own power. If we are going to catch her, it is going to be now."

The corridor opened onto a chamber of some size, which in turn served only as a balcony for a greater chamber beyond. Although it shared the same high ceiling, they could see that it dropped down at least one full level and appeared to be about forty meters wide by at least a hundred long. The three Starwolves could see little of the floor below, although they could make out a similar balcony on the far side and an entrance where the main corridor on this level picked up again.

"Security region," Velmeran remarked as they paused at the doorway. "We are on the far edge of the Kalfethki quarters."

"How do you know that?" Consherra asked.

"Airlock," he explained, pointing to the double doors immediately behind them. "We were supposed to be a level above this."

"Then what are we waiting for?"

"I prefer to meet them here," he said as he began to ready his weapons. Baress did the same, although Consherra was too surprised to do anything but stare in disbelief. He indicated for her to set the controls on her rifle. "Single shot, full power will be most effective. At least we have two chances to salvage this mission. The Kalfethki will not call up to the bridge until they have defeated us. Also, their weapons are kept under lock, so that all they will have to fight us will be their ceremonial swords."

"Why do we have to fight them in the first place?" Consherra demanded.

"They already have us cut off."

Velmeran advanced cautiously to one of the two sets of stairs leading down from each corner of the alcove. Towering Kalfethki warriors began streaming into the larger room below, stalking along in their awkward saurian gait with surprising speed. A smaller army was loping along the main corridor behind them, cutting off any retreat. All were armed with long, curved swords, with heavy blades two meters or more in length and quite capable of cutting a Starwolf in half, armor and all.

The three Kelvessan took up a defensive position on the steps, Velmeran at the bottom and Baress guarding the top. The Kalfethki continued to come, first by the dozens and then by the hundreds, until they filled the main chamber and overflowed into the alcoves. Velmeran knew their thoughts, and he could sense their eagerness and complete lack of fear. They had no concern for wars, for defending this ship or serving their temporary masters. They wanted either the honor of the kill or their own death, with a slight preference for the former.

Velmeran tried to keep this in mind, for this fight was to the death. Within himself there was a quiet shift of character, the coldly efficient killing machine he was designed to be replacing the true personality that was in itself incapable of violence. It was this duality of instinct that explained the puzzle of Kelvessan behavior, of how the most innocent and harmless of people in known space were also the most deadly warriors.

The press of saurian forms opened silently before him, forming a narrow corridor through the crowd. An older warrior, his battle harness decorated with at least two score badges of honor, advanced in slow stateliness, his weapon held upright. Behind him walked two more warriors and behind them a group of four. Others followed.

"A challenge," Velmeran explained to his companions. "The first challenge is given to the senior warrior. With each challenge, the number of challengers is multiplied by two."

"Quaint custom!" Consherra remarked. "What happens when you pass the challenges?"

"In theory, you do not survive the challenges. Challenge is issued only to a warrior who is hopelessly outnumbered, trapped, or otherwise doomed. They are not offering a chance to survive, just a chance for both sides to face death with all possible honor."

"Would it be foolish of me to ask if you have a plan?" she inquired.

"Yes. At my order, Baress and I will use our guns to hold them back long enough for you to blast a hole through the floor just large enough for us to slip through. If we can escape, the Kalfethki will be so dishonored that they will go back to their cabins and begin the ritual of mass suicide."

The crowd had gradually pulled back, allowing ample room for the combatants. The first warrior waited silently as a warrior from the second group came forward to present Velmeran with a pair of swords—a remarkable concession—one for each hand. Velmeran took the weapons, the smallest the Kalfethki could find but still as long as he was tall, and swung them experimentally. He handed one sword to Consherra, then removed his helmet to give himself a clear view.

Velmeran approached the seasoned warrior, the sword in his upper hands held in the same upright salute. The Kalfethki lowered his sword slightly in a gesture of recognition and dived in, suddenly drawing back for a vicious swing. Velmeran's major advantage was his speed, and he used it now, striking and pulling back faster than the mortal eye could follow. The Kalfethki paused and toppled backward over his massive tail. The Starwolf had slipped the blade between his ribs, through his heart, and on through his chest to severe his spine.

For the first time the gathered warriors broke their silence, muttering their surprise and approval before falling silent again. A couple of younger members stepped forward to retrieve the body, and the second set of challengers took his place. They had learned something from the mistake of the first warrior about underestimating the lightning-quick speed of their tiny adversary. Velmeran seemed almost to disappear as they swung their heavy weapons in unison, only to come up beneath their swords and fell them both before they had time to recover. The Kalfethki were impressed, to say the least.

"Three to nothing, my favor," Velmeran remarked quietly as he retrieved his second sword. "Stand ready, now. I count five challenges; that means thirty-two in the last. I believe that I can take them all—they are incredibly slow—and a Kalfethki carcass is quite an obstacle in itself. Thirty-two should be an effective barricade. You start to work on the floor at my signal."

"Are you sure that you can handle this alone?" she asked.

"I have to. Besides, this swordplay seems to come quite naturally. I should have been a pirate."

"You are a pirate, among other things," she reminded him.

"Captain!"

Maeken Kea and Donalt Trace both looked up and quickly identified the security officer standing beside his station to get their attention. Mystified, they hurried over to him as he returned to his seat.

"Trouble, Lieutenant?" Trace asked.

"Trouble, sir," the junior officer agreed. "The Kalfethki are fighting."

"Each other?"

"Yes, sir. They have someone cornered in a C Chamber on their level. They seem to be engaged in ritual challenge, and he must be holding his own very well."

"Seal their section," Trace ordered sharply.

"Yes, sir." The young officer hit a master switch. On the maplike schematic on his monitor, the handful of open doors in the Kalfethki section sealed and locked.

"Now what?" Maeken Kea demanded impatiently. "We are not very likely to get them back under control once they start fighting. And if they decide to come after us, not even airlock doors will hold them long."

"Yes, you are right. The Kalfethki are of no more use to us." Commander Trace turned abruptly to the security officer. "Vacate the entire sector."

Sixteen Kalfethki warriors were advancing to do battle when they stopped short to look around. Velmeran, helmetless, heard it as well. Airlock doors were being slammed shut. He thought that he could guess what it meant, while the Kalfethki knew beyond any doubt. They were about to die, suddenly and without honor, and there was nothing they could do about it. They stood, calm and silent, with their swords held in a final salute as they waited for death to come.

Their wait was not long. A slight breeze stirred within the chamber, the air whistling softly as it was drawn away. Soon even that quiet, ominous sound faded as the air became too thin. Decompression was usually a violent death, but the Kalfethki were too solid, their armored hides too thick, for them to simply explode. The only apparent damage was that their ears ruptured, leaving thin, red trails from the almost invisible holes in the sides of their heads. But their lungs were ripped apart in the growing vacuum. They began to fall unconscious within seconds.

Kelvessan were even tougher organisms. Their lungs did share the same vulnerability. However, they possessed by design a secondary valve that closed their trachea as tightly as an airlock. Since it was also an automatic function, Velmeran had no choice but to hold his breath until he was safely inside his helmet.

"What happened?" Consherra asked as soon as he could hear her.

"Somebody up there likes me," he said, indicating the front of the ship. "They obviously thought that the Kalfethki were fighting among themselves."

He walked over to the dead warriors and tried to pull one over to the area of the fight. His problem was not one of strength but a serious lack of traction in moving half a ton of inert weight. Baress realized what he intended and hurried to help. Together they pulled one back to the base of the steps and arranged limbs and weapons to suggest that this warrior had been fighting his fellows.

The three Starwolves made their way through the maze of saurian bodies and ascended to the alcove above the opposite end of the great chamber. Velmeran stopped before the closed airlock and began his remote manipulation of the controls. He had only begun when the doors snapped open unexpectedly, and a blast of air and a Kalfethki exploded outward at him. Although caught off-guard, Velmeran reacted quickly enough to catch the warrior by a massive arm and flip him overhead. The warrior crashed heavily on his back a good four meters away. His ears already bleeding from decompression, he rose shakily and staggered forward in a final charge. He made it only four uncertain steps.

"Inside!" Velmeran ordered them into the airlock and shut the door, immediately cycling air into the chamber. "Deliberate decompression of an airlock. You can bet that set off alarms all the way to the bridge."

"Why did he do it?" Consherra asked, still shaken by it all. "He could have lived."

"No, he would have been dead within minutes by his own hand anyway," he explained, pausing to trigger the outer doors and wave them through. "Honor, you know. But there was some honor to be won in at least trying."

Before they could scramble for cover, a lift door only three meters ahead opened suddenly and a sentry stepped out, no doubt on its way to investigate the disturbance. The automaton did not see the Starwolves until it stepped into the hall and turned to face them. Then it found itself eye-to-eye with Velmeran and paused in midstride.

"You did not see anyone," he told the machine.

The sentry made no reply, but neither did it open fire. Velmeran gestured the others past and slipped by the sentry when they were clear. They froze along the wall behind it, but the machine took no notice as it trotted awkwardly down the corridor the way they had come.

"What do you make of it?" Maeken Kea inquired.

The security officer shrugged. "I can only guess, but it was no malfunction. A Kalfethki was inside the airlock when they were sealed. Perhaps he tried to open the wrong door. Perhaps he simply wanted to die with his companions. Any survivor would not have been a willing one, knowing that his death was ordered."

"Just keep watch until the sentries have a chance to tally the dead," she told him. "I do not want any of those licentious lizards wandering about the ship. There is no telling what strange ideas some survivor might dream up."

Maeken Kea was not particularly pleased with the situation, nor with Donalt Trace. She had not liked the idea of two thousand Kalfethki on board her ship in the first place. She liked even less to have them decompressed at the first provocation, as much as she had to admit to the necessity. Needless to say, she still had no idea that Trace had ordered a nuclear strike on Tryalna; he had contrived to have her off the bridge at that time. As it was, she got along with him as well as she did because she was under the mistaken impression that he did not interfere with her command of the ship.

"Captain?"

Maeken looked over and saw that the security officer monitoring and directing the sentries had called her. The officer was one of several Faldennye who made up a third of the Challenger's crew. Maeken was not adept at reading their expressions, but she had the impression that this young lady had just been profoundly surprised.

"What is it?"

"Captain, I . . . I have just received a communication from a sentry," she explained hesitantly in her rich, purring voice. "It called in to report that it had just not seen anyone."

Maeken reacted to that with predictable mystification. "I take it that there is something unusual in this?"

"Captain, sentries relay reports only when called for, or when they have something definite to report. They do not make contact spontaneously to report nothing."

Maeken nodded in understanding. "I see what you are getting at."

"There is also a problem in syntax," the Feldennye continued. "The sentry said that it had just not seen anyone. As if it had seen something important enough to report, and that it was nothing. Something is wrong."

"A malfunction?"

She nodded in resignation. "That would have to be it, although a remote internal check reveals nothing. I have ordered another sentry to reinforce that one, in the event it is failing."

"Where did this occur?"

"Here, just as it came off the lift." She indicated the place on the map projected on her monitor.

Maeken drew back in surprise. "Not fifty meters from an airlock that was decompressed. And it is now standing guard outside that very lock."

"It is so," the Feldennye agreed. "Could the two incidents be related?"

"If you can figure out how, then you tell me. The airlock only opened on the other side." Maeken glanced at the ceiling, rubbing an aching neck as she considered the matter. "Keep your eyes open."

Maeken saw that Commander Trace had returned and hurried to join him on the central bridge.

"Did you see Lieutenant Skerri?" She asked.

"No, he wasn't there. He must have returned to his cabin. I didn't think to ask for him."

"Captain!"

She turned in time to see the same Feldennye officer pull off her headphones and throw them down on her console. The entire bridge crew stared in open amazement. Feldennye were extraordinarily calm, even-tempered people, and it took a great deal to frustrate them to the point of being upset. Maeken hurried to her station, the Sector Commander close behind.

"Captain, I was making a complete scan of the location and activity of all the sentries when I found one unit far from its assigned place," she explained. "It belongs near the middle of the ship, but found it as far forward as it can get. I asked it to explain itself, and it . . . it told me to shut up and mind my own business."

Maeken glanced up at Donalt Trace, but he had missed the previous report and was even more mystified. She turned back to the security officer. "That is no simple malfunction, is it?"

"No, Captain."

"I would guess that either this entire ship is cracking mentally under the stress of battle, or else someone is tampering with our sentries."

"That is the only explanation," the Feldennye agreed.

Maeken turned to the astonished Sector-Commander. "I have to remain here, so it is up to you. I suggest that you find four or five off-duty crew members and put rifles in their hands, take as many sentries as you can squeeze into a lift, and see if you can intercept them."

"Who?" Trace asked, perplexed.

"You have Starwolves on your ship."

"Starwolves? Are you sure?" He almost looked faint.

Maeken shrugged helplessly. "Not entirely. It might all be coincidence, but I doubt it. The Kalfethki were fighting when you killed them. Were they fighting among themselves, or were they defending your ship? Only a few minutes later an airlock in a decompressed area opened, and a sentry on the other side of that lock spouts nonsense."

"But how could they have gotten into the ship undetected?"

"Simple enough. They must have a device that activates the locks without alerting the master control. It failed once, and we got a light. A similar device stuns sentries." She looked up at Commander Trace. "Your ship is as good as you meant it to be. They couldn't hurt it from the outside, so they mean to wreck it from the inside."

Donalt Trace shook his head slowly. "Damned Starwolves. But what can they do?"

"Heaven only knows," Maeken said. "I will stay on the bridge and call in about fifty sentries to guard the passages in. You organize that hunting party and do your best to intercept them."

Velmeran stopped so suddenly that Consherra nearly ran into him from behind. Both she and Baress snapped their rifles to ready and prepared to shoot anything that moved.

"They know that we are here," he said at last. "Donalt Trace is coming to look for us."

"That hardly makes any difference," Baress observed. "This

is a very big ship, and they have only a general idea of where to look for us."

"They know what level we are on," Velmeran told him. "It might not be long before someone remembers that the auxiliary bridge is on the same level. I have to do something to turn their attention elsewhere."

Baress regarded him closely, a wasted gesture, since both of them were in their helmets. "I think I know what you have in mind."

"Then you know what you have to do, as well. Sherry, I am going to have to leave you for a while, to lay a false trail to lead Commander Trace away into some other part of the ship. Baress will watch out for you until I come back."

"But what about my part?" she asked. "I cannot get into this ship's computers without your help."

"Just call to me when you are ready," he told her. "I will be listening for you. Do not worry about me. All I intend to do is to make my way toward the main bridge tripping lights and upsetting sentries as I go. I can move faster than they can follow, then catch up with you when you are finished."

"You watch out for yourself," Consherra called after him as he hurried down the corridor the way they had come.

"Come on," Baress urged her gently. "He has done this type of work often enough to have learned how to stay out of trouble. And the sooner we finish our work, the sooner we can all get out of here."

Consherra agreed with the logic in that and reluctantly joined him as they hurried on their way.

Velmeran retreated back up the corridor about a hundred meters, where he had seen an access tube, and quickly descended five levels toward the center of the ship. The plan of the Challenger was as complicated as the map of several cities stacked one on the other, but he had committed the basic mechanical design to selective recall and he knew the trick of navigating the major corridors. Soon after reaching the lower level, he happened upon a sentry unfortunate enough to be facing the wrong direction and quietly slipped a heat charge on its back. That should be enough to shift any pursuit down to this new level.

After that he dropped two more levels and located a corridor that took him laterally toward the interior of the ship and the mechanical core that ran through the very center of its length.

All the power lines from the engines and turrets met here, merging with eighty additional generators before being channeled into the field drive and shield generators. Centermost, a hexagonal chamber two hundred meters across and running twenty-five kilometers from one end of the vessel to the other, it was the spine of the ship, a power core capable of containing and channeling the power of a small star.

Velmeran had to force the access doors to the power core, intentionally allowing an indicator to light on the bridge. He followed the core forward, looking for mischief. Soon the power core began to branch off, feeding field generators clustered on groups of four about the core in chambers large enough to serve as hangers for cargo shuttles. He began ducking into these chambers, setting heat charges on vital control mechanisms. He doubted that he was doing the Fortress any real damage, for there was too much redundancy for that limited damage to have any serious effect. On the other hand, the results of his handiwork should have the bridge in a frenzy.

Frenzy was a very good description of the state of affairs on the bridge. Marenna Challenger began to report damage to her innermost drive units. Maeken Kea pondered only long enough to establish exactly what was going on, then began shouting orders as she ran to her own console on the central bridge.

"Tie me in with Commander Trace's personal communicator!" she ordered as she ran up the steps.

"Maeken?" Trace inquired even as she arrived at her station. "Captain Kea, what is it? My sentries just took off at a run."

"Follow them!" she shouted into the com. "Starwolves are in the power core. I've relayed specific directions to your sentries, so they will take you straight there."

"Right!" Trace agreed simply. The destruction of a section of the core might not affect the ship, since that power could be recircuited through the outer power network. But it was better to take no chances. If the Challenger was unable to shield herself, even the damaged Methryn could rip her apart.

Then all the pieces of the puzzle fell into place with shocking suddenness, instantly and unbidden. Momentarily stunned by that revelation, Maeken sat down heavily in her seat to review the facts she knew. Nothing was certain, and she still did not know the full truth. But she was so sure that she was willing to gamble the success of the entire battle on it.

"Marenna Challenger!" she ordered sharply, leaping from her chair. "Reduce speed gradually to a full stop. Do you understand me? Ready all guns and stand by to shield engines."

"I understand," the ship responded. "Beginning deceleration now. All offensive and defensive systems standing by."

Not even Velmeran was aware for some time that the Fortress was slowing. The sudden shift of power from the rear engines to an equal number of forward engines running at the same level went unnoticed. His first hint came when he suddenly realized that the Methryn's own sustained, high-pitched pulse was almost on top of them. In the next instant the Challenger braked hard before executing a quick end-over pivot to face back the way she had come.

Tregloran, do you hear me? he called out with all his telepathic skills.

Yes, Captain. Tregloran's reply was distant but clear.

Warn Valthyrra! I cannot yet reach her.

I am already on my way! the younger pilot replied, for he had already figured out what was happening for himself. Unfortunately, he needed the more powerful com inside the fighter to call above the static inside the ring.

But it was already too late. Valthyrra Methryn had been skirting one of the larger moonlets, five kilometers across and large enough to have been rounded under its own gravity. When Tregloran's warning came, she began braking hard to stop. Suddenly the Challenger was there before her, emerging black and threatening behind the satellite. She opened fire on the smaller ship with every gun she could bring to bear. From a hundred kilometers, only four times her own length, she could not miss.

And from that distance, the Methryn's shields had little effect against those powerful bolts. A hail of brilliant shafts of energy slammed against her shields, and she could not turn them all. One and sometimes two scored every second, cutting deep into her hull and discharging with tremendous explosions. The entire ship rocked violently under the unrelenting impacts.

"They are trying for the bridge!" Valthyrra shouted above the confusion as she readied herself for the flight. With her own pack members clinging to the hull of the Fortress, she could not fight back. It would have been foolish, futile effort anyway.

Mayelna glanced at her impatiently. "They seem to have a damned good idea where it is."

A single bolt tore screaming with raw energy through the ceiling above the bridge, cutting through the heavy plating barely a meter behind the main viewscreen and striking at the front of the upper bridge, slicing through the front of the Commander's console and into the deck below. It discharged into the structural supports on the next level, and the force of the blast traveled upward, ripping out most of the upper bridge. Cargin, at the weapons station, was pitched from his seat and landed unharmed on the forward console to the right of the navigator's station. Mayelna was thrown against the ceiling with such force that her armor snapped as easily as the bones within. She fell amid the wreckage of plating and her own console in the center of the bridge.

Valthyrra's camera pod was nearly ripped free by the blast, and it turned reluctantly when she tried to bring it back around. Reacting to falling pressure, doors were slamming shut throughout the area to contain the break in the hull. Cargin, recovering quickly, hurried to the dented helmet he spied amid the wreckage. With this in hand, he rushed to Mayelna's inert form and gently lifted her up so that he could set the helmet over her head and clip it in place even as the last trace of air and smoke fled through the gaping hole overhead. Another crewmember arrived with pressure tape to seal the breaks in the Commander's armor, in case the suit underneath had not sealed itself.

Oblivious to the continued assault she was taking, Valthyrra forced her damaged camera pod around until she was looking down at Mayelna's silent, battered form. Cargin opened her chestplate for a reading. In spite of all their fears, it showed a feeble pulse of life.

"Dyenlerra to the bridge, now!" Valthyrra all but screamed over the ship's com. Then, almost as an afterthought, she opened a line through every speaker and suit com. "Stand by to abandon ship."

Mayelna stirred weakly. Surely she had heard! Valthyrra bent even closer, hoping that her suit com remained intact. "Commander?"

"Save yourself, you old fool!" Mayelna admonished in a thin, harsh whisper.

Valthyrra glanced up abruptly at the main viewscreen, a cold, determined gesture. The Challenger lay to her right and slightly above barely twice her length ahead, pounding the smaller ship with unrelenting fury. Swinging her nose around to face her enemy head-on, the Methryn opened fire with deadly accuracy as she accelerated straight toward the larger ship. Valthyrra concentrated her fire on the cannons of her very nose, kilometers forward of where Tregloran and the others watched in stunned terror.

The results were as she had anticipated. Neither the Challenger nor her captain knew whether the Methryn meant to ram or to fire her conversion cannon so close that nothing could deflect the flood of raw energy, even if it meant the destruction of both ships. Maeken Kea had to decide in a hurry. She diverted one quarter of the ship's power to the hull shields, enough to minimize the damage of a direct impact, sending the rest into the outer shield. The Challenger disappeared within its protective white shell of static force.

The Methryn struck that barrier nose-on and it parted around her in a fantastic display of blue and white lightning that rippled harmlessly over her hull and a fourth of the distance around the shell. At the same time she dropped her tapered nose enough to pass just beneath the blunt bow of the Fortress. Although she cleared the lower hull with fifty meters to spare, their great forms appeared to skim past with only the narrowest gap. The Challenger had dropped her outer shield and held her fire, her full power to her hull shields for nearly half a minute that the Methryn was beneath her. Then she was past, accelerating at her best speed along the decoy corridor laid by her own transports.

Now Valthyrra was safe and could flee out of range before the Challenger could pivot back around to bring her main battery to bear. She turned her attention back to her stricken Commander. Dyenlerra had arrived moments earlier and was bent over the diagnostic unit attached to her suit. She looked up as Valthyrra brought her camera pod around.

"I am sorry," the medic said softly. "It is too late."

For a long moment out of time, Valthyrra was too stunned to react. Then she did something that she should not have been able to do, something contrary to the programming that had brought her to life thousands of years before. Her capacity for both love and grief had grown far beyond what her initial design had allowed. In a blind fury, mindless of her own safety and forgetting her own crew members on the Challenger, she swung herself back around and began charging her conversion cannon. But the Challenger immediately sensed that rapid increase in power, and she knew what it meant. Without even waiting for orders, she threw up her shield.

No, Valthyrra! Velmeran called to her silently across space. *Run for now. I will call you when the time comes.*

That brought her fully back to her senses. She began to power down her cannon as she turned herself back around and disappeared into the ring.

Velmeran sat alone in the chamber just off the power core, beside a control console for a field generator that still smoked from the effects of a heat charge. One life had been required in payment for the successful completion of this task. He had known that from the first. But he had thought that it would have been his own, terms that he would have been willing to pay. In the end the payment had come suddenly and unexpectedly, the one life nearest to him that he had considered safe. If he had only known. He sat alone in the middle of the vast ship that he had come to destroy and grieved silently for what might have been.

So it was that he grieved too long, lost amid regret and self-recrimination, when Donalt Trace found him there minutes later.

15

When Donalt Trace first saw the single figure completely encased in Starwolf armor sitting on the steps of the inclined ladder leading up into the machinery of the field generator, he did not know what to make of it. Because the Kelvessa was helmeted, he could not tell who it was or why he just sat there in a decidely dejected altitude. He was aware that the Challenger had been in battle, having ambushed the Methryn and apparently won. And so he thought he knew from that who this must be.

Commander Trace checked his rifle a final time before moving in. Two other crewmembers moved in along converging paths, their own rifles ready. The sentries held back, too big and clunky to sneak up on anything short of a deaf thark bison facing in the wrong direction. As versatile as the automatons were, they were never subtle.

Three against one. Trace considered the odds slightly on his side because he had the element of surprise. He would have felt safer if he could have gone in shooting, but he desperately needed a live Starwolf.

"We have you surrounded!" he called out, a slight exaggeration. "Put down your weapons and move in this direction."

The Starwolf looked up, startled. Seeing the three rifles trained on him, he decided quickly. Moving carefully, he released his belt with its two pistols and remaining heat charges and laid it on the floor. Then he rose slowly and walked half the distance to where Trace stood.

The Sector Commander called in the waiting sentries, ordering them to surround the captive at a distance of only two meters and shoot if he made any sudden moves. Only then did he receive the abandoned weapons. The rifle was a greater burden than he cared to admit, and he hung it by its strap from the access hook on the side of a sentry and slipped the latch of the belt on the opposite side. He gave the Starwolf's armor a quick inspection but saw nothing he considered to be a weapon.

"Now, my busy little friend," he said, facing his tiny captive. "Why don't you remove that helmet so that we can see who you are."

The Starwolf released the throat clips and pulled off his helmet. As much as his kind looked alike to most humans, Donalt Trace recognized him immediately. What surprised him was to find that Velmeran had been crying. His triumphant look faded to one of sadness.

"Your ship?" he asked gently.

"You hit the bridge," Velmeran explained simply.

"I am sorry," Trace said, and his regret seemed very sincere.

"I never really meant to hurt you, not like I have. This is simply business. I do what I have to do."

"I am glad that you can appreciate that," Velmeran remarked. Trace looked at him sharply. "What do you mean by that?"

Velmeran only shrugged indifferently, as if he had a secret and considered it very secure.

"You've put a bomb in the power core, haven't you?" Trace insisted. "All this minor sabotage . . . you could work at this for hours and never get anywhere. Well, I know where you entered, about three-quarters of a kilometer back. Your bomb has to be somewhere between that point and here."

Velmeran shrugged again. "And how many tens of thousands of access plates will you have to check under in the next hour before it goes off before you find it? It is not a very big bomb, but it is more than enough to snap this power core in two."

"We can reroute the network around the power core. Besides, the Methryn is not going to fire on you—assuming she is still able—while I have you."

"The Methryn will do what she must," the Starwolf assured him. "And I will be gone by then, anyway."

Trace grinned in wry amusement. "You know, I more than half believe you will. That's why I'm hoping to make it very, very hard for you. If you'll excuse me, I'll leave you to my associates for a few minutes while I call up to the bridge."

Commander Trace sent him back to the steps where he had been sitting and put the three watchful sentries to stand guard over him, their guns charged and ready to fire. Then he withdrew around the corner, far enough to avoid being overheard by the sharp ears of a Kelvessa.

Velmeran, distracted from his grief by matters at hand, gave some quick thought to the immediate future. His claim that he could escape at any time was not an idle threat. At least he hoped not. For now he had to buy time for Consherra to reach the auxiliary bridge and complete her own task. As long as Trace was preoccupied with him and the crew of the Challenger was distracted by looking for a nonexistent bomb, Consherra was likely to remain forgotten.

Velmeran?

Yes, Sherry? he responded silently. *Are you ready?*

I am, she said. *Give me access.*

Velmeran concentrated his talent on forcing the Challenger to open her basic programming. He found it easier to control this ship than to force Valthyrra to recite Lenna's rank poetry, but he also had to be far more subtle.

Your access is open, he reported. *Take your time. I have found a way to keep this entire ship preoccupied for at least the next hour.*

Take care of yourself. Consherra admonished before quickly breaking contact. Velmeran was momentarily amused. He could guess what her reaction would be if she knew how he was keeping this ship preoccupied.

Commander Trace returned presently, looking very pleased. Velmeran could well imagine that everything must be going very well in his world.

"I thought that we might take a little trip up to sick bay," he announced.

"Sick bay?" Velmeran asked innocently. "Am I going to be sick?"

Trace laughed as he indicated with his rifle for the Kelvessa to precede his three mechanical guards out of the chamber. "No, but it seems about the best place to try to keep you. Even our security cells are made of ordinary floor and panel plating, which would not hold out very long against your strength. No, the surest way to keep you is set you down somewhere and surround you with more sentries than you can handle."

Commander Trace led the odd procession out of the power core and back into the main corridors of the ship, the unfortunate Starwolf packed between two sentries ahead and three behind. They soon came to the lift and Trace went on ahead with two of the sentries, sending the car back for Velmeran and the other three. The ride was not long, the lift going up four levels and ahead only a short distance. Velmeran thought that they could not be more than three hundred meters from the auxiliary bridge, a little more than twice that far from the main bridge.

The sick bay was clearly meant to serve a much larger crew; for the present needs of the Challenger, one physician and three automated assistants were more than enough for the single patient who waited for a plastifiber cast to cure out. Velmeran was led into a very large general diagnostic ward just off the main lobby. There he was set on a stool-like chair near the back wall, surrounded at a discreet distance by two of his dutiful guards.

The other two remained to either side of the door that was the only exit.

There he sat, looking dejected but not particularly frightened. Trace watched him with an expression of puzzlement as he conferred for a minute with the physician. Dr. Wriestler seemed to Velmeran to be a fairly typical military doctor, radiating an air of faint ineptitude. They spoke quietly for some time before the physician hurried off on some errand. Trace, looking as if he had just settled some major problem, walked slowly over to where the Starwolf waited.

"I am about to take a terrible liberty, so I want to explain," he began, pulling up a chair of his own. "As you might have guessed, I have gone into the ultimate weapon business. I already have a ship that has proven its ability against Starwolves. I intend to build more like it, certainly. But I also hope to build a smaller carrier version, a great deal faster but just as invulnerable. Naturally, I want my own Starwolves to go with it."

Velmeran looked startled. "Me?"

Trace nodded slowly. "As much as I would prefer, we cannot begin to design and create our own. But as long as we start with living genetic material, we can clone our own. By fishing out your recessive traits, and introducing genetic variables of our own, we can create an entire race out of you alone."

Wriestler returned at that moment, pushing a small cart that bore a collection of medical supplies. Two Velmeran recognized instantly. One, a curious boxlike device, was a suspension chamber, designed to keep organs alive in stasis indefinitely until needed for transplant. The other was a large laser cutting tool.

"You see, I do take you at your word," Trace explained. "I do consider it very likely that you will either escape or die in the attempt. This way, if you do part from our company, you will leave what I need behind. What do you think, Doc? A hand?"

"Yes, that is one item he has in redundant quantities," Wriestler agreed, regarding his subject appraisingly. Although far shorter than Donalt Trace, his thin, lanky frame made him appear taller than he actually was. "Yes, a hand would be quite sufficient. Which one do you favor?"

"I am quadrilateral ambidextrous," Velmeran explained, trying to look more nervous about the prospect than he actually was. "There is, however, an arbitrary order of importance. I should miss the lower left the least of any."

"So be it," Wriestler agreed. He took the hand in question, twisting the cuff to remove the glove. "Will you require any medical attention?"

"None at all. There will be no bleeding, since veins and arteries seal automatically, and healing will be complete in a few hours."

"If you will allow me, I have my suspicions about Starwolf reflexes," Trace interrupted. He had Velmeran to sit down on the floor, his wrist extended, then instructed one of the sentries by the door to brace both of its forelegs atop the armored sleeve. Wriestler regarded this procedure questioningly, but wasted no time as he adjusted the setting on the laser scalpel to maximum intensity.

There was a loud electric snap and the sentry somersaulted to land heavily on its back. Velmeran drew back his arm, swearing in his own language, but the pain faded almost immediately; Kelvessan nervous systems included a feedback mechanism that blocked unnecessary pain. By the time he looked up, Wriestler had already transferred the hand to the suspension box and was setting the controls. Trace was watching the uncertain movements of the sentry, undamaged but unable to raise itself without help.

"Are you all right, little fellow?" Wriestler inquired professionally, taking the injured wrist to look inside the open sleeve. He looked surprised and approving. "My, it really is healing up in a hurry. You people are remarkable."

"Take care of that," Trace said as the physician quickly packed up his supplies. "That hand means more to the final defeat of the Starwolves than this entire ship."

Wriestler made some impatient gesture of assurance as he pushed the cart out the door. Trace frowned, obviously displeased with the physician's indifference at what was to him a very important occasion. A threatening gesture from the sentries alerted him to the fact that Velmeran had risen and was returning to his stool. His almost festive mood returned instantly.

"I'm glad that you could give me a hand," he remarked glibly as he took his own seat, as if he expected Velmeran to appreciate his attempt at humor. He shrugged. "I do hate to see you so dejected, although I can hardly blame you for that. I guess that I was expecting to find the friend I last saw in that café in Vannkarn."

Velmeran glanced up at him. "What did you expect? This is business, remember?"

"As you say, this is business," Trace agreed. "Oh, hating you and plotting dire revenge enlivened those endless weeks while they made and installed new pieces of my back, and those endless months of pain while I learned to use those new parts. But, when it was all over, I realized that I hurt you worse than you had hurt me. Now it seems that I've hurt you again, and I honestly regret that."

"Why did you not die?" Velmeran muttered.

Trace laughed ironically. "Pure perversity, I assure you. Listen to me, Starwolf. We both have our duty. You have to destroy my fine, big ship, and I mean to destroy yours. I think that only one of us will succeed, and I do seem to be winning. I thought it was a purely human failing to imagine your enemies as cruel monsters devoted to the service of evil. I assure you that I am an honest man."

Velmeran glanced at him sharply. "The honest man who dropped a bomb on a city just to get my attention. It seems to me that you are the very monster you describe."

Trace shrugged indifferently. "It is of small consequence. You see, young Richart is a more practical man than Jon ever was. He's impatient with sending invasion forces to take planets, only to have them freed by Starwolves. He's instituted a new policy, one that even I find a bit severe. Just now, there are six conversion devices in orbit over Tryalna, four equally spaced in equatorial orbit and two in polar. The explosion would blast away the air, seas, and rip off at least a few kilometers of the surface itself, caught in the center of a concussion like that. The way I see it, the entire population of that world lives on my sufferance now. I simply called a small portion of that debt due."

"You are a monster," the Starwolf said, shaking his head slowly.

Commander Trace's calm indifference broke suddenly, turning with frightening speed to self-righteous fury. "Damn it, you four-armed freak, I'm trying to save my race and my civilization. Can't you see that our only hope is in the firm hand of a strong government to enforce selective sterilization on large segments of a dying population?"

"No, because that is not your only hope," Velmeran insisted. "There is a much easier way. In our worlds, the human population has already begun a program of voluntary screening of genetic defects at the time of artificial insemination. No genetic tampering is allowed, just a deletion of the faulty genetic variables so that the sound genetic variables have a better chance. That protects the complete freedom and individuality of the offspring. And it allows the positive aspects of evolution to remain in effect so that the race does not stagnate. In fact, five hundred years should completely eliminate the overload of genetic defects that have accumulated. And potential parents are very eager to make use of genetic screening, when the alternative is a forty percent chance of some mental or physical defect."

Donalt Trace sat in silence for a long moment as he considered that. His one virtue was that he was indeed an honest man. But fairness and honesty were by no means the same thing; he knew that he was not always fair, and he was less fair than he believed himself to be. He proved just that.

"You are right on one thing," he agreed. "That is a simpler, more effective idea. I'm sure our planners thought of that and rejected it. Your mistake must be in thinking that we are too backward and shortsighted to know better. You and I both know that we intend to eventually breed whole races of workers designed for specific tasks.

"I know all about this great democracy that your Republic values so highly. Wonderful theory, but it works only on paper. It is a shaky, effectual form of government at best. Man was barely able to govern himself at his height; he certainly cannot now, in the days of his decline. The fact remains that there is an inherent flaw in any system that tries to reciprocate political power back into society at large. Power is used effectively when it is concentrated into the hands of those who have been trained to use it. And do not think that the sector families look upon our civilization as a society of slaves to serve us. We are not the masters. We serve just as anyone else, and we have bred ourselves thousands of years to be what we are."

Velmeran sighed at the hopelessness of the situation. "Donalt Trace, I did not come all this way to discuss philosophy with a tyrant. But I will tell you this. I am in control of this situation. I will escape, and I will destroy this ship in the process. And if you want to escape with your own life, you will abandon this ship within the next half hour."

Trace only laughed. "You sound so sure of yourself, you almost have me worried. Unfortunately for you, I do know the value of a good bluff."

He paused as his communicator beeped imperiously, and held the small device to his ear for private listening.

"Right away," he responded tersely before putting away the device. He turned back to his prisoner. "I have to go up to the bridge for a while. I know that you won't mind me leaving you in such fine company."

"Not at all."

He turned to the sentries. "If he so much as gets off the stool, you are to shoot to kill. Is that understood?"

"Understood," the sentries agreed in a ragged chorus, including the one still lying on the floor. Trace left, locking them inside the room.

Nearly three-quarters of an hour later, Lenna Makayen was concluding her sixth act of judicious sabotage. She would have liked to have done more, but she was running out of time. Lieutenant Skerri stood well to one side, watching her closely. His obvious concern told her that she must be doing something very right. He had been very reluctant to cooperate, but he also had shown very little tolerance for the minor beating he had received at her hands. Bill, the sentry, stood at the door leading into the weapons chamber, watching his prisoner while he listened down the hall. His electronic patience was inexhaustible.

"There's the last one, all set," she said to herself with satisfaction.

"Damn it, don't you appreciate the seriousness of what you're doing?" Skerri demanded, resuming their previous argument. "Sabotage of a Union warship is a very serious crime. You would do well to give yourself up now."

"I would, now? And why is that?"

"Because what you've done is more than illegal, it's treasonous!" he declared. "You're obviously not a Starwolf, but you are in league with them. Your crime is punishable by death. You should surrender yourself immediately and accept your punishment."

Lenna set down her socket wrench to stare at him. "That has to be the most damned foolish, illogical argument I've ever heard. 'Give yourself up, and we'll thank you before we kill you.' You're in no position to make threats, boy."

She turned back to her work of securing the inner access plates, hurrying now because she was afraid that it might be getting late. She had a long trip back to her fighter yet. She had no desire to be inside this ship when the Methryn attacked, especially after her own tampering.

"Where are you from?" Skerri asked almost politely.

"Scotland," she snapped.

"Sounds like a frontier planet."

"It is. Named after Sir Walter Scott, the first colonist."

"How did you happen to fall in with Starwolves?"

"Answered an advertisement in the paper, just like everyone," she replied absently.

"But why?"

She afforded him another of those impatient stares. "Because I think your Union sucks rotten eggs. At least my new friends don't pitch nuclear missiles at defenseless planets just to get your attention."

Skerri remained silent, lacking a ready answer for that. His arguments were not going very well, so he finally admitted to himself that he was not going to convince this girl to surrender. Instead he now thought it best to allow her to conclude her business so that she would let him go in time to warn the ship about the damage she had done. He really was a trusting soul, and not particularly bright.

"You will be leaving when you finish here?" he asked guardedly.

"Of course. And you . . ." She paused to look at him. "I can't take you with me, and I certainly can't just let you go. I really cannot risk your getting free if I left you tied up somewhere, and you'll be dead soon enough anyway."

She looked over at Bill, and Skerri knew that she meant to have the renegade sentry shoot him. Lenna turned back to her work unconcerned, but he watched the motionless sentry. After a moment the machine moved for the first time since they had arrived, turning its head to look out the door.

"The lift door just opened," Bill reported. "I also hear a sentry approaching from the other direction."

"Check it out, Bill," Lenna told him. "I can keep an eye on Captain Dauntless. I'll blow his head off if he makes a sound."

Although she had been addressing the sentry, Lieutenant Skerri was quite aware that her final statement had been for his benefit. Nor did he doubt that she meant it, and he had nothing to lose except a couple of minutes off a severely limited life expectancy. As soon as Lenna returned to her work of securing the outer access panel, he launched himself directly at her. She saw him coming at the very last moment and threw herself well to one side, unfortunately in the opposite direction of the gun that she had laid handy on top of the launch tube. Skerri knocked the gun off the top of the tube as he landed against it, and it disappeared into the shadows beyond.

The two combatants came off the floor at the same time, ready for battle. Lenna had three distinct advantages: she was much stronger, quicker, and Skerri was under the mistaken impression that both of those advantages were his. She was more than a match for him, at least until he snatched up the long-handled socket wrench. That put her on the defensive from the start.

Skerri advanced menacingly, swinging the wrench in a wide horizontal sweep as if it were a club or battle-ax. Lenna avoided it easily, but his tactic was simple; each swing drove her half a meter toward the wall at her back. After the second attempt she followed his swings with a quick rabbit punch to the jaw. Skerri endured three of these dizzying punches before changing his tactics, lifting his swing high enough to make her duck. While bent over, she delivered one more vicious punch to his stomach, ducked under his arm, and followed with a joint-snapping two-fisted thump in the middle of his back. The combination so thoroughly knocked the wind out of him that he nearly passed out and was forced to retreat.

Skerri returned to the battle with a little more respect for his opponent. He held the wrench in one hand, leaving him freer to hit and kick. That helped a bit; he did not score any hits on Lenna, but at least she was scoring fewer hits on him. But Skerri was clearly on the defensive, and Lenna knew that she only had to bide her time until Bill returned.

After a minute of this a sentry ambled into the chamber and paused just inside the door. Lenna glanced over her shoulder and realized that this was not Bill. There was no heavy rifle strapped over his left shoulder. While Bill had been checking the lift, the second sentry had heard the sounds of the fight and hurried to investigate. She was also trapped with Skerri in front and the hostile sentry behind. Then she realized that it was confused by the sight of two Union officers. Skerri was just as quick to recognize the problem.

"I am Lieutenant Captain Denas Skerri," he stated authoritatively. "This is an imposter. Shoot to kill!"

The machine did not respond immediately; perhaps it was checking his visual identification against the file to confirm his claim. Lenna turned back to him and did her best to kick his balls off, then slipped behind him to put his bent form between herself and the sentry. Skerri recovered with surprising speed, turning to face her. Lenna drew back and launched herself at him, kicking with all her strength into the very center of his chest. Skerri was thrown backward, actually leaving the ground for most of his three-meter flight. He crashed back-first into the front of the sentry's head, the pencil-thin barrels of its two smaller guns driving ten centimeters into his back. But he was dead already, his chest crushed by her kick.

Lenna had fallen sprawling to the ground, and she rolled to one side as bolts from the sentry's larger cannons deflected off the floor where she had been. It shook its head violently to free itself of the burden of the body penned there. Lenna had hoped to slip around behind it, but now she was hopelessly trapped between the two launch tubes. The sentry tracked her darting movements with its head until it had her, and fired.

The protective flarings on both of the sentry's forward guns were blocked with thick blood, and the bolts discharged within the focusing lenses before they could cut through those barriers, causing the head of the unfortunate machine to explode. However, as Velmeran had discovered a couple of years before, that was only a minor complication to the normal function of a sentry. The headless machine staggered blindly as it sought its prey by the infrared scanners on its chest.

Lenna dived over the top of the launch tube, using that for shelter as she searched for her gun. The sentry fired two short bursts over her head as it continued to seek her. Then Bill was there, ramming the stricken sentry from behind to knock it off balance before discharging a round of bolts into its vulnerable lower hull. Lenna waited for the shooting to stop before she peered cautiously over the top of the tube.

"Thank you, Bill. Nice work," she said, climbing over the protective barrier. Then she saw the broken body of Lieutenant Skerri where it had been tossed aside. For a moment she allowed herself the privilege of turning pale, just as she had those times in the chilly streets of Kallenes. Half of it was from the sudden awareness that she had killed this man herself, half from the realization that it had nearly been herself. For a moment she wanted to sit down and cry, but this was hardly the time or place. You wanted to be a Starwolf, Miss Makayen, and so you are, she reminded herself. This is just the ugly part of the business.

"They are dead," Bill said helpfully, no doubt meaning to be reassuring.

"Sure, and that's what bothers me about it," Lenna said. "I'd better seal this up to make sure that it works the way we want, then we'll be on our way. Think you can get us back to the airlock where we first met?"

"Yes, that is a simple matter."

"Don here," Commander Trace responded, speaking into his com unit as he sat down wearily on the step. "Is that you, Kea?"

"Yes, Commander. Fifty minutes from your mark."

Donalt Trace sighed and nodded in dismal agreement to no one in particular. "Wait five more minutes and order a general evacuation from the power core. Seal up the core completely, from one end of the ship to the other. We haven't found the slightest hint of tampering, much less a bomb. No wonder he was so sure of himself."

He paused a moment to watch the workers swarming over the surface of the power core, surrounding it in a ring that moved slowly forward. There were fifty live workers and twice as many automatons. In the last three-quarters of an hour they had removed nearly two thousand access panels.

"Go ahead and bypass the power core for the secondary power grid," he continued. "That way we won't be caught by surprise when the core blows. If I guess right, you'll see the Methryn show her broken nose just about the time the thing goes. Draw her in as close as you can; this time we don't want her getting away."

"Right," Maeken agreed. "By the way, that stunned sentry just attacked and destroyed another down in the lower decks. I would like to know how the Starwolf did that. Do you have the device?"

"Well, I . . ." Trace looked as stunned as the automaton in question.

"Surely you did search him for the device?" Maeken asked.

"I was too preoccupied with worrying about that damned bomb!"

"No wonder he was so sure that he could escape whenever he wants. No doubt he's been waiting for the core to blow. I suggest . . ."

"On my way!" Trace assured her as he jumped from the steps and headed for the nearest lift, suddenly very afraid that the little Starwolf had escaped him again. He was actually startled to see Velmeran still seated impatiently on his stool, the alert sentries still standing guard. He stopped short, regarding the mildly surprised captive before arrogantly walking over to hold out an impatient hand.

"There is the matter of the little device that you use to stun my sentries," he explained. "You should have used it when you had the chance."

Velmeran's first reaction was one of complete confusion, but that demand had been fairly self-explanatory and he needed only an instant to figure things out. After a brief hesitation he opened his chestplate and removed a small rectangular device, nine centimeters by five and just over two thick, with several clip-in leads in the back. It looked very impressive, smaller than Trace had anticipated. Unfortunately for him, it was only the emergency power unit for the suit.

"Does this have the same effect on the airlock controls?" Trace asked.

"It has the same effect on a number of electronic devices, including such things as lifts and navigational guidance systems," Velmeran answered truthfully. Of course, it had no effect on anything as far as he knew.

"Clever little machine," Trace commented as he tucked it into his pocket. "Are you in any pain?"

"A little discomfort," Velmeran answered. "An unavoidable part of rapid regeneration. I have nothing to take for it."

"Oh? What would you need?"

Velmeran thought for a moment. "You might ask Dr. Wriestler if he has any pyridoxine."

"Right away," Trace promised as he left on his errand.

Velmeran watched until the door closed behind him, then quickly focused his thoughts on a nearby portion of the ship. *Sherry?*

I am just finishing, she responded immediately. *I will be ready as soon as you can get here.*

Then I am on my way.

At least Velmeran hoped so. He closed his eyes as he concentrated fully on directing his talents. Half a minute passed before anything began to happen. Suddenly he felt his way begin to open. The lights dimmed, and the sentries reeled momentarily under a loss of power. And Velmeran simply vanished.

Only a matter of seconds passed before Commander Trace returned. He was halfway across the room before he noticed that the five attentive sentries were guarding an empty stool. He nearly tripped in his astonishment. There was only one way in and out of the room, and he had not been out of sight of that door. The sentries continued to stare at the stool as if their prisoner was still seated there, and Trace, startled and confused half out of his wits, walked over to the stool to confirm that the Starwolf was indeed gone.

"How did he escape?" he demanded of the nearest sentry. "You were ordered to shoot to kill if he left the stool."

"I am aware of my orders," the sentry reported concisely. "The prisoner did not leave the stool."

"Well, he sure didn't take it with him! Where did he go?"

"He vanished."

Trace blinked in bemusement before realization set in. Velmeran must have had another device, stunning the entire group. This vanishing act sounded too much like that 'I did not see anyone' business. He turned and stalked from the room, only to be intercepted at the door by the physician.

"Here you are!" Wriestler said, thrusting a small plastic bottle containing several pills under the Sector Commander's nose. Trace took the bottle and stared at it.

"What the hell is this?" He demanded.

"What you asked for," Wriestler explained triumphantly. "Pyridoxine. Vitamin B$_6$."

16

Rifle in hand, Baress advanced cautiously to the single door leading into the auxiliary bridge and peered out. Consherra, seated at the main computer console, frowned without looking up. Baress was as regular as clockwork; in the last fifty-five minutes he had checked that door exactly fifty-five times.

"Velmeran should be coming in a few minutes," she remarked. Her four hands were moving over two separate keyboards with lightning speed. "I just told him that I am finishing this up."

"Right on time," Baress remarked, consulting the chronometer built into one of the sleeves of his suit. "I wonder what Velmeran has been up to. Whatever he did, every sentry in this end of the ship took off at a run a long time ago and they never came back. For that matter, I wonder where he is."

"Right behind you."

Baress was so startled that he spun around and fired two shots from the powerful rifle into the ceiling overhead, and even Consherra nearly fell out of her chair. Velmeran, looking very pale and worn, sat in the Captain's seat, staring apprehensively at the smoking holes in the ceiling immediately over his head.

"I do not know whether to compliment you for not shooting me, or just be glad you missed," he remarked, then turned to Consherra. "Close your mouth and get back to work. I want to get out of here."

Consherra admitted to the logic in that and returned to work.

"But . . . but how did you get in here?" Baress demanded. "I never left that door."

"I did not come through the door, I teleported."

Consherra glanced at him over her shoulder. "I would sooner believe that you put yourself in a box and came through the mail."

Velmeran shrugged. "Believe what you will. Now that I consider it, I am known for entirely too much wizardry as it is."

That was the wrong answer, of course. By denying it, he had inadvertently forced Consherra to feel obliged to believe in him. She glared at him. "What have you been doing, anyway? You look about half dead. What happened to your helmet and weapons?"

"Don has them," he explained. "I have spent the better part of the last hour as his guest."

"Then you were the grand diversion that brought every sentry on this ship at a run?" Baress asked.

"Only at first. I hinted to Don that there is a bomb in the power core of the ship, and that he had an hour to find it."

Baress grinned mischievously. "I can imagine how that made them hop!"

"Exactly," Velmeran agreed. "He was so generally delighted to have me, and so nervous about finding that bomb, that it never occurred to him that there might be other Starwolves on his fine, big ship."

"That does it," Consherra announced suddenly. "Now we can go home. What about your weapons and helmet?"

"Nothing I can do about that."

"Well, you can at least have a gun," Baress said as he offered a pistol.

"I can do better than that," Consherra said as she began to removed her belt. "Let me keep one pistol for reassurance and you can have the rest. It will do you more good."

"Drop those weapons!"

The three Starwolves glanced up to see Commander Trace and two crewmembers standing at the door, rifles aimed to fire, as five additional crewmembers filed in to take up positions surrounding the prisoners. There was no question of escape or fighting back; this could not have come at a worse time. Baress's rifle stood beside the door, while Consherra's was lying beside the console. Velmeran had no weapons, Consherra was holding her weapons belt with the pistols clipped in their holsters, and Baress had laid both of his pistols on the console. Consherra looked questioningly at Velmeran, but he indicated for her to comply.

"Damn it all, anyway," he muttered in disgust. "If I had not been so tired, they never would have been able to sneak up on us."

"Now, move away from that console," Trace directed. "Out into the open."

The three Starwolves did as they were told.

"Might I ask how you managed to find us so quickly?" Velmeran asked.

"That was a very simple matter," Trace said, lowering his weapons now that the Starwolves were safely surrounded. "The ship reported a partial power loss in that diagnostic room in the sick bay and here at the same time. Whatever the cause, it suggested where to find you."

Velmeran shrugged indifferently. "I guess that I need to work that out before I try it again."

"There will be no next time," Trace said ominously. "I will not risk having you escape a second time. That is why I took that little memento out of your hide, remember. I knew at the time that I would probably have to kill you."

"Do not be a fool," Velmeran said sharply. "I am still in control of this situation. If you want to live, then you will get out of here now."

"Whatever else happens, I will have the pleasure of killing you first," Trace declared, unimpressed, as he aimed his gun. "Fire!"

The auxiliary bridge was rocked as every gun exploded at almost exactly the same instant. Flames and thick, black smoke enveloped each of the gunners, and pieces of the white-hot metal pelted the nearer half of the bridge like hailstones. The fire alarms rang shrilly as the ventilation to the area shut down to suffocate a possible fire as the single door to the bridge snapped shut; had they possessed a sense of smell, the Starwolves would have been overwhelmed by the odor of burnt flesh. A few seconds later the ventilation came back on at full power, drawing away the thick curtain of smoke to slowly reveal eight blackened, lifeless bodies.

The door reopened a moment later. The Starwolves assumed that it was an automatic function, and so they were caught by surprise when a sentry ambled through at its best pace. Baress dived for Consherra's gun, while the other two prepared to dodge.

"Sentry, halt!" a voice commanded sharply, and the machine pulled itself to a stop. A moment later a tiny human peered cautiously through the doorway. "Don't shoot, please. I'm not armed."

"We will not fire," Velmeran assured her.

Maeken Kea entered cautiously, glancing apprehensively at the bodies that were still smoking lazily. "So you got him at last. I assume that you have some way of causing guns to explode when fired?"

"On a small scale," Velmeran answered evasively. "Am I correct in assuming that you are Captain Maeken Kea?"

"I am. I assume as well that you are Velmeran." She did not make a question of that as she came to a stop three meters away.

"Of course. You do not seem particularly worried about the fate of your late Commander."

"Bastard!" Maeken spat viciously. "I've only just found out about how he liked to play with nuclear weapons. I'll not apologize for anything I've done to try to win this battle, but I am sorry for some of the tricks he pulled. For that, most of all. And for what he did to you. He's paid for it all, I suppose. I'm just sorry that I had any part of it."

"I am also sorry that you had any part of this," Velmeran added. "Any other captain would have given me less trouble. But it is over now."

Maeken frowned. "That is what I wanted to ask you about. It seems to me that you people have been a great deal busier than anyone first thought. I suppose that there is no question that you have done enough damage to assure the destruction of this ship."

Velmeran nodded. "You could not stop it at this point even if you knew what to look for."

"So I had assumed." She paused a moment to glance at the charred bodies. "If you don't mind, I would like very much to get my crew away from here. All I have are children with fresh commissions and harmless Feldenneh . . . technicians, not soldiers."

"My mercenary common sense tells me that I should eliminate such a capable Commander as yourself," Velmeran remarked frankly, and paused only a moment to consider the matter. "As soon as I leave this chamber, I am going to instruct the Methryn to attack in fifteen minutes."

"Thank you, Commander," Maeken said as she hurried to the communications console on the lower portion of the bridge to relay the order to abandon the ship. The Starwolves collected their weapons and left in a hurry. Velmeran was already in telepathic contact with Tregloran to relay his orders to the Methryn.

They now had to use the lift to get away in time, and he doubted that he had the strength left to get himself out of the Fortress otherwise. It no longer mattered how many lights they tripped on the bridge.

Lenna, you have less than fifteen minutes to get yourself back to the fighters, Velmeran warned. She lacked the ability to reply in clear words the way the Kelvessan could, but he received the impression that she was already well ahead of them.

The lift accelerated quickly, the computer control compensating for the longer run with greater speed. It had completed most of the distance when the car began to break to a sudden, jerky stop. Velmeran appeared to listen to some distant voice.

"The Challenger knows where we are," he explained. "She means to hold us here until a group of sentries can arrive to investigate, Baress, you are young and strong. Pop open those doors so that we can take a look."

"I might be stronger than you at the moment, but I remind you that I am nearly twice as old," Baress said as he took hold of the edge of each door and pulled them apart. They parted easily, revealing a blank wall of gray metal just beyond. "Definitely a wall. Is that what you expected?"

"I am afraid so. Give it a punch and see how thick it is."

Baress drew back an armored fist and put it through the panel, then peeled it back like foil. Baress tore open a way large enough to climb through in a matter of seconds, then slipped through to the other side to receive the guns and helmets that Velmeran passed to him. Soon they were all assembled in the corridor beyond.

"Sentries will be coming from every direction, so we had better hurry," Velmeran warned. "The stairs leading down are about two hundred meters ahead."

They found the stairs quickly and descended to the level of the outer airlock. Baress now led the way, assuming the role of vanguard since it was obvious that Velmeran would be lucky just to get himself out of the ship. They soon came to the access conduit that served as a channel for a maze of pipes that ran the length of the ship. The corridor that led to the airlock intercepted this a hundred meters farther down. Baress was about to step out onto the wide walkway that ran above the river of pipes when Velmeran pulled him back.

"Sentries," he explained. "At least five. They are waiting for us."

To prove the point, he broke off a half-meter section of hand-rail from a nearby service ladder and tossed it out onto the walkway. A barrage of powerful bolts centered on that target. Then the fire shifted to the entrance of the passage as the automaton tried to bounce bolts down the side corridor to their unseen targets.

"We have to work our way around," Velmeran decided reluctantly.

There was a sudden, unexpected explosion from somewhere around the corner, followed by a steady hail of bolts that gave the Starwolves the distinct impression that the sentries themselves were under attack. When yet another exploded, Baress was overcome with curiosity and cautiously peered around the corner. He drew back instantly, looking decidedly astonished.

"So what is it?" Consherra prompted impatiently.

Baress shook his head slowly. "I still find it hard to believe, but I think the cavalry has arrived to save us."

Velmeran looked for himself, and was met with the most incredible sight he had ever seen. Bill, the sentry, was running at his best awkward pace along the walkway behind the ambushers. Lenna Makayen was perched on the very top of his back, her rifle in hand, and both of them were firing for all they were worth. The other sentries, mystified at the unexplainable attack of a Union officer and one of their own, did not even fight back as they fell quickly under the assault. They shot their way through the line of attackers and drew to a stop before the three startled Starwolves.

"Hurry up!" Lenna urged. "We've cleared the passage, but more are on their way."

"Lead on, then," Velmeran answered as they fell in behind Bill's protective bulk. "How did you know where to find us?"

"Bill did," she explained. "He's been listening in as the Challenger has been ordering her sentries about trying to find you. The first ambush is here, and the second is at the far end of the long corridor leading to the outer hull. You need to call Treg and the others and have them catch those sentries from behind. How many are there, Bill?"

"Three," the machine replied, typically concise.

They were about halfway down the tunnel to the outer hull when a short, rapid burst of cannon fire echoed loudly through the length of the passage. No bolts lit up the interior of the long corridor, however, and at its end they found Tregloran standing with his rifle in hand, surrounded by the smoking hulks of three sentries.

Tregloran turned without a word and led the way to the airlock. They stopped at the door and Lenna handed down her rifle before hopping off Bill's towering back. She headed immediately for the suit room, already stripping off her clothes at a furious pace.

"You people go on and get yourselves out of here," she ordered, her accent thickening as she tried to sound firm and authoritative. "It'll take me a couple of minutes to get into this suit. I can't go outside without it, and I'll get it on no quicker with you waiting for me. It would be foolish of you to get caught here with me."

"So who's arguing with you now?" Velmeran asked, imitating her perfectly. "I have to go. Valthyrra needs me. But you get yourself out of here."

"I'll be just fine," she assured him. "Bill is here to watch out for me."

"The Challenger has left the ring for open space," he added. "That might give you a little more time."

He herded the others into the airlock and indicated for them to put on their helmets. Since he had none of his own, he began taking deep breaths until the air in the lock began to thin. Moments later the lock opened on the blackness of space and not the boulder-strewn surroundings of the ring. Trel and Marlena were there immediately, bending over the opening and reaching down to lift them out. Velmeran went first. Speed was critical for him, since he was now without an air supply and too tired to last for very long without one. He felt the intense cold of open space immediately, cold enough here in the shadows of the ship to have frozen dry ice, and perhaps even nitrogen, temperatures that would begin to affect him within minutes. He hurried to the fighters, the others only a moment behind.

He also could not hear their warnings, because he was completely deaf without the medium of air to carry sounds from the com built into his collar. He was suddenly aware of the presence of a warship immediately behind him, and turned to see a destroyer emerging from a concealed lock perhaps seven kilometers ahead. As soon as it slipped from its rack, it began to drift rapidly toward them as the Challenger continued to accelerate past, skimming the black hull of the larger ship with just meters to spare.

Velmeran stood beside the fighter as he watched. The smaller ship was facing in their direction, and he was able to see the guns open and charged below the extended bridge. Suddenly it stopped, or rather it fired its forward engines to match speed with the Fortress and hover alongside not fifty meters from where they stood. Then the destroyer began to move laterally away from the hull of the larger ship until it was clear to navigate.

As the tension of the moment passed, Velmeran felt himself begin to grow cold and dizzy and broke contact with the hull to pull himself in free-fall into the cockpit of his fighter. Maeken Kea had rescued her crew from the doomed Fortress. If she had seen Velmeran's party on the hull, then she had returned the favor. Even so, he left one of his own behind. The Methryn was closing, and Lenna had run out of time.

Officers hurried to take their places on the Methryn's auxiliary bridge, a smaller copy of the one that lay in ruins. Cargin paused on the way to the weapons console to catch a bright orange cord and jerk loose the pin that freed Valthyrra's camera pod. The boom immediately dropped down to a comfortable level and the twin lenses spun in unison as they focused. She turned to Cargin, who remained waiting.

"I am going to charge to eighty-five percent of overload on the conversion cannon," she explained quickly. "Back me up on the gauges so that I do not exceed that."

"Right."

The Challenger had turned abruptly to head straight out of the ring, running for open space where she could shield effectively. Valthyrra accelerated rapidly, closing quickly on the Fortress after its initial gain on the smaller ship after leaving the ring.

The Challenger was building to speed barely ten thousand kilometers ahead, trying to get up to a speed where even minor shifts in field-drive steering would throw her tremendous bulk into wide, evasive turns, making her a difficult target for the Metryn's conversion cannon. It might have been that she was trying to survive long enough to get into starflight. But that was a poor defense at best, for the smaller, quicker Starwolf ship could follow her in and shoot out her exposed engines. She had to stay and fight.

The Methryn leaped forward as she unshielded the aperture of her conversion cannon and began charging the powerful weapon. There could be no hiding such a tremendous surge of power. The Challenger scanned it and cut acceleration as she made ready to divert her full power to her shields.

Valthyrra could wait no longer, even though she was still three thousand kilometers short of her target. She aimed herself quickly and fired. The Challenger threw up her shield, full and strong from the first instant, forming a misty white sphere around the ship. Only a fraction of a second later that concentrated blast of raw energy struck squarely in the middle of the shield and parted around it, like a wave breaking over a rock. For three full seconds the Methryn turned the power to destroy a world against that shield, and it was still intact when she found nothing else to throw against it.

For a moment Valthyrra was at a loss to know what to do. She could not fire the conversion cannon again; although undamaged, the thick walls of the containment chamber and the kilometer-long throat of the weapon glowed white-hot. Then the dense shield came down and she saw that the Challenger was already pivoting to face her, and she knew that she had no choice. Even as she closed to attack, she turned sharply to head away at a right angle.

As it turned out, that was perhaps the only thing that saved her. The Challenger altered her path to follow the fleeing carrier, opening fire while her target was still in range. In the next instant she turned into a rapidly expanding nova of blinding light and heat and millions of tons of vaporized metal. The Methryn all but leaped into starflight to stay ahead of the shock wave that put a sizable dent in the ring and for a short time added a white glaze to its normal dirty brown as the haze of trapped ice crystals was vaporized by the stellar heat.

Within minutes the Methryn was setting herself into a wide, slow orbit around the planet well outside the ring. Six of the seven fighters of the special tactics team closed quickly on final approach to her landing bay. Velmeran brought his fighter in quickly, landing in the center of the bay. He leaped out as soon as the canopy was open and ran for the lift that was waiting for him, landing-bay crewmembers moving silently out of his way.

Even though he knew what had happened, he still was not prepared for the destruction he saw on the deserted bridge. Temporary patches had been set in the hull so that the atmosphere could be restored, and all of the loose debris had been cleared away. Most of the bridge showed some damage; both of the stations of the middle bridge were in ruins, while the blasted pit of the upper bridge was lost in darkness. This was the worst shock for Velmeran, even above the sight of the Methryn's wrecked nose. His earliest cherished memories were of his privileged visits to the place, the Methryn's heart, when his mother had still been Commander-designate and the best pack leader on the ship.

"Valthyrra?" he called hesitantly.

She brought her camera pod around to look at him, the twisted hinges of her boom creaking. Only one lens focused in on him, the leads of the damaged camera hanging loose.

"I am sorry," she said softly. "I let you down."

"No, not you," he assured her as he walked over to join her. "It was my fault, if anyone's. My careful plans simply were not good enough."

Velmeran collapsed wearily into the nearest of the two seats of the navigational console. Valthyrra brought her camera pod in closely to look at him. "There is a matter of truth that I would discuss with you. I suspect that you knew that this fight would cost a life. You meant it to be your own."

"I wish that it had been," he said despondently. "I guess I believed that I had made some bargain with fate, that I could trade my own life to protect a world and save my ship. If nothing else, I have been taught that fate is only a word for what will be, and that I cannot bargain with chance. And that, for all my special talents, I cannot see the future, only hints of what might be. I would rather see nothing at all."

"No, you are wrong," Valthyrra insisted. "Twice now you have been warned, and twice you have used that warning to shape a future of your own making. But shaping a future and controlling it are two very different things. It is only natural to blame yourself when something goes wrong, but that really does not make it your fault."

Velmeran said nothing, nor would he even look up at her. Still, she thought that he had listened to her, and that his grief would not turn inward to guilt and self-doubt.

"I feel very alone just now," he said at last.

"I think you know that you are not," she told him. "You are surrounded by a great many people who love you and think very highly of you. There is a girl down in the landing bay just now who is crying as much for you as for her former Commander. I hope I do not have to tell you how much you mean to me."

Velmeran sighed heavily with regret at the mention of Consherra. He had not told her and the others, saving that bad news for when they were clear of the Challenger. He had meant to be the one to tell them upon their return, but he had forgotten in his haste to reach the bridge.

He shook his head slowly. "What have I won? Mayelna is gone. My ship is wrecked. I had to leave Lenna in that ship after she came back to help us. Donalt Trace is dead, and even that gives me no satisfaction. I am tired of war and destruction. For once I would like to know that I have done something positive, something of value."

"But you have," Valthyrra insisted. "In years to come you will make an end to this war, and free the Kelvessan to seek worlds and lives of their own. Before she died, Mayelna spoke these final words. She said that we must not grieve for her, for her life was long and full and nearly all that she had ever hoped to see had come to pass. She said that I must watch over you, and help you in every way I can to use your special talents to make the best future you can imagine. For no one has ever done a tenth as much to shape a new future for the Kelvessan as you have."

Velmeran looked up at her suspiciously. "Did she really say all that?"

"Well, no," the ship admitted reluctantly. "All she said was, 'Save yourself, you old fool.' In her own way, that meant very much the same thing."

Velmeran made an odd noise, and Valthyrra glanced quickly away in the thought that he was going to cry. Then, to her astonishment, she realized that he was laughing softly. She turned to stare at him, and then the humor of that struck her as well.

"Commander?" she said gently.

Velmeran glanced up at her, momentarily shocked to receive that title and its awesome burden of responsibility for the first time. Then he found that, while the title might be new, the mantle of responsibility had a familiar, almost comfortable feel with little power to frighten him. He rose and shrugged the shoulders of his armor into place.

"Progress report."

"I have already sent the packs to assist the Kalvyn in breaking the invasion force over Tryalna," Valthyrra reported. "Capture ships and other support vessels are also on their way to assist."

"Donalt Trace said something about conversion devices in low orbit."

"I will consult with Schayressa on the matter immediately."

"Call me a lift, then."

"I left it waiting for you," Valthyrra said. "By the way, Schayressa reports that she discovered the conversion devices quite sometime ago and quietly removed them."

"Send her my compliments on being so alert," Velmeran said as he entered the lift. Privately, he wished that those devices had not been there.

He found Consherra and the members of his special tactics team waiting for him in the corner of the landing bay where the lift opened. Consherra had been crying; even the boundless energy and optimism of Tregloran was subdued by sadness and a sense of defeat, and he had been crying nearly as much as Consherra had. They looked up at him expectantly as the door opened, and he could guess their thoughts. An age in the history of the Methryn was passing. Mayelna had been the last of her pirate commanders. Velmeran was a warrior, not a pirate, and he required a warship to serve him.

"I am sorry for not telling you at the time," he began. "I wanted you to concentrate on watching out for yourselves."

"Of course, Commander. You had the success of the mission and the lives of your crewmembers to consider," Trel, the oldest, answered for them all.

The lift doors snapped open again and Keth stepped out to join the small group. "Commander?"

"Yes, I need your help," Velmeran said. "I believe that you have students who are ready to join the packs."

"Yes, Commander. Ten in all."

"I will take them off your hands right now," Velmeran said, and turned to Barress. "I want you to take Gyllan, Merkollyn, and Delvon with five of those students to form a new pack. The remaining five will serve as replacements for our old pack. Treg, do you think you can handle that?"

"Can I?" The younger pilot seemed about to jump for joy, but caught himself and attained an exaggerated air of mature dignity. "I would be happy to oblige."

"It is a bother, but someone has to do it," Velmeran agreed, and turned back to Keth. "You know your students best, so I will leave it up to you to divide them between the two packs."

"And what of the special tactics team?" Baress asked.

"That stays exactly the way it is," Valthyrra insisted, cutting Velmeran off, as her camera pod pushed its way to the middle of the group. "Meran, the better part of your business is conducted through special tactics. And you have to admit that you could not very well sit back and direct a special tactics team from the bridge."

"That is true, but Commanders are not allowed to fly," he protested.

"Allowed? Where is that written? You kept a special tactics team in addition to your pack for two years, and there was no problem with that. Who is going to say you cannot?"

"Treg and I will be busy with our own packs, but we have no intention of giving up special tactics," Baress said.

Consherra frowned. "I suppose that I would even be willing to go out with you again, if you ever need me."

"Which brings us to the subject of lost members," Valthyrra said, drifting slowly into the bay while bending her long neck to peer out the rear door. The others looked as well; they saw nothing, but they could all sense the approach of a single fighter.

"Lenna?" Velmeran asked as he came to stand beside the probe.

"Who else?" she asked in return. "She accepted landing instructions but says that she is too busy to talk. I am going to signal a crash alert and summon Dyenlerra to the bay."

The three demanding beeps of the alarm sent the bay crew into immediate action, securing fighters in their racks so that they could be carried away. Half a minute later the incoming fighter ducked beneath the Methryn's tail as it began its final approach. At the same time that it dropped its landing gear, the watchers in the bay noticed something unusual about the little ship. A curious white object could be seen standing upright in the hull between and just ahead of the two vertical fins. Velmeran's first thought was that the fighter had been transfixed by a piece of wreckage hurtled from the explosion of the Challenger.

Then the fighter slipped smoothly into the bay and the strange object was revealed to be a passenger. Bill, the sentry, stood atop the ship, his powerful legs braced with his magnetic pads locked to the metal hull. Lenna brought the fighter to the front of the bay and landed gently, and Valthyrra immediately brought in a set of handling arms to pluck the automaton from atop the ship. Lenna opened the cockpit and climbed out just as Velmeran walked over to join her.

"I will not ask you why you brought that machine back with you," he said slowly. "I will not even ask you if you are crazy, or simply foolish. But I would like to know how you managed to get it on top of your fighter and still get away in time."

"Oh, I sent him on ahead," Lenna explained as if it was some trifling matter. "In free-fall like that, the hardest thing was for him to climb out of the lock. He just walked up the sloping part of the wing and was waiting when I got there. And it was a near thing, I can tell you. The shield went up just as I was about to light out of there, so I had to wait it out or risk being caught in the Methryn's fire. But I had to run for hell when that shield came down because I knew that the Fortress was going to blow in a matter of seconds when it did. Scared me half to death when it did, too. Even Bill commented on it."

Velmeran turned to look at the sentry, which had just been lowered to the deck. Sentries were not known for their personalities, which rated somewhat above a toaster but well below a Starwolf carrier. Bill did seem to be developing one, but Velmeran was not sure if it was really his own or just a reflection of what Lenna believed him to be.

"He did save my life," she added defensively, having noticed his stare. "Besides, I thought that I might use him in my spy work. Especially if he can always scan the security frequencies the automatons are linked on. He was very helpful."

"The two of you have more than proved your worth," Velmeran agreed. "But I want Valthyrra to completely rework his hardware to make him more intelligent and versatile."

"Do I have a patient here?" Dyenlerra asked as she pushed her way to the center of the group, closing on Lenna.

"Not her, but you might have a look at Bill."

"Bill? Who is Bill?" the medic asked. She glanced over her shoulder, and nearly jumped out of her armor.

17

As soon as Tryalna was secure and the remains of the human invasion force sent running for home, the Methryn and the Kalvyn made a short journey together. Surrounded by their packs, they dived side by side toward the fiery heart of that system. They came uncomfortably close to the warm yellow sun before they veered away, leaving behind an old friend on her brief sojourn to her final rest.

Commander Tryn carried Mayelna to her last rest, her broken body encased in white armor donated by Dyenlerra to replace her ruined armor. Nearly four thousand Starwolves, every crewmember of both ships who had a suit, crowded onto the broad platforms over the shock bumpers of the two ships, while those who did not watched from the windows of the observation decks.

It was a very hard time for Velmeran, and he was privately grateful to be spared the need to carry his mother to her final rest. He never looked upon her again after his return from the Fortress, preferring to keep as his last memory of her their final words in the landing bay. He had been so happy then, thinking that he had accomplished something good for her in his offer to command the Methryn in her place. Now the Methryn was his, but all his hopes and good intentions had been for nothing.

Velmeran was distracted from his grief afterward when his return to the crowded observation deck became an unexpected reception for his confirmation as the Methryn's new Commander. All of the officers, pack leaders, and various other crewmembers, including many from the Kalvyn, presented themselves to offer their condolences and quietly affirm their loyalty. Tryn slipped away early, responding to Schayressa's subtle pleas for his return, and Consherra disappeared with Lenna and Dyenlerra soon after. At least Valthyrra's probe stayed dutifully at his side the entire time.

"It is normally the case that you appoint a Commander-designate younger than yourself," he told Baressa privately as the crowd began to thin. "That is not very practical for me, under the circumstance. And, since I am keeping my special tactics team, I do need to have a replacement ready. As far as I am concerned, you are the only choice."

"For now, perhaps," Baressa answered. "Treg will never be your equal, but he is quickly becoming a reasonable facsimile."

"And I plan to begin his training immediately," Velmeran agreed. "But I do have other plans for him."

She looked at him questioningly. "Other plans?"

Velmeran shrugged. "The Vardon will be coming out of construction airdock in a few years. I might not have the authority to make such an appointment. . . ."

"But who would dispute the recommendations of Commander Velmeran of the Methryn?" Valthyrra inquired.

Velmeran looked annoyed. "You be discreet about how you use my name—or your own—with your sister ships or home base. Where did Consherra get to?"

"Oh, Dyenlerra appropriated her and Lenna several minutes ago," the ship replied. "She told them to get out of their armor and report for a medical scan."

"I think that I should join them," he decided. "Can you call me a lift?"

"On the way. I will put away this remote and join you there."

Velmeran returned to his cabin and removed his armor for the first time in well over a day. He dressed quickly and hurried to the medical section, where he found Consherra and Lenna occupying separate diagnostic beds in the same room. Valthyrra had commandeered another probe and had arrived with Baressa, Tregloran, and Baress just before him. They stared at him in surprise as he entered, and he could imagine why. He was now dressed in the white of an officer, clothes that Valthyrra had hurriedly prepared for him. His thick, shaggy mane of wood-brown hair tumbled over his shoulders and halfway down his back, his large eyes glittering behind the fringe of that brown curtain.

Dyenlerra afforded him only the briefest glance before turning back to the readout for Lenna's scanner. "You seem to be well, for all I can tell. These readings mean nothing to me. I am not a veterinarian."

"Then how do you know that I'm well?" Lenna asked as she sat up on the edge of the bed.

"Because they are the same readings I got a couple of days ago."

"I have a very good question to propose, if this is the time," Consherra began suddenly.

"This is not the time," Dyenlerra insisted. "But ask, if it will shut you up long enough for me to run a scan on you."

"What happened to the Challenger?" she asked, ignoring the medic. "My reprogramming was an obvious failure, so what did cause that ship to explode? I am sure that it blew several seconds after Valthyrra fired."

"Oh, that was Lenna's work," Velmeran explained, and continued when he saw five astonished stares. "While you were playing with her programming, Lenna was running about the ship setting nuclear missiles to explode. How many did you set?"

"Six in all," Lenna explained, blushing slightly in uncharacteristic modesty. "I set them on a ten-second delay after the ship brought up its full shield. Good thing, too. About the delay, I mean. I was still inside the shield when the Methryn fired. I guess those warheads caused a chain reaction through just about every generator on that ship."

"But the Challenger had already shielded once," Valthyrra pointed out.

"Yes, but I had only just started. It was a near thing, too. Half a minute more and it would have exploded in my face. Scared the . . . devil out of me, so it did."

Consherra was practically speechless. "You mean that I did an hour of reprogramming for nothing, while Lenna just walked in and destroyed that monster of a ship with no trouble at all?"

Lenna glanced at her. "No trouble at all, did you say? Remind me to tell you how much trouble it was to have someone swinging a wrench at my head on the one hand while a sentry was aiming all its guns at me from behind."

"Well, you're a real Starwolf now, even if you have only two hands," Velmeran said. "Which is only one less than I have. That is what I needed to talk to you about."

Dyenlerra glanced up from her monitor. "What is it. Did you hurt yourself?"

Velmeran stepped over to her side and held up his handless lower arm for her inspection. It was the first time the others had realized that the hand was actually missing, since he had kept the glove of his suit on earlier. Tregloran made some exclamation of outrage; Consherra, who was lying on the table next to him, reacted even more sharply. Ignoring her, the medic pulled back the sleeve for a closer look.

"How did this happen?" she asked with professional detachment.

"Donalt Trace wanted it," he explained. "The ship's medic took it off with a laser scalpel."

"He did? What did he want it for?"

"He wanted to make lots of little Starwolves."

"*Rashah ko veernon,* what a horrible thought!" she remarked softly. "Just imagine Donalt Trace surrounded by half a million Velmerans. Sounds like something from his own worst dreams."

"Donalt Trace is dead, and the hand was destroyed," Velmeran said. "Can you make me another?"

"I could, but I'm not going to. All Kelvessan can fully regenerate skin, muscle, teeth, and any organ, but my studies of mutant genetic structure indicate that you can replace missing limbs as well. This is my first chance to test this. If it does not work, well . . . you know that you can always come to me for a hand."

Velmeran was spared the need to answer that when the medical scanner beeped imperiously and Dyenlerra turned to the monitor. She nodded in satisfaction. "The two of you are perfectly well."

"I could have told you that," Consherra remarked, then paused when she saw that Velmeran was staring at her. He bore a look of deep hurt and disappointment—even betrayal—that she had not expected.

"It is true," she said simply, cautiously. "I am sorry, but I did not know how to tell you."

"Well, yes," he stammered uncertainly. "But I had just thought that when you wanted . . . that you and I . . ."

The sudden realization of what worried him was nearly enough to knock her off the table. "Dearest ass! You are the only mate that I have had in several years now. How could you possibly imagine that you are not the father?"

"But we had not planned . . ."

Dyenlerra laughed aloud. "This is one of the little things that may happen when two people fool around for fun. Has no one ever explained these things to you?"

Velmeran was startled by some sudden revelation. "Mayelna started to have that little talk with me just as I was about to leave. It was not the best time, and I had no idea what she was talking about."

"So now you do," the medic remarked. "And while we are on the subject, you owe me a duty mating."

Velmeran began to make some evasive reply, but he was distracted by Lenna as she leaped from the bed in her excitement. "Hey, I'm a Starwolf now! How do I get in on this?"

Dyenlerra regarded her tolerantly. "We are not the same species. Velmeran cannot get you pregnant."

"Who cares?" Lenna demanded. "I just want to screw around!"

Consherra regarded her for a moment, then took Velmeran by one hand and led him off to one side of the room, as private as they were going to get in such close quarters. "Are you pleased?"

"I could not be happier," he assured her.

"And no regrets?"

Velmeran frowned. "Only one, and we can do nothing about that."

Consherra nodded slowly. "She knew. And I believe that she was pleased. I know that I am. He will be just like you, I am sure."

"She," Velmeran corrected her gently.

"She?" Consherra asked, and looked questioningly at Dyenlerra.

The medic shrugged helplessly. "She."

"*Varth!*" Consherra muttered. "I do all the work, and yet I am the last to know."

"Is it really so necessary?" Dr. Wriestler asked in feeble protest in response to the request.

"Yes, it is," Maeken Kea insisted. "You have saved his life, but it won't be worth a damn unless I can save his career. I must speak with him before we reach port, and he has to remember what I tell him. You indicated that he is alert enough at this time."

"Yes, he will understand and remember what you tell him,"

the physician agreed reluctantly. "If you consider it absolutely necessary..."

"It is so ordered," Maeken said with enough firmness to make him understand that she was not offering him a choice. "If you would care to go up to the galley for something to drink, I will call you when I'm finished. This will not take long."

Wriestler recognized the implicit order that he was to make himself scarce in a hurry and withdrew. Maeken watched until he was gone before entering the room that he had been guarding bodily. The cabin was small, dominated by a curious apparatus that was half plastic bed and half low-walled tub, fed by a maze of opaque plastic tubes connected to a series of machines and tanks. A dark figure lay in the tub, encased in a cocoon of microscopic tubes that covered the burnt upper half of the body like a pelt of long white hair. She braced herself and approached slowly.

She could not imagine how Commander Trace could have survived. Dr. Wriestler had plucked the bits of metal out of his chest and face and had set him in the tank to regenerate his burnt skin. Once that was done, teams of specialists would be able to concentrate on making replacements for his right eye and the arms that had been quite literally ripped to shreds in the explosion of his gun. Maeken had not been able to look upon him when the medical automatons had come to collect him on the *Challenger's* auxiliary bridge. At least most of his body was now mercifully hidden within the machine.

"Commander?" she called softly.

He responded more quickly than she had anticipated, opening his one good eye to stare up at her.

"My ship?" he asked weakly, his voice a faint, hoarse whisper.

"I lost the *Challenger*," she replied simply. "The Starwolves had her fixed too many ways. Velmeran gave me fifteen minutes to abandon ship."

Trace closed his one good eye and nodded weakly. "He fooled us both. You did what you had to do. How . . . how did you get me away from him?"

"I recalled something I had heard about Starwolves being gullible," she explained. "I told him a sad, sad tale and he bought it. Of course, neither of us had any idea that you had actually survived. As far as that goes, he probably still thinks you're dead."

She paused a moment, leaning even closer. "Listen carefully, now. The High Council might be ready and willing to descend upon you like scavengers for losing that very expensive ship, but we can still turn this into a victory. We lost the Challenger, but the experiment was a success. The Starwolves could not destroy a Fortress from the outside, and we sure as hell won't give them a second chance to destroy one from within."

"Very encouraging," Trace remarked. "What about . . ."

"Wriestler brought it," she assured him. "Now this is the plan, at least as we will present it. We continue to build Fortresses but hold them back, adding to the fleet and using the ships only to defend the inner worlds. We build our own big, fast carriers full of quick little fighters. And in about twenty years we will have thousands of our own Starwolves grown up and ready to fight."

Donalt Trace sighed heavily. "Twenty years. At this rate, I should last so long."

"For now you stay well away from Starwolves," Maeken said firmly. "You have no good sense where Velmeran is concerned. Twenty years, and you can retire successfully. You let me do the talking, and I'll start talking as fast as I can as soon as we reach port. You rest now. We'll talk again as soon as you're up to it."

"Do the best you can," he answered weakly.

Maeken withdrew quietly and hurried to the galley. After the spaciousness of the Challenger, the compactness of the destroyer was confining. There were no lifts, but the galley was less than half a minute's walk from the cramped sick bay. She found Wriestler seated at a small table, leaning over the hot drink he had ordered.

"Finished," she said as she took the opposite seat. "Shouldn't you hurry back?"

Wriestler shrugged. "He's in no danger now that he's on the machine."

"Then why were you so reluctant to let me speak with him?"

"Just being the proper doctor," he said. "A large part of your internship is just learning to be a self-important ass. They teach the same thing to officers, although you seem to have missed the point."

"It never did anyone any good, as far as I can tell. But there is one extraordinarily tall ass that needs to be back to work as soon as possible."

"Half a year at most," Wriestler said, and smiled at her reaction of surprise. "Yes, it took him the better part of two years to recover from that last one. But, in a strange way, he's not in nearly as bad a shape. The machine will have new skin on him in two weeks. The eye should be no problem, and we can fit him with a pair of mechanical arms as soon as a pair his size can be made."

"Mechanical?" Maeken asked.

"He asked for it and, under the circumstances, it's the best way to go. There's a limit to how many regenerated parts you can stick in a person, and he's pushing the limit right now. I once had a young officer who was half a year from receiving two legs, half an arm, and a rebuilt face. Halfway to nowhere he began to reject his new skin, and nothing would stop it. He screamed every waking minute . . . which I kept to a minimum."

"In pain?" Maeken asked cautiously.

"In terror. I could block the pain."

The Methryn remained with the Kalvyn over Tryalna for another day and a half until the Karvand arrived and the freighter Lesdryn had slipped unobserved into the fringes of the system. The Starwolves could not keep a ship in this system for very long, since the twenty remaining carriers had to adjust their patrols to allow for the two damaged vessels. The Lesdryn would be back in a couple of weeks, her caverous holds filled with rebuilt destroyers and battleships to replace the system fleet.

Daelyn was understandably shocked and saddened to hear that her mother was dead, although the rare opportunity to visit with both her father and brother distracted her from her grief and she went away with more good than bitter memories. Both she and Commander Schayranna thoroughly approved of the new Commander, but the strange girl with two arms who sat familiarizing herself with the helm controls on the auxiliary bridge took a little getting used to.

Lenna was at the controls when the Methryn, the Kalvyn, and the Lesdryn left orbit, an occurrence that took more than just a little getting used to for the ship, the regular helm, and the new Commander. The auxiliary bridge had no commander's console, which gave Velmeran the excuse to loiter about and watch her every move. Since it was Consherra's responsibility to teach her young assistant, she also made it her business to watch over the girl. And since Valthyrra's camera pod was mounted overhead, she had the best view of all. Besides that, she had the reassurance of having an override on every control.

Once she got the Methryn out of orbit and accelerating to starflight along the proper flight path, however, they began to relax. Lenna had grown up with the desire to be the helm on a starship, and now she had her hands on a bigger, faster ship than any Trader had ever hoped for.

This scene was repeated several days later as the three Starwolf ships decelerated in their approach on the planet Alkayja. They moved out of starflight together, the Methryn and the Kalvyn flying side by side with barely their own length between them while the freighter Lesdryn followed at about three times that distance.

Everyone on the bridge watched the viewscreen expectantly for their first glimpse of Alkayja and its immense orbital base. For many, like Velmeran and Consherra, this was the first time that the Methryn had been in port in their lifetimes. Valthyrra's earliest memories were of this place. Her first run under her own power had been in this space, executing experimental trajectories around the four smaller and three larger planets. And yet even she had spent less than a score of years out of her eighteen centuries here, most of that time in refitting. Carriers never returned home except at need.

"Alkayja control, this is Methryn accompanied by Kalvyn and Lesdryn," Lenna hailed at Valthyrra's direction. "We are closing at twenty-two point eight million kilometers and anticipate Alkayja orbit in just over four minutes."

"Affirmative, Methryn," the reply came immediately. "We have your course projections and clear you to proceed as you are. Do you require assistance?"

"Negative, control. All systems are secure. We anticipate normal approach and docking."

"We understand, Methryn. Table for three, right this way please. You are to take refitting bay one. The Kalvyn is directed to refitting bay two. The Lesdryn is to take berth five. Do you comply?"

All three ships responded, and Lenna continued the approach. She would not attempt to slip the Methryn into airdock; even Consherra would have hesitated to try that, although she could have. At least having Lenna to watch the helm freed Consherra to attend her own duties as second in command; Velmeran was beginning to appreciate just how much she did to keep this ship running. She spent an average of twenty hours a day to her work, spending at least half that time visiting various sections of the ship. Not only did she keep track of the physical condition of the ship itself, she also knew every member of the ship by name and kept track of their affairs.

Braking hard, the Methryn was upon Alkayja within minutes, dominating the left half of the viewscreen. Lenna brought the ship completely around the sunlit side of the planet, holding the tight curve by force at several times the required velocity of that low orbit. As they neared darkness, the station appeared over the black horizon.

Alkayja station was not the largest that Velmeran had seen, smaller in fact than the Rane Military Complex above Vannkarn, the difference being that this was a compact structure. The main body, twenty-five kilometers across, consisted of a thick ring studded by the large rectangular modules that were the carrier bays. Twenty-two were docking bays, their wide, low openings enclosed only by containment fields, while the two construction bays and four refitting bays had actual doors. Above this was a thinner ring with bays for ordinary freighters and regular military forces. The thick inner hub of the station, completely filling the rings, contained the city itself and an industrial complex. The hub tapered quickly to blunt ends above and below, housing generators and clusters of large engines. Home Base was a mobile station, although it had not left orbit after arriving from Terra fifty thousand years before.

Valthyrra resumed direct control as the three ships closed on the station, each one moving toward its individual bay. She edged her shock bumper into the bracket designed to receive it, the meters-thick shock pistons attached to the frame of the station and those within her nose catching her tremendous mass and bringing it to a gentle stop. The pistons relaxed, pushing her into the parked position as two additional sets of brackets moved in from either side to lock into catches within the hull grooves at the tips of her blunt wings. Docking tubes telescoped out from the forward wall to fasten against her major airlocks.

With docking complete, the Methryn began the process of shutting herself down for the first time in a hundred years. Some basic systems had to remain in operation, such as internal gravity and atmosphere, as well as all of Valthyrra's essential computer systems. But she did shut down her generators to shift over to station power. This was the only painful part of the process, although strictly from a moral and philosophical point of view.

"All secure," Valthyrra reported.

"That's it?" Lenna asked, still at her station. "So what do you do now?"

"Do?" the ship asked. "You leave. You do whatever you can find to keep yourself amused and out of trouble."

"No, I mean, what do we do?" the girl protested. "Where do we go?"

She looked at Velmeran, but he only shrugged. "I have no idea."

"*Aval den tras etrenon!*" Valthyrra exclaimed. "You still live here, in your own cabins. The pilots are still answerable to their pack leaders—that includes you, two arms—and they are expected to practice. And the other crewmembers have their regular duties to perform This is not indefinite port leave."

That had not been directed solely at Lenna, and the young Starwolves who had not been through this before were relieved to hear it. They had somehow been under the collective impression that repairs and refitting meant that a carrier and her crew of Starwolves became a damaged machine and a couple of thousand unemployed Kelvessan.

"However, you have all earned a vacation," Valthyrra continued. "This is your first port leave, so you should have one of your new friends show you how to sell your trade goods."

"Trade goods?" Lenna asked, confused.

"Yes. We support ourselves with acts of piracy, and our crewmembers are paid with various items taken from the capture cargo. Did Dyenlayk not pay you for your good work on the Challenger?"

"Pay me?" Lenna asked, mystified. Then realization hit like an exploding star. "Oh, so that was why he gave me a silver tea service!"

Valthyrra stared. "What did you think you were supposed to do with it?"

"Hell, I was going to give a party!"

Valthyrra's camera pod shot up in surprise, then spun around in a complete circle and beat itself three times against the ceiling. Once that was out of her system, she brought it back to where Velmeran was standing. "Fleet Commander Laroose is on his way to the bridge."

"Fleet Commander?" Velmeran asked in obvious confusion.

"Yes, the Fleet Commander," the ship insisted. "Your superior. The guy who gives you your orders."

"My orders?" he asked, even more confused. "No one gives me orders."

"I doubt that he would dare to. Nonetheless, he does have the theoretical authority."

Velmeran had little time to speculate on the type of person who would undertake the task of directing the entire Wolf Fleet. He did have some idea of what he expected of such a person, something very different from the tall, broad-chested human of middle years who entered the bridge half a minute later. His initial surprise was seasoned with mild indignation that the Republic would keep a human in the position of leadership of its Starwolves like a gesture of ownership, coupled with his inner belief that a human was not morally or intellectually capable of such a task.

Commander Laroose obviously knew his way around a carrier's bridge. But he approached the middle bridge almost reverently, like an admirer in the presence of an idol for the first time.

"Commander Velmeran?" he asked tentatively.

"Yes?"

"I cannot tell you how glad I am to meet you," he said enthusiastically, shaking the Starwolf's hand vigorously. He noticed but politely ignored the missing hand, indicating that he had read the report on the incident. "You've done some amazing things, and you'll find that quite a reputation has preceded you. In fact, you're the first true folk hero of the Kelvessan. And something of a hero of my own, as you might guess. Every Kelvessa I know has taken up playing cards with the faces down."

Velmeran smiled at the comic image that Laroose drew for him with such obvious enthusiasm. These tactics, even if they were not intended as such, were not without their results. Velmeran was not flattered, since his ego did not operate in that manner. But he was more than gullible enough to be taken in by such charm.

"Before we begin work on the Methryn, there is an important matter that I must discuss with you and your ship," Laroose continued, now serious. "There have been a lot of changes here at Alkayja Base these last two years. Your own exploits have forced us to realize that we have to do more to serve our own ships. I now have four refitting docks in full operation; we can now overhaul a carrier in two months. We can even have the Methryn repaired and back out in only three. And it is important for you to be back out as soon as possible."

"Of course," Valthyrra answered pointedly before Velmeran could reply.

"But I would like to convince you to stay six months. You see, we have a new generation of bright Kelvessan scientists. Mutant stock, I daresay. Anyway, since we started work on the new Delvon, they put their minds to the task and came up with improvements for our engines. Maximum power output is up by over one-third. We have dampening fields that work a full fifty percent better than before. And we have successfully tested an operational jump generator."

"What?" Valthyrra demanded breathlessly, in spite of her inability to breathe. "The Delvon is going to be a real terror."

"Yes, well, we have all these new engines and units ready to install two decades before we can put them in," Laroose explained. "So, when I heard that you were coming in, I thought that we might want to strip out your old engines and give you all these toys, where they will do the most good. In fact, we mean to refit all the carriers and freighters as fast as we can bring them in. What do you say?"

"I do not consider that my decision to make," Velmeran replied, and looked up at the dazed lenses of the camera pod. "Val, do you agree?"

"Do I agree?" she asked incredulously. "I beg!"

18

Commander Laroose's assertion that Velmeran was becoming quite a hero to his people was no exaggeration; if anything, it was an understatement. Kelvessan had begun to arrive even before the Methryn was docked, watching the procedure through the wide bank of windows just above the docking bracket. The crowd continued to grow as hours passed, hundreds and then thousands. Velmeran was appalled, but finally felt obliged to put in an appearance. Kelvessan were very polite and quiet admirers, but they were also very blunt with their affections. Since the crowd was constantly changing, he was required to make these appearances every four hours for the next three days. Someone observed this routine and actually posted a schedule.

Actually, the term *hero* was not a completely accurate definition of what Velmeran represented to the Kelvessan. He was a leader, a symbol of Kelvessan presence and unity, a representative for a race that was emerging into its full maturity and looking at itself with a new sense of awareness. He came to accept this role because he believed in that and because, in a curious way, it comforted him. He had come away from this last battle feeling very much like someone whose gifts lay only in destruction. He was pleased to discover that, in the judgment of his own people, he was a builder of dreams and worlds.

Curiously, the one who was most unhappy was Lenna Makayen. She was caught between three races, not entirely human, not really a Trader and certainly not a Kelvessa. She had been quietly depressed since learning of Consherra's pregnancy. That reminded her only too sharply, for the first time in her life, that she was a sterile hybrid of two races and alien to both. She considered herself alone, a freak of nature. And yet her problem resolved itself very quickly; there was a perfect companion even for her.

Repairs began on the Methryn at a pace that kept even Valthyrra happy. In spite of her professed dread of refitting, Velmeran soon began to suspect that she actually liked the attention. She was certainly enchanted with the thought of acquiring a functional jump generator, allowing her to throw herself vast distances interdimensionally. Earlier tests of jump ships had not been successful, the carrier *Valcyr* having leaped out of time and space in the early days of the Starwolves, never to return. The problem with the system had finally been solved, and Velmeran confirmed the data before installation began. He was, after all, the resident expert on interdimensional jumps, having the ability to do it himself without the aid of machines.

After the first week Velmeran began to think that all the surprises were over. He was sitting alone in his cabin one evening, ship's time, reviewing data on a new weapon he was trying to design to crack quartzite shielding. The door announced a visitor, for what seemed like the fiftieth time that day.

"Come in!" he called without looking up, and the door slid open.

"I am sorry to disturb you, but I have come very far," a voice that was a rich, warm purr stated in Tresdyland, accented in a way that he had never heard. Velmeran glanced up.

The Aldessan were the true parent race of the Kelvessan, but there had been little contact between the two since. In Union space they were dismissed as creatures of legend, and Velmeran was naturally surprised to have a legend pay him a call in his own cabin. She was large, dwarfing him in comparison. A long, snakelike body was supported by a spider's cluster of appendages, four triple-jointed legs in back with four arms in front, each one longer than he was tall. She was furred in a plush brown velvet, a shaggy mane running from the top of her head to the tip of a thick tail two meters in length. A meter-long neck supported a fox's head with a long, tapered snout, vast cat-slit eyes, and tracking ears. Three pairs of breasts lining her belly identified her sex, although there was a curious delicacy to this oddly graceful lady.

She was also a Venn warrior-scholar, as he could tell by the body harness that was her only clothing. The harness supported two long swords and a clutch of throwing knives. As large and powerful as she was, she could not match a Kelvessa for strength and speed. Even so, she would be more than a match for twice as many Kalfethki.

"No, please come in," Velmeran insisted, hurrying to greet his guest. She towered over him on her long spider's legs, so tall that she risked bumping her head on the ceiling.

"I am Venn Keflyn," she said simply. "I am very pleased to meet you, but in truth I must admit that I was sent."

"To me?"

"To instruct you," she explained. "Word has reached us of mutant Kelvessan, and of the things that Velmeran can do. But after reading the report of your last battle, I think that you should instruct me."

"No, I need all the help I can get," Velmeran insisted. "We have been bumbling along as best we can. If it is all the same to you, I would just as well start over again with someone who knows what is going on."

Keflyn nodded. "In truth, with all matters concerning the psychic arts, we must all be our own teachers. We learn by example, and an example is only a model, a pattern that is not complete until you learn how to adapt it to your own use. I profess to be a teacher of such things, which is to say that I am experienced at setting good examples. But even I do not have your powers, some we had not even believed could be possible. You have caused quite a stir in the hallowed halls of the Venn Academy."

"I am sorry. . . ."

"No need to be concerned," she assured him. "It is, I assure you, a most delighted agitation. Such things I may not know, but I still hope to be of some service to you. As we say, those who cannot lead may at least stand behind and push in the right direction."

Velmeran was soon given to wonder if Aldessan were naturally given to understatement, or if Keflyn was simply too cautious to promise results. She knew exactly what was needed. He soon discovered that philosophy, not science or metaphysics, was the foundation for the study of the psychic arts. She never tried to explain how such powers worked. She was more interested in exploring the question of why.

"Many have talent but lack the self-awareness to make use of it," she explained once as they sat on a ledge overlooking the removal of damaged plates from the Methryn's battered nose. "Some stumble through life only half awake, not aware enough of either themselves or life around them to make use of what they possess. We are all limited by our beliefs, and that applies to more things than just the exercise of any gifts we might possess. Indeed, it might be that belief is the only limitation that is placed upon us."

And so they spoke together, sometimes exchanging only a few words, sometimes conversing for hours on end. Sometimes they volleyed questions back and forth in gentle exchange. Sometimes they speculated together on the same question. She never gave him some repetitive psychic exercise to do or drilled him in use of his talents. But from time to time curiosity would lead him to try something new, or he would try something he had already done with greater ease and accuracy than ever before.

"I assume, then, that our talents do not strengthen and grow with use," Velmeran said. He was becoming used to Keflyn's company. With her meter-long neck, it was not unlike talking to Valthyrra.

Keflyn curled the end of her tail forward and sat back, balancing a portion of her weight on its thicker, stronger upper half. "It seems that the only thing that strengthens and grows is our skill with the tool that is the individual talent, while the tool itself remains always the same. A psychic talent is not like a muscle that develops with use. Say, rather, that your talents are the eyes and ears—and in some cases the hands—of your soul."

"And is there such a thing?"

"Oh, of course," Keflyn insisted. "Anyone trained in his talents can feel the souls of those about him. Indeed, a person of your talent can manipulate a lesser spirit, although for obvious reasons we consider that the worst offense that anyone can commit by the use of talent. We may even transfer the essence of a person out of a broken body into a cloned replica. Even the body I wear is not the one I was born in."

Velmeran looked at her in open amazement. "You?"

She smiled gently. "I am Venn. Like you, I fight whenever there is need. It happened that when I was still very young, some four centuries ago, I was not as cautious as I should have been, and not as lucky as I would have liked."

Another time, weeks later, they were standing in the vast cavern created by the removal of one of the Methryn's four main drives. The repairs were proceeding in three steps. First the damaged portions and the old engines were removed, then the new field generators and jump generator were installed during the general refitting and overhaul, and finally the new engines would be installed and new hull plates set into place.

"Did the Aldessan make us?" Velmeran asked quickly, the question that Kelvessan had pondered for hundreds of years. It took a certain amount of courage for him to ask that, and even so it was not the question that he wanted most to ask. The only question that he might not have the courage to ask, because he was so afraid of what the answer might be.

Keflyn regarded him closely but without expression. "What do you think?"

"I believe that you must have," he replied. "But . . ."

"But why?" she asked when he faltered, asking the question for him. "Again I ask, what do you think?"

"I know only the obvious answer to that. Because the Terran

Republic asked, and the Aldessan agreed. Perhaps we were only an experiment, from your point of view."

"But you also know better than that," she said, sitting back on her tail. "We did not make you for their use. This has only been your childhood, your time of maturing. Soon you will leave them to seek your own worlds and lives. We made you because we wanted you, as one might seek a friend in one's loneliness. We made you because you are the thing in most ways like ourselves. Perhaps you are even what we wish ourselves to be."

"And that is the reason?" Velmeran asked.

She smiled. "Were you expecting some great oratory to express some inescapable argument of logic and practicality? I have none. Your lives are your own, to live as you will."

"And the humans?"

"They have problems that you cannot solve for them," the Aldessa insisted. "They have found the best solution for their genetic deterioration, but even that cannot save them forever. We have seen too many races come and go for us to have much hope. There is a chance, but if they do survive they will be the first of half a hundred such cases we have observed. But that is not your problem. You cannot keep them alive, and you should not try to take their place when they are gone. Rid them of the Union before it begins the process of turning them into genetic machines, and that is all you can hope to do for them."

"These are the general specifications for the jump drive," the young Kelvessa explained as he began handing over microdisks, sheets, and booklets. "This is the helm manual, what your helm and navigator need to know to set up jumps manually. And these are the specifications, detailed enough for you to repair the generator or even—fortune forbid—build a new one."

"Can you read that?" Consherra asked Lenna as they looked over the helm manual. Lenna was now very conversant in the Kelvessan language, although she still had some trouble reading technical material.

"Big words," Lenna answered, a vague reply at best.

Commander Laroose entered the bridge at that moment, and Velmeran left Consherra and her assistant to work out matters themselves. Laroose was watching Lenna closely, still unsure of what to make of her after all this time.

"I see that you are using your new hand," Laroose remarked

"I am trying to remember to," Velmeran amended, demon strating the hand that he had grown. "It works now, even if it a bit small yet. At this point it will only continue to get larg for another week or so."

"That is amazing. And speaking of getting bigger . . ."

Consherra afforded him a tolerant stare. She remained on th ship now, where no one noticed—or pretended not to notice— that she could no longer button the lower half of her tunic over round belly. With only days to go, she would not get any large Nor was she nearly as large as humans got, since Kelvessa young were born half the size of their two-armed counterpart nor even as large as a Feldenneh, whose cubs always traveled pairs.

"At least I can now be sure of having this over with befo we leave airdock in four weeks," she said. "Obviously, natu does not take into account that we have ships to run."

"I can appreciate that," Laroose agreed. "The joke around th station is that all pregnant Kelvessan must be from the Methryn It's a purely inside joke to ask who the father is."

Velmeran looked uncomfortable, although it was hardly h fault that over a third of the Methryn's female population wa pregnant. Baressa had brought forth a son only days before, an those few who knew conveniently forgot that Baress was n the real father. But Valthyrra made no attempt to hide he amusement.

"What became of your long-legged friend?" Laroose asked "It occurs to me that I haven't seen the Valtrytian in quite som time."

"Keflyn left about seven weeks ago to collect some thing she needed, although she should be back any day now," Ve meran explained. "She has decided to stay with us. She say that she has more to teach than she could even begin in only si months. And we can use another teacher."

"Can she handle life with the Starwolves?"

"She says that she can handle the accelerations as well a Lenna can, and the cold bothers her even less. She certainly ha more fur."

"On the other hand, she wears no clothes." He shrugged "It's your business. It just seems to me that she's changing yo into something I can no longer understand. The truth be known I probably understand you better than I used to think I did. An

Tregloran only a second behind. "I have to get back to the Methryn."

Keflyn perked her ears and started to follow.

"Wait!" Laroose called after her. "What did he say?"

"Vey von schess," the Aldessa replied. "It is here."

"What is here? What does it mean?"

"I have no idea, but it must be very important," she called over her back as she trotted out the door.

The construction bay was over a third of the way around the huge station from where the Methryn was moored. There were no convenient lifts, and the small trams were slow and had the habit of stopping every half kilometer. The quickest way Velmeran knew to reach his ship, short of teleportation, was to run. At a sustained speed of seventy-five kilometers per hour, he and Tregloran covered that distance in half an hour. Keflyn, with her two-meter legs and tremendous strength, could match that with difficulty. Commander Laroose, who knew a few tricks from long experience, commandeered a tug and arrived slightly ahead of the others, catching up with them at the Methryn's airlock.

The mystery was revealed when the lift let them out at the Methryn's medical section. Velmeran rushed into the main reception room just as Dyenlerra stepped out of a smaller room.

"Where? Where?" he demanded frantically.

"There! There!" she exclaimed mockingly, jumping and gesturing to the room she had just left. "You wait here."

She disappeared into the room, leaving the astonished Velmeran standing in the middle of the main foyer. A moment later Consherra emerged from that same room. It was the first time in three months that she had been able to button a shirt all the way down.

"Where are you going?" Velmeran asked, mystified.

"Back to the bridge," she replied. "I was supervising the repairs when this began, and I thought that I should be getting back."

Keflyn twitched her ears but said nothing. After all, anyone who could lift six tons would not consider this anything more than a half-hour diversion from one's normal schedule. Consherra had been expecting this for half a year, so the novelty had certainly worn off. But that was not the case for the rest of the crew. Lenna arrived at that moment, and Baress was only seconds behind.

Then the almost tangible sense of anticipation was transformed into an audible sigh of relief as Dyenlerra returned bearing a tiny patient cradled in her four arms. Tiny was indeed the word, for young Kelvessan seldom weighted more than a kilo at birth. Nor did they look any more alien from their human counterparts than at this time of life. She was in most ways a miniature of the adult, a tiny body with long, slender arms and legs and a large head with immense eyes. This remarkably advanced state of development included a full set of teeth and a thick, disheveled mane of brown hair that extended just past the upper shoulders. She sat upright in Dyenlerra's hands, staring about in a bemused but curious fashion.

"Congratulations, Commander," the medic said as she transferred the little one into his arms. "It's a wolf."

Father and daughter stared at each other with the same vacant mystification. The little Kelvessa's curiosity was insatiable, reflected in vast eyes that peered out in wonder beneath an unruly shock of hair. She stared up at Velmeran with special interest, as if she sensed a closer tie with him. She reached up and took hold of his nose with a hand too small to fit around it and made an inquisitive chirping sound. Velmeran smiled.

"What a wonderful, wonderful thing this is," he said softly. "What an incredibly delightful young lady she is. Of all the wonders I have seen, this is surely the greatest."

"Privately, I have to admit that I could not be more pleased," Consherra said, moving close beside him to brush the hair out of the little one's eyes. "And nothing makes me happier than to see how happy you are."

"I cannot get over how fully developed she is," Lenna commented, stepping up for a closer look.

"A matter of necessity," Dyenlerra explained. "Our young have to be born hardy enough to endure the demands of life on a warship. She will be walking in a few hours, and speaking simple words by the end of the week. She will be starting to school in three months."

"Our babies must sleep their first few months, but she doesn't look sleepy."

"Sleepy?" the medic asked in astonishment. "Kelvessan do not sleep."

"Then pity the poor mothers!" Lenna declared. "Does she have a name?"

Velmeran looked at Consherra, who smiled gently. "I have

not given the subject any thought, to tell the truth. So I thought that I might leave that to you. If you wish. I thought that you might want to name her after your mother."

Velmeran shook his head slowly. "It would not be fair to expect her to relive a memory, especially a memory that is not her own. But I would like it very much if Venn Keflyn would lend her name to the cause."

"My name?" Keflyn asked, momentarily astonished. "I would be honored, to say the least. But how would that come out in the way you often adapt our names to feminine use. Keflenna?"

"No, just Keflyn," he said. "That is a purely human conceit that we acquired long ago, this idea that males and females cannot have the same names. If that is all right with you."

"I like it very much," Consherra agreed eagerly.

"Then Keflyn it is," Velmeran proclaimed as he passed the tiny Kelvessa into Venn Keflyn's hands. Then he placed his arms around Consherra's shoulders as he led her off into a quiet corner of the room, leaving the others to admire the Methryn's newest crewmember. Unnoticed for the moment, Tregloran and Lenna slipped their arms around each other comfortably.

"Do you still feel quite so lonely?" Consherra asked.

"No, not hardly," he assured her. "It never occurred to me that I could mean so much to so many people, or that so many people could mean so much to me. But the most important thing that I have found is that I could never be alone as long as I have just you with me. Your love is exceeded only by your patience."

Consherra smiled and settled comfortably into his arms. "Is that what you like about me, that I am the only one with the patience for you?"

"I love you for just being you. Patience is just one of your many virtues, and the one that you should be most grateful for. Why in the name of sanity did you ever decide to love me?"

"It was decided for me, so I have never given it much thought," she replied. "True love, with no reasons or excuses. How could I not love you? Still, if it is all the same to you, I would rather not go through this more often than once every fifty years."

They wrapped their arms tightly around each other and kissed warmly and gently, without a thought for the tight knot of visitors gathered around the tiny object of interest.

"Eee-yow!"

They glanced up in surprise at that unexpected howl of pain. Little Keflyn, now in Lenna's firm but astonished care, had wrapped a small hand around Venn Keflyn's finger and was unknowingly applying bone-crushing pressure.

"Get her off, please!" the Aldessa pleaded to the astonished onlookers. "Do not hurt her, and for pity's sake do not hurt me! Just do something to loosen that killer grip. *Varth, val trenon de altrys caldayson!*"

"Half a moment," Dyenlerra promised, and gently pried her loose. Everyone was surprised by the sight of a newborn Kelvessa bringing an Aldessa—and a Venn warrior—quite literally to her knees. The only thing stronger, it seemed, was an adult Kelvessa. Lenna, looking a bit dazed, eagerly transferred the bundle of joy and brute strength into Baressa's waiting arms.

"Talk about a bouncing baby!" Commander Laroose remarked.

"It might be wise for the non-Kelvessan to restrict themselves to looking until she learns to control her strength," Valthyrra said. She had entered unnoticed during the excitement and now brought her probe forward to face Laroose. "I would have been here sooner, but the station is on full alert and the system fleet has been mobilized. You promised when you ordered these things that you would discover the cause and report back."

"Oh, my word!" Laroose exclaimed. "When Velmeran turned and ran yelling who-knows-what, I just assumed that he had some premonition of immediate danger. Where can I find a com to Station Control?"

"On that desk," Valthyrra said, indicating with her camera pod the desk beside the outer door.

Trying his best not to look contrite under the stares of the others, Laroose walked over to the desk and sat down, studying the com unit for a moment before pressing a button. "Station Control? Commander Laroose here."

"Yes, Commander," the eager reply came. "What is wrong?"

"Wrong? Nothing is wrong!" he declared. "Issue this report. Commander Velmeran and First Mate Conpherra, the Methryn's helm, now have a young daughter by the name of Keflyn."

"Glad to hear it, but why did that require the mobilization of the system fleet?"

"Why, to celebrate!"

Taking advantage of his mistake, Laroose ordered the fleet to pass in honor formation, firing their cannons in salute while packs of fighters executed fantastic maneuvers. Then the station, clearly visible in the night sky of the world below, flashed its bright exterior lights for a full rotation of the planet so that the entire population of Alkayja could observe the spectacle. If Velmeran and Consherra considered that a little much for such a common occurrence, they soon learned that it was indeed a cause for celebration as thousands gathered outside the Methryn's refitting bay and millions more throughout the Republic sent messages of congratulations and various small gifts during the next week. All in praise of the smallest Starwolf in the fleet.

Velmeran paused at the entrance of the bridge. In spite of the fact that his office and cabin were immediately behind the bridge, he had honored Consherra's and Valthyrra's entreaties to stay away until the repairs were complete. Now he returned for the first time since he had spoken with Valthyrra there after his return from the Challenger. At first glance he could tell no difference, except that everything looked shiny new for the first time in nearly a century. A second glance merely confirmed the first.

"Well, what do you think?" Valthyrra asked anxiously, hovering at the limit of her boom.

"You look beautiful," he told her honestly. "But you made such a big deal of your reconstruction, you led me to expect major changes."

"Ah, but there are major changes beneath the surface," she insisted. "Come over and take a look at this."

Velmeran strolled slowly through the bridge, approaching from the right wing. He paused briefly to admire the clean, bright fabric of the seats and the adjustment mechanisms beneath the frames that were bright silver rather than dark with accumulations of dark oil. The floor and consoles lacked the numerous scratches and dents from objects dropped or shifted during high-G accelerations. As he came nearer, he saw that Valthyrra's camera pod and boom had never looked so neat and clean. The servos, designed to hold the long boom steady through accelerations as high as several hundred G's, no longer hummed noticeably when she moved.

"Is that a new boom?" he asked.

"Actually, nearly everything you see is new," Valthyrra said.

"Everything in the middle and upper bridge is completely new. The helm console is a third again as large to accommodate the jump-drive controls and a fully independent navigational computer. One person at the helm can now start the generators and power up the shields, run the ship on any of the four drives, and direct the cannons by computer control."

"You are now the fastest ship in known space," Velmeran observed. "How do you feel?"

"Very much the same as always, although I will not be able to tell anything until I get out and run under my power. But I do feel very new. Very young, you might say. I had forgotten how it feels to have all your systems working perfectly and without complaint. I felt very strange when we powered up the jump drive yesterday, like a balloon at the end of a string."

Velmeran laughed. "You make one very big balloon. Are you worried about testing the jump drive?"

"A little, I have to admit. I cannot forget the story of Quendari Valcyr and how she jumped, never to return. But we will not let that happen."

She watched quietly as Velmeran ascended the steps to the middle bridge and took the seat at the helm station to inspect the new controls. The actual jump-drive controls occupied a fairly small section of the right-hand side console, as well as a lockout shift lever among the manual controls.

"Would you like to try out your own station?" Valthyrra asked.

"Have they changed it greatly?" he asked, and she moved her camera pod in a negative gesture. "Then it can wait."

"I thought that you might like to try it on for size," she suggested, then glanced away as she recalled a painful association. Mayelna had used those very words when she had surrendered her station to him during the attack on the Challenger.

Velmeran reached up and laid one hand gently on one side of her camera pod, a touch that she could feel only in her heart. "What I meant was that I want to wait until we are back out in space before I try out my new chair."

"I understand. It fits you just fine, I am sure," she agreed. "But what of you? Are you happy?"

"Yes, I am," he replied, leaning back in the seat. "That might seem strange, after all the trouble we went through to get me here, but I am. This is my place now. My days as a pack leader seem like years ago, much more than just the six months that we have been here. I actually look forward to going back out to fight again. Union space has been very quiet since Tryalna, but that cannot last much longer. Still, things are going to be very different from how they used to be."

"That is so," Valthyrra agreed. "Usually very little seems different after a change in Commanders, just someone new on the upper bridge. But I feel different, and I am not referring to my parts. Another age of my life is gone, and a new one has begun. It is the first time, however, that I have been aware of that change as it happened."

"I thought you said that you do not feel your age," Velmeran observed.

"No, not really. I am young again, like I said," she concurred, and her lenses unfocused slightly as she turned to her deepest memories. "I was born a fighting ship. For my first five thousand years it seemed that I always had a few dents in my nose. Then I was a pirate ship for so long. Now I am a fighting ship again."

"Do your memories fade in time?" Velmeran asked softly.

"The sense of immediacy fades with the passing of the years, so that there is always a sense of time to my memories. But I can never forget any detail that I do not want to forget." She paused, and her lenses took on an even more distant look. "The pain of a loss fades, but it is never completely gone. Mayelna was more like me than any who have come along in a very long time. She was a better friend than any I have ever known, and I will always miss her. And I do not want you to ever leave me. I do not think that I could bear that. I love you more than I have ever loved before."

Velmeran smiled gently, reassuringly. "So many years. So many terrible memories of past hurts."

"No, those hoarded memories are my dearest possession," Valthyrra insisted. "Terrible? They are beautiful!"